BLACKSHIRT REBELLION

BLACKSHIRT REBELLION

AN
AGENTS OF ROOM Z
NOVEL

JASON MONAGHAN

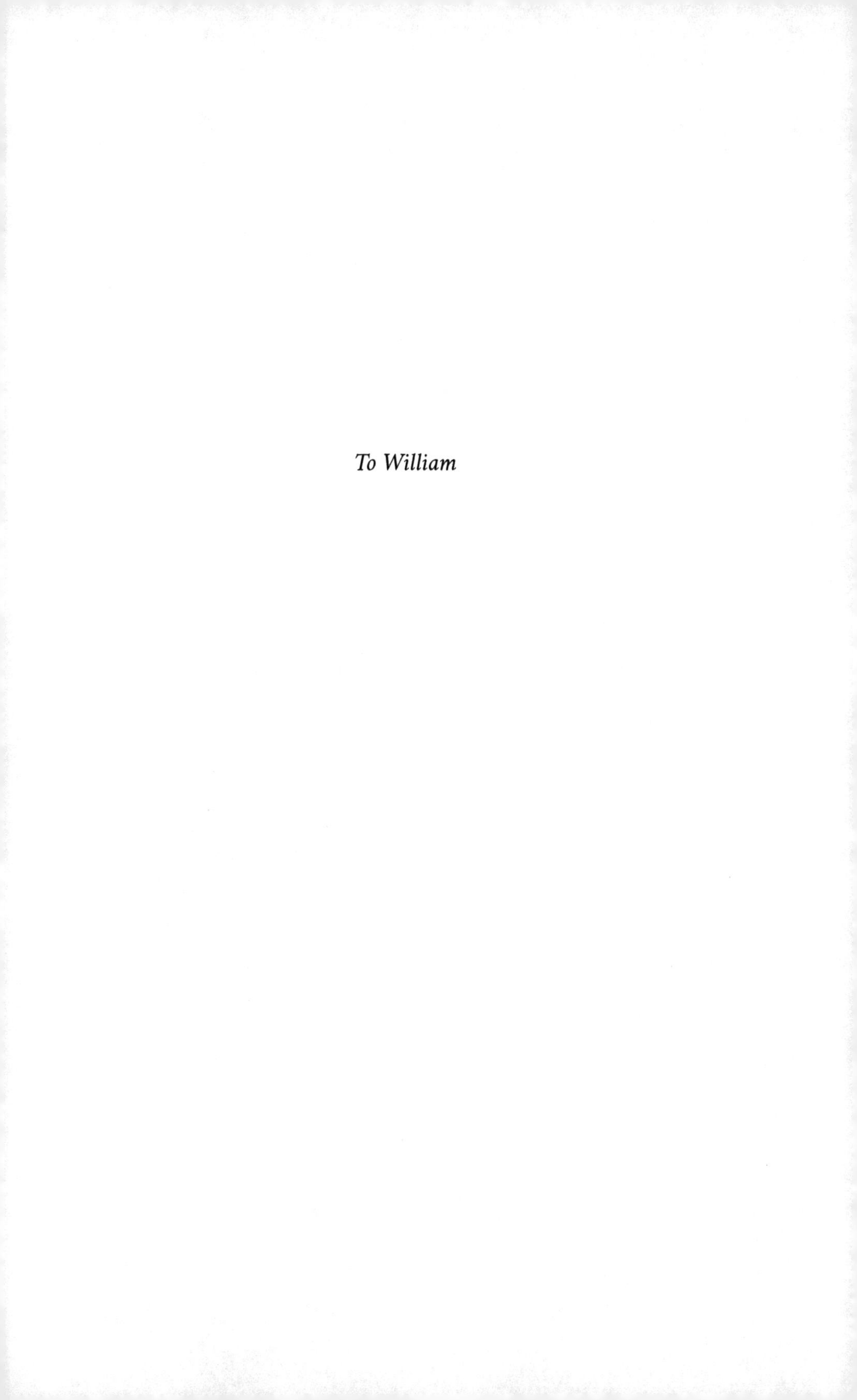

To William

Dramatis Personae

Department Z was the intelligence unit of the British Union of Fascists and National Socialists, which by 1937 was known simply as British Union. In this alternative history, the fascist movement and with it, Department Z, have grown to be larger and more powerful than they remained in reality. Characters and organisations listed in italics are based on real historical figures, modified in the interests of fiction.

Department Z
Hugh Clifton, Commander Z3 Confidential Investigation Section
Sissy Poe-Maundy, Section Leader
Julian Thring, Section Leader
Danny Hills, Unit Leader
Lucy Parmentier, Unit Leader
Eleanor Fitzherbert, an ex-debutante
Jimmy Walsh, Hugh's driver
Dr Valentine, Director of Intelligence, Department Z
Commander Blake, Z1 Internal Security Section
Commander Parker, Z2 Special Action Section
The Chelsea Wives, Lucy's unit of administrators

British Union (British Union of Fascists and National Socialists)
Sir Oswald Mosley, 'the Leader'
'F-H' Neil Francis-Hawkins, Director-General of Operations
William Joyce MP, Commissioner for Propaganda
Melissa Thring, Woman Section Leader, wife of Julian
Dowager Baroness Rockwell, Sissy's mother

Fuller J F C, Commissioner for War and Munitions

Security services & police
Marcus Calhoun, Head of *the Security Service (MI5)*
Detective Inspector Renton, *Special Branch, Metropolitan Police*

Other characters and organisations
'Verity', former MI5 agent
'Ruth Fritton', former Department Z agent
Bruno Vogel, *German Embassy*
Leonora D'Auville Clifton, 'Leo', Clifton's wife
Young Britain Club, an exclusive London gentleman's club
Arnold Alexander Thorne, 'AA', Young Britain Club
Philip de Vere Challenger, Young Britain Club
Frederick 'Dougie' Douglas, Young Britain Club
J E B 'Jeb' Baxter, an adventurer
King's Party, a cross-party coalition of MPs supporting King Edward VIII

Historical characters
Winston Churchill, First Lord of the Admiralty
Admiral Sir Barry Domville, former Director of Naval Intelligence
Kim Philby, a reporter
The myriad of historical extreme right wing organisations that existed in the mid-1930s are listed on Hugh's blackboard in chapter 8.

Chapter One

Spring, 1937

A man would be very foolish to ignore a tommy gun pointed in his direction, even a man who finds fascism not extreme enough and needs to fall further into darkness. I hoped not to use the weapon resting by my knee, but anyone who resorts to donning a white cloak and hood to push a racialist agenda has clearly left logic behind.

Sissy was driving my Alvis tourer towards the setting sun, and two colleagues rode behind us. A baker's van followed at a short distance, and last came one of the allegedly armoured black vans from the motor pool. A dozen armed fascists rode in those vans, believing they were working to build that shiny new Britain the Leader promised. Most were aged under thirty, and all had been carefully filtered without knowing they were being filtered. Racialists, Nazis-in-waiting, and street thugs had no place in my section. The agents of Room Z were an adventurous bunch, easily bored, and I needed to keep them busy. Too easily they might be drawn down darker alleys.

We knew both the time and the place precisely. It was rumoured Department Z had spies on every street corner, which was nonsense, but I did nothing to discourage the myth. Even without being all-seeing, all-hearing, enough intelligence came our way by both regular and irregular means. Tip-offs, bribe-taking, score-settling, and petty jealousy were rife in the uneasy spring of 1937.

Dusk fell in rural Berkshire. The scarred side of Sissy's face was closest to me, and no matter how she curled her dark hair forward, it couldn't conceal the damage to her jawline. From the back seat of the Alvis, red-haired Eleanor Fitzherbert held her Oxford spectacles in place as she used a map to navigate our route to the rendezvous. At her warning, Sissy made the turn into a narrow lane. After a few hundred yards of twists and turns, we saw Unit Leader Hills stepping out of the cover of a hedge, and Sissy slowed the car to a halt. I wound down my window.

'Two hundred yards on the right, boss,' he said. 'High wall, and they've padlocked the gate. No guard on the gate, no dogs, but there's a man by the house door. He can't see the gate from there; the drive curves a bit to hide the house from the road. I counted six cars and a small charabanc; we could be outnumbered.'

All three vehicles were pulled into the kerb, and drivers killed the engines lest we announce our arrival. Hills collected the second tommy gun from the bread van. With a reputation built up by American gangster movies, they always made an impression. Our pair used straight magazines, unlike the dramatic drums employed by film villains, which in practice were rather heavy. The rest of the men carried revolvers or automatic shotguns while Sissy and Eleanor drew Walther PPK pistols. If there was to be trouble, it would be at close range.

The country mansion was owned by the Challenger family, industrialists with interests in steel and chemicals, and was home to the elder son. A bolt cutter made short work of the padlock on the main gate, but the gravel of the drive crunched underfoot, so we split into groups on either side where a grove of Scots pines shielded us. Beyond this point, the drive ran arrow-straight, so to get closer to the house unobserved, we dodged from shrub to shrub. Up ahead, a man in a snap-brim hat stood watch under a porch supported by four Doric columns. The house was similar in size and style to my father's pile up in Yorkshire, a sign of new wealth and pretentious aspiration. Leaving two of the newer recruits to watch our escape route, Hills took three men to work around the right-hand side of the building. Another four were to creep up to the front via the rank of parked vehicles on the left.

I allowed two minutes for both groups to get into position, then burst from the cover of a rhododendron at the head of my pack. Sissy was to one side of me, Eleanor to the other. Once the laziest member of my team, the murder of her school friend had turned Eleanor into the most dedicated.

He was not a very effective watchman, reacting slowly, wasting time to throw away a cigarette before spinning round and making for the door, oblivious of the weapons aimed at his back. Thank God neither of my women shot him as they ran within range. The door spilled yellow light as it opened, but his warning yell was cut off as a scrum of us heaved on the door and threw him back into the hall. Rolling onto his haunches, he shuffled back as far as a suit of armour. Eleanor advanced on him, her pistol muzzle daring him to move again.

Muffled chanting came from the back of the house where the ballroom should be. A ritual was in progress. It was an initiation at which praise was heaped on Edward the First, the king who had once expelled the Jews from England. A servant in green livery threw up his hands, wide-eyed.

'Open the door,' I ordered.

'But sir, I'll lose my position.'

'You'll lose your balls if you don't.'

He opened the ballroom door with a flourish, as if to announce us. The room beyond was in half-darkness, lit by only candles that gave the air an oily scent. Two dozen white-hooded men sat in chairs arranged in a horseshoe, their long white gowns flowing onto the floor. Swastika flags advertised their political philosophy.

'Department Z!' Sissy yelled, rather shrill, betraying her nerves. 'Nobody move.'

Whatever litany was being recited came abruptly to an end. The White Knights of Britain stared at us.

'Hoods off, gentlemen,' I commanded. A tommy gun makes its own case without need for elaboration.

The first hood to reluctantly slide away revealed an army colonel I recognised; the next was one of the BU regional inspectors who started to protest loudly. Glass broke as Hills forced his way in from the garden door.

'Come on, gents, don't be shy.' Hills strode into the light. 'Let's see your pretty faces.'

'Damn and blast it!' A Conservative MP threw off his hood and stared at the floor.

That made at least three careers terminated.

My heart leaped as the hood slipped away from the face of Phillip de Vere Challenger. At Christmas, I'd retrieved the membership lists of London's Young Britain Club by unorthodox means, and Challenger was listed as a member of its committee. Behind the scenes, the inner circle of committee members exerted a benign influence on British politics. Without the political meddling by the Young Britons, Eleanor's friend would be alive, and Sissy would still have an intact face. The club may be still too powerful to destroy completely, but I could take down their members one by one.

'Perish Judah!' cried the chief wizard or whatever fanciful title the Knight's leader had assumed. 'You'll pay for this, Hugh Clifton!'

Hills tapped the barrel of his submachine gun on the shoulder of the wizard's rather comical white gown. 'Off.'

Wizard no more, the man let his hood fall to the ground and I was surprised not to find someone more important behind the disguise. He was too old to be a Young Briton, and I didn't recognise him at all.

'By the powers vested in me by the Public Order Act, 1936,' I bawled, 'you are all under arrest.'

The Act had originally been drafted to curb the rise of the Blackshirts but had been completely amended to hand authority to Sir Oswald Mosley's paramilitary forces. For the first two years I had masqueraded as a member of Department Z we could only play at being secret policemen, but now that Mosley was in power, we could arrest who we pleased. We didn't even need a warrant.

One by one, the men in gowns were ushered towards the exit. We'd use their own charabanc to take them in for questioning. I'd take an hour or two to explore the house, open desks, remove letters and incriminating memos, and confiscate the inevitable antisemitic tracts. The White Knights of Britain would ride no more.

Chapter Two

Some said I was abusing my newly gifted powers, and some dared say it to my face. Perhaps I was turning into that thing I'd once been fighting, but ever since being talked into infiltrating the Blackshirts my only option was to be carried along with the current. I'd watched people die who'd over-estimated their chances of swimming against the tide of history. Extremism was a disease spreading from the fringes at a time when few wanted to be seen as a moderate, a democrat, a softie. By pinching out the most extreme groups, I might just prevent British Union members from drifting their way, or at least prevent the antisemitic, jingoistic creed of the far-right taking over the narrative. Being so visibly heavy-handed may also help convince Middle England of the arbitrary and dangerous nature of fascism.

Away from the violence, the orchestrated black-clad parades, and the sheer deceit of my pretending to be a fascist, Sissy and I maintained what in normal times would be a scandalous relationship. Tonight, we were staying at her Chelsea flat, tastefully-appointed with minor artworks and art deco lamps. It was a warm evening, and Sissy stood before her cheval mirror wearing just a camisole and a sleek French brassiere. I wish she'd simply been admiring herself.

'I'm hideous,' she said.

'No, you're as beautiful as ever.'

'With this?' She half-turned and displayed the rip on her left thigh, which had healed well but still carried redness. 'And this?' She adjusted her underwear so I could more easily see the smaller wound forming a pink-purple teardrop on her lower left midriff.

I was lounging on her silk bedsheets, still in my dinner shirt with my jacket and tie draped across a chair and my shoes kicked haphazardly beneath the bed. She came closer, her face cleansed of all makeup. Since returning from France in the new year, she'd habitually applied heavy foundation she'd not needed before.

'How about this?' In the fleshy part of her left cheek had been a triangular puncture which the finest surgeons family money could afford had done their best to make good.

'I can hardly see it now.'

'Liar,' she said. 'You've become a very good liar, Hugh Clifton. What are your orders now, from those people you work for? Did they order you to disband the White Knights?'

I gave a laugh. 'The White Knights are clowns, dangerous clowns. You don't want their ideas infecting the Party. And the people I once worked for, and the people I once worked against, are now serving the same master, so my conflict of loyalties is solved, mission over. Which is what I wanted to talk to you about over dinner before you brushed me off.'

We had dined at Veeraswamy, London's premier Indian restaurant located in Regent's Street. Apart from the excellent cuisine, one reason I enjoyed going was I knew that the racialist wing of the British Union wouldn't be seen dead eating foreign food. Unless it was French or Italian, which were at least European and carried snob value. I'd wondered why one of the plate glass windows was boarded up until the head waiter was pleased to inform me there would be no charge for our meal.

'Mr Clifton, we're honoured to have you eat here.'

'Who broke your window?'

He hesitated for a moment, rather as a schoolboy is wary of telling tales to the beak. 'Last night, at this time, young men threw stones.'

'Were they wearing uniforms?'

He fell silent, clearly embarrassed.

'Black uniforms?'

'Grey. With hats.' He mimed the style of a kepi.

I drew in breath. 'I'll have a word. But I insist on paying for our meal.'

'And the manager insists you eat for free.'

Sissy met my glance. I could be a prig and continue to insist or allow myself to be corrupted as if this was Chicago and I was running a protection racket.

'Thank the manager very much. We look forward to dining here again.'

Our meal should have cost around ten shillings, so allowing the same for the wine and adding a suitable tip would bring the cost of my soul to just over a pound. We were brought our coats, and as he helped Sissy into hers, the head waiter smiled. I tipped him a pound and two shillings.

'For your service,' I said.

* * *

Sissy slumped onto the bed, ensuring her unblemished right cheek was towards me. Her *good side*, as she'd refer to it eternally. She'd also lost a tooth to a grenade fragment that so easily could have severed an artery or taken out her eye. The replacement glinted gold as she challenged me.

'So talk.'

'I repeat, mission over. And as Mosley is now in power, I'd venture to suggest that your mission is also over.'

'It's not over,' she stated.

'But Mosley is the Prime Minister. Yes, propped up by the King's Party and Churchill and the others, but isn't that enough? It's not a dictatorship, but frankly, do you want a dictatorship?'

'That's not what I mean.'

'Look, the raid went off well, nobody got hurt, but it won't always be the case. Why don't you and I just go away now? How about Canada, with all that space? Or Australia, South Africa. Nobody will chase us; they're too busy chasing each other, scrabbling for power in this glorious new fascist Britain.'

'Don't mock—you're mocking.'

'I've done my bit—you've done your bit. Let's walk away. Hasn't this cost you enough?'

She glared at my lack of tact, but I wanted to ram the point home that victory for Oswald Mosley's British Union of Fascists and National Socialists was never going to be bloodless. And without doubt, the bloodletting had only just begun.

'Sissy,' I said as gently as I could. 'It's over.'

'Julia is dead. I brought her into the Party, I trained her, and I saw her die.' Her lips quivered. 'I had a piece of her bone stuck in my skin.' She jabbed a fingernail towards her scarred face. 'And whoever is responsible for this is still out there, so it's not over while they're still breathing.'

Chapter Three

William Joyce MP, Commissioner for Propaganda, was a scruffy dresser when in civilian clothes. Pale and thin, ever conscious of the razor scar down his left cheek, he slouched with one elbow on the table.

'Of course, we considered you as the new Director of Department Z,' he said, 'but you lack...' He moulded his hands around the shape of an imaginary ball. '...sufficient political commitment. You are the embodiment of the National Socialist ideal, yet you don't project it; you don't carry your loyalty on your sleeve.'

Even when putting me down, Joyce was heavily overestimating my zeal for fascism, national socialism, or any other excuse for suppressing free thought and free will. Perhaps he was being ironic and had seen through my charade from the start. It was a dangerous state of affairs when a part-time English teacher had risen to become the second most powerful politician in the country. And having just turned thirty-one, he was only a few months older than me, if six inches shorter.

'I've never wanted the top job,' I said. 'I'm content to play my part in Z3.' By pretending to have no ambition, I might just stay immune from the petty jealousies that ran through the Party like so much fat in streaky bacon.

We sat in the small meeting room at Black House, Chelsea, now given over almost entirely to Department Z. British Union's political hub had moved to Westminster, the printing presses migrated to Fleet Street, and the Blackshirt stormtroopers now had barracks all over the country, so only a security squad were now based in the former teacher training college.

As the Party changed and grew, Joyce and the populist fascists were being progressively sidelined by what Joyce called 'the heel-clicking petty militarists'. It was the Blackshirt commanders who claimed to have taken control of the streets and saved the country during the abdication crisis of 1936, and it was they who confronted strikers and anti-fascist demonstrators in the cities of Britain every day since. Joyce's first wife had even left him for the commander of Mosley's personal bodyguard. Soon after his divorce, he'd married a young northern typist called Margaret, who struck me as being far too pleasant for him. The couple lived not so far from Sissy, curiously sharing their home with Joyce's previous flat mate.

'Oh, here they are,' Joyce said.

Into the room came Commander Parker, Dr Valentine, and Valentine's new weasel-faced minion Blake, who he'd bumped up to Commander Z1, in charge of internal security. Blake was a qualified solicitor, and his appointment underlined Valentine's move to staff his intelligence department with diverse talents. It would make Department Z more dangerous than when it was mostly populated by thugs such as Parker.

None of us were in uniform. Perhaps the others had taken my point that strutting round dressed like Hitler's SS was not the smartest thing for a secret police force to do. It also emphasised the growing distance between Department Z and street-fighting Blackshirts.

Valentine noticed immediately that Joyce and I'd been engaged in conversation. 'Has the meeting begun?'

'We're just filling time, Dr Valentine,' Joyce said. 'Parker, take the floor and explain where we are with Dragon North.'

Parker had little new to say. As soon as the stormtroopers were ready to storm the last socialist enclaves in the industrial cities, Special Action section Z2 would move in to root out the communist ringleaders.

'Until then, it's business as usual.'

'Containing the Jewish threat,' Joyce said with satisfaction. 'And what progress are you making?'

Parker enjoyed ten minutes extolling what 'special actions' Z2 had been carrying out against Jewish interests. Closure of businesses for any infringement of regulations plus mysterious fires destroying those whose legal slate was clean. Arrests where cause could be proved in court, intimidation where it could not. Deportations on the slightest pretext and a few accidental deaths along the way. Parker was the alcoholic given the keys to the wine cellar and revelled in every act of malice his men could deliver.

I could stand no more and interrupted his flow. 'Parker. About Veeraswamy restaurant in Regent Street.'

'The wog place?'

'You know the one. My agents use it regularly to dine incognito—it's the last place anyone would expect Department Z to be meeting contacts. And while India remains in the Empire, we must expect to see Indian restaurants in London. If it's your men trying to close it down, please desist.'

'He has a point,' Valentine said. 'Two points, in fact.'

Parker shrugged. 'It's not us; we've better things to do.'

'Grey uniforms?'

'Cadets perhaps, letting off high spirits.'

'This is more than high spirits. For God's sake, we're running the country now; there's no need for crude vandalism.'

'It could be the Nordic League,' Parker said, clicking his fingers. 'They wear grey.'

'And kepis? How many private armies do we want running round the streets?'

'You're defending your Indian friends, Clifton, but saying nothing about what you are doing against the Jews. Are you defending them next?'

For two years, I'd been a moth orbiting a candle, spiraling inward, and the heat was growing.

'Section Z3 was set up to investigate,' I said. 'Which is what we do. Almost all our investigations are directed towards threats to the state. Mostly communists.'

'How about Jewish communists?' Parker teased.

'We're a nationwide network, and there are hardly any Jews outside London.'

'So why not start rounding up gypsies,' Parker suggested. 'They're everywhere. Everyone hates them, no one will miss them. We'll win a lot of support.'

He knew I was not cast from the same mould as him and delighted in pushing my reasonable argument to its limits.

'People may think we have eyes on every corner, but we don't,' I said. 'We need to shepherd our resources and concentrate on the genuine threats.'

'Clifton, we are under attack from the twin pincers of Jewry,' Joyce said, forming his arms into crab claws. 'Rich, international capitalist Jews controlling our industry.' He advanced his right claw. 'Foreign communist Jews in their millions filling our cities.' His left claw closed the trap.

It made no sense to me, but it was a neat way of explaining the contradictory logic of antisemitism to those who wanted to justify it.

'Parker is leading the battle on the streets, but you find time to dine in west end restaurants.' Fired up now, Joyce's tone made me uneasy. 'And persecute the White Knights.'

'The anti-state activities of the White Knights contravene the Public Order Act.'

'That is true, strictly speaking,' said Valentine, and Blake nodded his support. 'But are your actions a good use of our precious resources?'

'We need to start rounding up fascists.'

I could hear that proverbial pin drop.

Valentine fixed me through those piggy little spectacles. 'What do you mean?'

'I mean, I've read your latest research paper, Dr Valentine: *Follow the Leader*. The one in which you argue that despite your earlier essays on the true path to fascism, you now fall in step precisely behind the Leader's vision.'

'As do we all,' Valentine asserted.

'The Party grew from, what, thirty members in October 1932 to fifty thousand two years later, and to how many now—two hundred thousand?'

'More,' said Joyce.

'The Nazis have a name for their latecomers—March violets. People who only joined the party once it was firmly ensconced in power. Because it was good for business, or they wanted the prestige of being a Brownshirt but waited until there was no longer a risk of being shot down by the police.'

'You're saying we should freeze recruitment?'

I opened my hands. The fewer people who signed up for Mosley, the greater the chance for the return of democracy.

'We've never checked who we are letting in.'

Blake broke his silence. 'What do you think Section Z1 is for?'

'Locking the door after the horse has bolted. We had at least three spies in Black House last year, and one of my agents was killed because of it.'

'Department Z was run by a traitor,' said Valentine, the traitor's replacement. 'Not anymore.'

I wouldn't wind Valentine up any further in case it encouraged his paranoia.

'We're not freezing recruitment,' Joyce said. 'But what did you mean about rounding up fascists?'

'Well, consider Parker's comment about the Nordic League. We're not the only fascist party in the country.'

'National socialists,' Joyce corrected. 'We are national socialists—fascism is a foreign creed.'

'Exactly my point,' I said. 'There are at least a dozen parties in Britain claiming to be one flavour of fascist or another. How many do we need? Now that Special Branch and MI5 have lost interest in hounding the right, they can devote their whole attention to hunting Moscow's spies. So, from now, Z3 will be doing the hounding.' I concluded with a nervous cough.

'We've more important things to do,' Joyce said.

'Yes, with Dragon North coming up, we've better things to do,' Valentine hacked out. 'Stop it, Clifton.'

* * *

Chastened, I returned to Room Z in an angry mood. Perhaps I'd overplayed my hand, and that could be dangerous not only for me but for those who followed me. If I was stuck in this role, there must at least be a moral objective, one that justified my collaboration with the fascists. I checked my watch and picked up *The Times* but was too irritated to take in anything I was reading.

The internal telephone rang. I stared at it in annoyance, then grabbed it. 'Yes.'

'Joyce here. From a Party point of view, what you said at the meeting makes a good deal of sense. The Knights were of no importance, no relevance, but I've instructed Dr Valentine you're to be given a free hand in removing some of our rivals. Selectively, of course.'

So, not a free hand.

'I will choose the groups you purge. I have no problem with the Nordic League, but Arnold Leese is mad and dangerous. Dissolve the Imperial Fascist League.'

Chapter Four

If masquerading as a fascist came with a perk, it was I now had the whole of the top floor of Black House for my operations, keeping Room Z for myself as it had good light and a view down on King's Road. Section Z3 also maintained an outstation at Fulham Bakery for activities best kept well away from the eyes of Valentine, Parker, and their underlings.

Julian Thring had become my friend in the summer of 1935 when he was still a target of interest to the Security Service. Old hands referred to it as MI5, and although I'd never officially worked for them, my old army comrade Viscount Wickersley had talked me into becoming an informer. He'd almost dared me in the manner of a senior boy leading a junior into mischief, offering a sense of purpose after I'd been court-martialled and dishonourably discharged.

It had been unwise to form any personal bonds within the movement, but friendship came naturally and is hard to fake. Julian had little enthusiasm for jack-booted repression, rather his father had schooled him to be excited by the possibilities presented by a corporate state unhindered by the dead hand of democratic politics. Still in his late twenties, he'd asked me to be the best man at his wedding earlier in the year. I could hardly refuse, even though his wife's political views both bored and appalled me.

If I was doomed to remain a spy, I may as well be a comfortable spy, so the functional needs of Room Z had given way to it being my personal sanctuary. Seated in one of the cosy leather chairs I'd been leafing through papers retrieved during the raid on the White Knights when Julian put his head round the door.

'Hugh.'

'Jules, have a seat.'

He eased down into the second leather armchair.

'Are those the White Knights papers?'

'Yes, I presume you've seen them?' I asked. 'The wizard character turns out to be called Rowe—an importer of German goods. He doesn't have any political clout, does he?'

'I've never come across him, so no,' Julian said. After a moment's hesitation, his purpose in visiting me became clear. 'But Phillip de Vere Challenger does.'

He waited for me to respond, but I said nothing.

'He's on the Heavy Industry Commission, for goodness sake.'

'Then he should have known better than to flounce around in a white frock like the flipping Ku Klux Klan.'

'And he's on the committee of the Young Britain Club.'

'Ah, but there's the rub,' I said. 'One of the inner circle, which makes him the prize catch.'

Julian frowned, clearly not wanting a confrontation. 'I say, old man, I know what the Britons did last year and how you have this Italian-style vendetta against them, but can't we just drop charges against Challenger? I'm being pressured by the other chaps over this.'

'Not AA Thorne, by any chance?'

'Well, AA is the chairman, so naturally, he's upset.'

'Oh, what a pity.' I was pleased to hear AA Thorne was upset. 'Do you want to live in a country where membership of an exclusive gentleman's club makes a *chap* immune from the law?'

'Well.' Julian shuffled in his chair. 'It's always been the case that if you know the right people, you can swing things with a word in the right ear.'

'*Opportunity for all, privilege for none.* You've quoted the Leader's words yourself, more than once.'

Mosley was a Baronet and enjoyed moving in the upper crust of society, but his rhetoric was aimed at people who did not.

'Challenger is only being bound over with a fine he'll have no struggle in paying. Your chum should take it on the chin.'

'But he'll be dropped from the Commission; he's been made to look ridiculous. And he can't possibly stay on the club committee.'

I smiled. It felt like hitting a six at the start of a new inning.

* * *

British Union's original recruits were an odd mix of disillusioned socialists and restless conservatives impatient for solutions to the nation's ills. The party's key policies merged old-fashioned patriotism with socialist concern for the masses, capitalist love of profit, and modernist yearning for efficiency. If he had a redeeming feature, Mosley didn't bang on about leading the nation to victory or making foreign conquests, as did Hitler and Mussolini. With a third of the world under its sway, the British Empire was already big enough to satisfy any ego.

Not everyone on the right of British politics thought as Mosley did, and new right-wing organisations were sprouting up like nettles in a badly kept garden. I kept my team entertained by having them sign up as members of the new groups and infiltrate their meetings. My secret hope was I might be able to identify genuine opposition, a conservative grouping who could nudge the country back towards democracy without the shock of a revolution. The January Club and the Other Club had basically turned into the Cabinet, and there was nothing I could do about the Nazi-sponsored Anglo-German Fellowship beyond using my own membership to keep an eye on them. As information came in, I chalked the different parties, groups, and factions onto a blackboard down at the bakery, and files were opened on each. Joyce had at least given me the next target.

Arnold Leese was an energetic speaker, and Sissy joined me to hear one of his lectures in a hall off the Edgeware Road little more than a stone's throw from the West London Synagogue. The former veterinary surgeon was framed by flags of the Imperial Fascist League—a union flag contaminated by a swastika at the centre. He was guarded by his own version of black-shirted stormtroopers wearing khaki breeches and armbands following the design of the IFL flag. Leese was possibly fifty years old, affecting a little Hitler moustache. He ranted about the Jews and little else, trotting out long-debunked myths about the ritual murder of Christians in Jewish rituals, which provoked some of the finer ladies in the audience to catch their breaths.

Eventually, inevitably, he started to praise Adolf Hitler. 'Germany is a great country because Hitler has identified the true enemy! The Imperial Fascist League offers three solutions: kill them, sterilise them, or segregate them.'

Acid rose in my throat.

Sissy turned to me, mouthing *what?*

Not even Joyce on a bad day went this deep and this dark.

'Heil Hitler!'

'Heil Hitler!' his supporters echoed, rising to their feet and making the salute.

This was not an England I knew or ever wanted to know. Audience members who were simply attending through curiosity remained seated, glancing to their friends with varying degrees of disquiet, amazement, or embarrassment. A few rose to their feet following a moment's consideration and raised their right arms, straightening them. I'd felt a complete idiot the first time I'd faked that salute, but I gave Sissy a wink, and we joined the circus, saluting with the rest. Neither of us went so far as to heil Hitler.

I'd written Leese a letter on R R Clifton Ltd notepaper inviting him to dine with us at the Cumberland Hotel afterwards. As he tucked into lamb chops, he continued the theme of his lecture between mouthfuls. Leese was only recently out of prison after serving six months for circulating particularly vicious anti-Jewish literature. Not for the highly charged racialist tone, but for causing a public mischief through insulting the British armed forces.

'You mentioned segregation,' I ventured.

'We ship Britain's Jews off to Madagascar.' He went on to give a little detail on how this would work in practice.

'But what if they don't want to go?'

'Then we have them humanely killed,' he replied, as if the proposition was entirely reasonable.

'There's a quarter of a million Jews in Britain,' I said.

'That's a lot of bullets,' Sissy added.

'A quarter of a million.' Leese mimed, placing a pistol against his head. 'Poof! Even if it's a shilling a bullet, it's a bargain. Put them down as you would a lame horse or an old dog. But using gas chambers would be more economical; we'd have to look into the practical considerations, where to site them, what gas to use.'

Sissy looked down at the tablecloth, clearly unsettled, which cheered me no end. Julian's new wife would have been paying rapt attention by this point and chipping in her own suggestions.

Leese leaned closer. 'Are you joining us, Mr Clifton? You mentioned your family has mining interests. We need money. Now Britain is seeing the light at last, the people need a push. The people deserve better than Mosley and the British *Jewnion* of Fascists.'

If not mad, Leese was certainly confident. Insulting Mosley in the wrong company was a sure way of being beaten black and blue in an alley. I could see Sissy curling up a knuckle in readiness.

'There's no future for kosher fascists,' Leese added.

'Shall you tell him, or shall I?' I asked Sissy casually.

'You will do it with so much more tact,' she said, finally raising her eyes.

'So, Leese, the Imperial Fascist League is hereby dissolved,' I stated.

'What?'

'Dissolved, banned, closed down.'

'Clifton...Clifton, I should have known that name! You're that bloody assassin. You're spies for Mosley—I should have guessed.'

'Department Z,' I said, taking out my brass badge. 'Arnold Spencer Leese, you are under arrest for offences under the Public Order Act, 1936, as amended.'

He stood straight up. 'This is outrageous.'

'I suggest you come quietly. Or my men outside will ensure you come extremely quietly.'

'I've got important friends, you know.'

'We'll be speaking to them too. My agents are visiting your house as we speak and will be taking your papers, your letters, in fact, anything which shows you are conspiring to undermine the state.'

He curled his chin, lips quivering. 'What's Britain coming to?'

'If you don't like it, I hear Madagascar is nice.'

Chapter Five

A flurry of parties followed the coronation of King Edward VIII, offering a busy social calendar despite the rain that marred many events. Many aspired to greet the new king himself but he refused all invitations, retreating to Fort Belvedere in a gloomy mood after taking the throne without a queen at his side. Von Ribbentrop, the German ambassador, was particularly disappointed, as he'd cultivated the king's former mistress as a route to win Edward's ear.

The Nazi swastika flag flew over the German Embassy, and two guards in SS uniform and shiny black helmets flanked the door. I made a point of attending every gathering staged by the Anglo-German Fellowship; indeed the prospect of mingling at high-class parties had been part of my original motivation for signing up to the spy game in the first place.

I made a beeline for Bruno Vogel, supposedly the cultural attaché but who I was certain was an agent of the *Abwehr*, German military intelligence. We enjoyed what passed for a friendship in our world and met for lunch or dinner most months.

'Do you know *him*?' Bruno twitched his little finger that was holding a wineglass stem.

I certainly did, but made no comment.

'Marcus Calhoun,' Bruno continued. 'He's the new head of your Security Service. His predecessor had to retire, of course, after last year's failures. But everyone was surprised when Commodore Calhoun took the job.'

My former handler had received an honorary promotion to commodore when appointed to head MI5 and I'd seen much less of him since. He'd risen a long way, quickly, and I was wary of the company he was now keeping. We kept our relationship secret as it would not be beneficial to either his career or my health, but Bruno seemed intent on nudging us together. Perhaps he was toying with me.

'I could introduce you.'

Even though I no longer strictly reported to Calhoun, we met from time to time in obscure cafes or quiet parks. I kept him fully informed of the machinations within the BU, and in return, he would throw crumbs of information to me rather less generously than he'd toss bread crusts to the ducks.

'I'll catch him later; I've just seen my wife, and I ought to say hello. Honestly, Bruno, you do insist on embarrassing me at these affairs.'

'Oh, that's what these parties are for my friend, bringing together the unlikely. Building bridges, forging new alliances.'

'I'll go and do some forging.' I nodded to Bruno and made my way across the room.

Leonora was wearing a lilac satin gown with short, gathered sleeves. I recognised the string of pearls she was wearing because I was the one who bought them.

She turned in mock surprise at my approach. 'Hugh, fancy seeing you here.'

'You're looking well, Leo.'

'And you, Blackshirt hero, the man who saved the king. That scar healed nicely.'

It hadn't. A white line above my eyebrow was a permanent souvenir of the dark December night when I'd dodged bullets and flying glass.

'You don't have your friend with you tonight?' she observed.

'No, she's indisposed.'

'How is she, honestly?' Leo sounded positively concerned. 'She was terribly badly hurt, was she not?'

'She was, but she's bouncing back.'

In truth, Sissy possessed too much bounce to risk taking her to the party, knowing that Arnold Alexander Thorne was likely on the invitation list. Not only was he chairman of the Young Britons' Club committee, but also one of the bright young men who'd emerged as the winners after the abdication debacle. One who I suspected orchestrated the whole thing.

'Are you here with AA?' I asked.

'Indeed I am. And you'll be pleased to know that you were correct in your assertion that his motivation for inviting me to such events is mostly to annoy you. I'm only brought along when he wants to parade me. He's younger than me, for goodness sake.'

'I'm younger than you.'

'I know, and it makes me seem a sad and desperate old hag. A man in his position needs a wife, a young, pretty one.' She paused. 'One who can have babies.'

'Leo.' I touched her forearm.

'I know; I've had my bite at the cherry I should be happy even to be invited along to drink Nazi champagne. It's his, you know, Von Ribbentrop's, his family are wine merchants. Honesty, the world is run by upstarts.'

'Like me.'

'Look, I'm sorry. I've been the most useless of your agents.'

At Christmas, I'd alerted her to the reality of Thorne's power games.

'I've tried, honestly, but AA never shares secrets. He travels abroad; he mixes with ambassadors. And look, he's cultivating another friend of yours.'

Across the room, I saw the figure of A A Thorne, Germanic in look with a blond Hitler parting. He was talking to the Philby's, Kim and Litzi. Sissy and I had enjoyed drinks and dinner with the couple a few times.

'AA's been to Spain, imagine that, with all that's happening over there.' She rolled her eyes. 'It sounds terrible.'

'Philby's been to Spain too, but then he is a reporter.'

'I don't know how anyone can go out there and just watch.'

The very fact of Kim Philby's conversation with AA made me uneasy.

'Philby's an enthusiastic chap, Sissy gets on well with his wife.'

'Sissy. Now she could give you a family.'

'Oh, stop it, Leo. Her opinion of babies is the same as yours.'

'But she has the option. She has the option, Hugh. And given I'm firmly on the shelf, I could divorce you now…if that would help you make things decent. I love gossip about scandals, but not when it involves me.'

I nodded. 'I'll have the lawyers talk money.'

She took a deep sigh, then drained her glass. This was a sad, deflated Leo. Not one I was familiar with.

'I'm going to get another one of these with the aim of ending the evening squiffy. Please don't cause a scene with AA; he only wants to taunt you.'

The man looked my way and gave one of those smiles that's not really a smile. So long as he only wanted to taunt me, I could live with that.

Chapter Six

I followed Marcus Calhoun from the Embassy into Belgravia Square in the cool of the late evening. He'd given me the nod and walked straight past waiting taxis and official cars, crossing the road into the green of the square.

'Bruno Vogel wanted us to get acquainted,' I said.

'The crafty dog sees straight through you, Clifton. Be careful with him.'

'He's had a chance to see me dead before now.'

'If it suited his masters, you would be. Was that your wife on the arm of A A Thorne?'

'Yes, he has a habit of escorting Leo to public events—more to annoy me than flatter her.'

'She looks like a fine woman; it was a shame what happened.'

'We're getting divorced.'

'Oh,' he said. Then added, 'I'm sorry. Did she tell you the news about Thorne? Though if your wife is merely window dressing she won't know. It won't become public knowledge, but Mosley has appointed Thorne as the new C, the head of the Secret Intelligence Service.'

I felt a thump in my chest. I'd suspected that was where the career of AA had been heading, but this was ominous news. This was the prize won through all his maneuvering.

'I saw him talking to a friend of yours, Kim Philby. He and I had a little chat later. He spoke well of you, dropped your name. In his guise as a reporter, and your guise as a top fascist, of course.'

'Top fascist.' I groaned inwardly. 'And how is Philby linked with AA?'

'We can never make assumptions about who is working for who, but Philby is making a name as a foreign correspondent. He travels here, travels there. He'd be a fine catch for SIS.'

'Someone else to watch,' I said, disappointed.

We turned the corner to walk the north side of the square. Even if May's weather was proving dull, it was a pleasant evening, and birds serenaded the sunset.

'Any news about what the socialists are up to?' Calhoun asked.

'The ones who dare put their heads above the parapet are organising strikes and demonstrations against Mosley,' I said. 'But the covert operatives are being very quiet, which is worrying.'

'Agreed,' said Calhoun. 'The illegals, the NKVD agents, have gone to ground. One's been recalled to Moscow, most likely shot in recognition of his service. Stalin is purging the Trotskyites.'

'Perhaps the others are keeping their heads down so they're not the next ones to be purged.'

'No, the Russians are up to something.'

I'd cultivated a very good source among the communists, who had also been one of Calhoun's sources until her murder had been arranged. She was still very much alive as far as I hoped, but she'd also dipped out of sight in the past months.

'If it helps, we've picked up a few whispers about a certain address in Holland Road.' I started to share details, but Calhoun stopped me.

'Kindly forget about that house,' he said. 'And whoever lives there, visits it, or watches it. M Section will have a busy summer.'

So it was either the base for an MI5 operation, or a communist safe house that was no longer as safe as they thought it was.

'Very well, I'll step away from communists to keep your field clear,' I said.

'But I'm sure you'll be able to pick up a lot of information during Operation Dragon North we'd find mutually useful.'

'Don't get your hopes up, because my section won't be involved; Parker's taking his gorillas up there. And I've different priorities at the moment.'

'*You* have different priorities?'

'The spy game has always been more of a hobby to me, but I need to keep my people away from sliding down the same path as Parker. So to fill the time, we're mopping up the nastier right-wing groups.'

'I've read the headlines, and it sounds more like a crusade than a hobby.'

'So any information you can offer would be appreciated, say about the Nordic League. Joyce suggested I leave them alone, which is precisely what I'm not going to do. During our raid on the White Knights, we found papers which show they share a London office.'

'Lamb's Conduit Street,' Calhoun said immediately. 'Above the pub. I'd also be interested to know what they're up to. Nordic suggests Germany and we must always keep one eye on the Germans no matter what our new leader says and however splendid their parties are.'

'I've tried to get one of my men on the inside, but they're a secretive bunch. League members we've identified are mostly toffs, so it's not for the likes of us.'

Calhoun smiled. 'All the money in the world can't buy a pedigree. If you pay the League a visit, do it at night, by the back door. Nobody in their right mind will miss Arnold Leese, but your raid on the White Knights has stirred people up.'

'At the Young Britain Club, by any chance?'

I knew Calhoun had been invited to join.

'I'm my own man, Clifton. I don't sell my country over brandy and cigars.'

'But by now, you know the way the Britons work.'

'And they know how you work. Thorne and his friends are aware that if they put a foot wrong, you'll kick down their door with twenty men and half a dozen amazons. The Security Service operates quietly and patiently, but Department Z rushes in with machine guns.'

'So no matter how many brandies and cigars they ply you with, and even if they promote you to admiral, promise you'll never expose my charade, Calhoun. One day, when Sissy comes round to the idea, we're going to up sticks and leave the country.'

'And go where? Mosley is cultivating Irish Catholics, America has its Bund, France has Francisme. There are fascists everywhere; run and they'll find you.'

'Promise you won't expose me,' I insisted. 'And for good measure, I have well-funded plans which will swing into motion in the event I should meet a suspicious death.'

'For the record, you're not a man I ever want to get on the wrong side of,' Calhoun said. 'I sometimes fear I've created a monster.'

Chapter Seven

The monster and his brood raided the Nordic League the following night. Lamb's Conduit Street is a narrow thoroughfare in Bloomsbury, only a short stroll from the British Museum, and, as it happens, not far from my apartment. One of my favourite small bookshops was located there, together with a café where I'd met Calhoun once or twice and a pleasantly quiet pub. The rooms above the pub were now the Nordic lair.

Any yards or gardens at the centre of the city block were wholly enclosed by buildings, making it unlikely the Nordic League office even had a back door. If it did, it was not freely accessible, so our only option was to enter by the front. I brought a small team along for the actual raid, including the ever-reliable Danny Hills plus the somewhat less reliable Eleanor Fitzherbert. Even in Mosley's Britain, burglary of private property was still frowned upon, and Eleanor's top shelf *my father knows people* accent might just be enough to brush off inquisitive policemen. She'd come into the Party as a young, bored, aristocrat tugged along by her friend Julia, who'd been the one with a firmer grip on doctrine. The one who had been shot in the back then blown apart by a grenade.

A safecracker and burglar named Rinker was the fourth member of our incursion. We retained the slight, starved-looking man on the payroll for this very purpose and to deter him from being arrested by pursuing his normal trade. As a usual precaution against surprises, my driver Walsh and three others loitered nearby in a bread van.

The presence of the Nordic League was marked by a tiny brass plate beside a separate, black-painted door. At just past midnight, we might conceivably have been walking home from a party or heading down to Theobalds Road seeking a cab. Eleanor and I halted and feigned flirting, while Rinker got to work, and Hills stood guard. We were inside in moments.

I wouldn't say burglary had become routine, but I was getting used to it.

'Nazis,' Hills said as he cast his torch around a meeting room draped with swastikas.

If he'd been German, the square-jawed and well-built Hills would have been an easy recruit for the Nazis. He had no ideology, but the former police sergeant had been dismissed from the force in disgrace and desperately needed a path back to self-respect. He'd be in the Gestapo now, following Himmler's lead, rather than in Department Z following mine.

The League was keen not to advertise its activities to the public so employed heavy drapes. We could afford to snap on the electric lights.

'More Nazis,' Rinker echoed, running a gloved finger over a small bronze statue of Hitler.

'Nazis are bad, huh?' Eleanor said.

'Foreign power,' I said, moving into a side office.

'But the Germans are our friends.'

'Today they are. But back in the last war, the Russians were our allies and see where we are now.'

I unlocked a filing cabinet with my lock pick set, and Eleanor set to work searching it, while I opened another.

'Militant Christian Patriots?' she asked, holding up a file.

'Never heard of them.'

'Liberty Restoration League?'

'Make notes. Names, addresses. Who is writing to who.'

The United Empire Fascist League and the National Socialist Worker's Party were also in regular touch; more names for my blackboard and more fodder for the files.

'Here's the White Knights.' Hills was into another stack of drawers. 'Member lists and addresses boss.'

I was tempted to take every piece of paper, but that would show my hand

and the men running the League would have little difficulty in working out who had been busy in their office. Over the past months, I'd begun to relax, comforted that communist agents had better things to do than kidnap, torture, and kill me, and I'd prefer not to build up new enemies on the right.

A naval man named Commander Cole was signing documents as 'Chancellor' of the Nordic League as if willing himself into Hitler's shoes. I spotted the name of a leading financier who was most likely filling their coffers.

'Make notes, as quickly as you can.'

I suddenly wished there were more of us; a couple of Lucy's quick-thinking women from the office would be a boon here.

'We'll risk two hours, then get out before the milkmen start on their rounds.'

I flicked through letters from the German Embassy signed by the Nazi ambassador von Ribbentrop. Baron Fritz von Nidder seemed to represent Ausland, a society for expatriate Germans living in Britain which looked to be little more than the Nazi party abroad. The Anglo-German Fellowship was also in correspondence, but they worried me less as Bruno had invited me into that organisation. Kim Philby had joined at the same time as me, and I'd seen AA Thorne at their meetings, so that put SIS on the inside too.

I scribbled as fast as I could, as well as I could. My handwriting was irregular at the best of times, so I hoped I could read all this in the morning.

Admiral Domville's name kept coming up in relation to an organisation called The Link. He'd been the head of Naval Intelligence until, according to rumour, he'd been forced out for being too pro-German. The Nordic League's membership included General Fuller, now Commissioner for War and Munitions, and a couple of other senior names in the British Union. Why, I asked myself, why bother? So many men frittering their energies on these Heinz 57 varieties of fascists.

Hills was copying facts down very slowly, but Eleanor, by contrast, worked furiously as if cramming for her finals. The office contained no pamphlets, no posters, and no manifesto. The Nordic League held no public meetings, and every activity took place behind closed doors. A small library of reference books was of predictable nature, including a signed edition of

Mein Kampf in German and a hand-bound copy of the fraudulent antisemitic libel known as the *Protocols of the Elders of Zion.*

'Have you seen any accounts, ledgers? It would be good to know where their money is coming from.'

'Berlin, Berlin,' Eleanor muttered.

'Honestly, you've found proof?'

'No, just teasing. The Nazis are the bad boys, and we are going to root them out.'

'Eleanor, don't be sarcastic, this is serious.'

'German.' She held up one sheet of paper. 'Florian Kahn, Hamburg.'

I almost snatched it out of her hand.

'Banker?'

'Shipping agent. A friend of both Sissy's mother and Julian's father.'

She waited for me to expound on what I knew. 'And? You know more about him.'

'We've a thin file on him.' After a moment, I thought she should know the truth. 'He may have channeled money from the Nazi party to our party in the early days.'

'The Party has never taken any money from the Nazis.'

'No, of course it hasn't.'

'Hmm. You'll get into hot water if ever you put that allegation into the files.'

'That's why it's not in the files.'

'I bet you know a lot of things that never make it into the files.' She began searching the drawer again, then gave me the most innocent of smiles. 'But I suppose we all do.'

Rinker occupied himself by walking round the rooms with one hand in his pocket, sizing up trinkets that, in another life, he would have dropped into his swag bag.

'Rinker,' I warned. 'Don't take any souvenirs.'

He froze, then darted to a window. 'Squire! Lights off!'

Hills killed the lights, and I followed Rinker to the window. He shifted a curtain open by just a crack. In the narrow street below stood two groups of men. Three of mine faced five others.

'Game's up,' Rinker said. 'Them's not coppers, though.'

Eleanor pushed a cabinet drawer closed and folded her notepad.

'No,' I said. 'But if we've been rumbled, we may as well grab everything and hang as wolves instead of sheep. Be quick about it.'

Hills switched his torch back on. In a few minutes we had bundled as many files as we could into the satchels we carried. From the corner of my I eye I noticed that bust of Hitler had also vanished.

We bustled down the stairs, all pretence at secrecy gone, with me leading from the front. From outside came shouts and threats. As I pulled open the door, one of my men was shoving away one of the strangers. Our antagonists wore kepi-like hats, grey in the low light. Two carried iron bars.

My team of burglars burst into the narrow street.

'Go home!' I commanded, striding towards the group.

One balled his fist. 'We're going to do you.'

I'd grown tired of street brawls with bricks and cudgels. I drew my Walther. Eleanor needed no more excuse and drew hers while Hills pulled out a Webley revolver.

'You want to play at being Nazis?' I challenged. 'Dressing up as if you're stormtroopers, kicking Jews and smashing windows—'

'Jew-lovers,' one spat.

At that moment, I trembled with the power of what I'd become. Of what I could become.

'You've no idea what it takes to be a true fascist. Go home, little boys.'

They didn't see my doubts, only the myth and the three gun muzzles. All five grey-shirted men began to edge away, one step at a time.

One pointed at me. 'We know who you are.'

'Then you should go home,' I said. 'Now.'

Chapter Eight

They knew who I was, but for all my dark reputation, I'd never, in fact, killed anyone. As in a good detective novel, the killers in our midst were the least likely suspects. Men had died the first time boy-faced accountant Julian Thring had used a tommy gun in anger, but he was still regarded as a quiet desk-commander totally in my shadow. Julian had been appointed to one of the working parties of the Commerce Commission, possibly due to the influence of his father, or possibly through Commission members wanting to keep in the good books of Department Z. At the start of June, he was ordered away on some secret mission, which was a shame as the paperwork was piling up.

Lucy Parmentier had been promoted to the rank of Woman Unit Leader, a typically clumsy British Union title. She ran the Z3 office at Black House and the parallel one at the bakery where a group of married women known affectionately as the Chelsea Wives were still going through the papers we had lifted from the Nordic League and White Knights. Information flowed in from the towns where Z3 maintained agents, and my chalkboard soon displayed a daunting list of organisations that could be placed to the right of Churchill's King's Party.

- Air League of the British Empire
- Anglo German Fellowship
- Ausland (the Nazi Party abroad)
- British Array
- British Fascisti

- English Mistery
- Imperial Fascist League
- League of Loyalists
- Liberty Restoration League
- The Link
- Militant Christian Patriots
- National Socialist League
- National Socialist Workers Party
- National League of Airmen
- Nordic League
- Other Club
- United British Party
- United Empire Fascist Party
- Young Briton's Club
- White Knights of Britain

A few more had already been crossed off as defunct, and I could now safely draw a line through the two we had closed down. Nothing had been heard of the United British Party for a while now, and if also dead, it would not be missed.

The rump of the original British Fascisti were patriotic right-wingers— 'reactionaries, not revolutionaries' in the words of Mosley when they refused to unite with him—but their leader Rotha Lintorn-Orman had drunk herself to death, so was no longer a problem. The west country fascist Gwladys Knight had been found dead in suspicious circumstances in the autumn, made more suspicious by the fact her husband ran M Section of MI5. Other former Fascisti were either joining the BU or drifting elsewhere. The remainder of the list promised an awful lot of investigating to come.

Agents of Room Z across the country had by now penetrated most of the groups. Sissy's mother joined out-of-touch feudalists English Mistery without even knowing she was an agent. Hills joined the National Socialist League, while Sissy pulled Lydia Vectis-Hunt away from Lucy's Wives and tasked her to join the League of Loyalists. Julian, of course, already trod a delicate path as a member of the Young Britain Club.

I was called down to Valentine's office the week after the Nordic League raid, expecting to hear some reaction. Men who wielded influence, or who thought they wielded influence, would be alarmed by our poking around in affairs they thought secret and would be yanking every string in their grasp. I expected to be ordered either to desist harassing Nordic League and their ilk or to use the information we'd seized to carry out arrests. The Public Order Act was not there to safeguard public order, but to impose order on the public.

Valentine made no mention of the raid at all.

'Has Thring told you about his orders?'

'Only that he has a secret mission.'

'And he keeps secrets even from you?'

'We are the *confidential* investigations section.'

Valentine nodded. 'He's heading to Sark in the British Channel Islands to set up a fascist radio station at the Leader's express request. It has been suggested you accompany him for security.'

'Is there a threat, a risk?'

'There's always risk with whatever we do, the Party has enemies everywhere.' His wide forehead glinted as he tipped back his head. 'But no, Sark is a tiny place in the middle of the Channel, closer to France than England. It's sunny, I hear, and there's nothing but cows, fishermen, and a few tourist hotels. The local people even have their own language.'

'Do we need a translator?'

'No, they speak English. Or French. What makes it ideal for this project is that the island has a curious, almost feudal government. It's not answerable to Westminster or any other national government for that matter. Thring is taking his new wife as cover, pretending it's a honeymoon.'

For a moment, I felt regret at being pulled away from the undercover operations in train against the far right, but the excursion would be a chance to escape London and the realities of fascist rule for a week or so.

'Rather than play gooseberry on Julian's honeymoon, I could ask Sissy along too. It would look more natural, and if you want a bodyguard, she's a crack shot.'

And we could also make a holiday of it.

'A good idea.'

Valentine added that once finished with our business in Sark we should take a boat to nearby Alderney, which was being considered for the site of an internment camp for undesirables.

'Parker is doing so well our prisons are running out of space. We'll need to set up detention camps, especially after Dragon North. Islands are ideal. The Isle of Man is a favourite, but Alderney offers possibilities. Scottish islands are still too troublesome.'

I'm sure the locals would be less than thrilled at the prospect, and I shuddered to think who might be sent to an island prison. Good reasons must be found not to recommend the idea. I then thought of Eleanor—lonely and directionless, looking for affection in the arms of a stormtrooper commander.

'I'm going to take Eleanor Fitzherbert too. She's a fluent French speaker.'

'Very well, but don't over-man it. Or over-woman it. This is a secret mission, *confidential*.'

Chapter Nine

The Radio Plan had been the brainchild of a failed businessman named Allen, who was a close crony of the Leader. We already held a file on him, and I had doubts about his *bona fides*, his loyalty, and the company he kept. But he claimed money was to be made in offshore radio, and Mosley was ever in need of money. A new fascist radio station would carry advertising to raise revenue and play popular music to attract audiences.

Although the BBC was fast turning into the mouthpiece of Mosley's party, it had since inception been the standard bearer of Britishness throughout the world, so the changes in its output were more nuanced than drastic. As the BBC was funded by the taxpayer, it did not carry advertising, but Air Time radio would belong to Mosley, Allen, and a few associates. Tweaks would be needed to the Post Office Act, but the King's Party government had become adept at tweaking legislation since it cemented its hold on power in January's snap general election. It still maintained the fiction of being the 'King's Party' despite the gradual drift of Conservatives who stood on the king's ticket into the Mosley camp.

Sark lay just off the Cotentin peninsula of France. A radio station placed there would be immune to the vicissitudes of British politics and be very difficult for Mosley's left-wing enemies to shut down by force. A son of the Dame of Sark was said to be an enthusiastic supporter of the BU and had more than one finger in this particular pie.

Julian invited his new wife, Melissa, in lieu of a honeymoon they hadn't yet enjoyed, and I invited Sissy. Eleanor was now the one playing gooseberry, but I took her along not only due to her aptitude for French but because I wanted to keep her firmly in hand. More than once since Christmas, Sissy and I had to extract her drunk and weeping from a bar and chaperone her back to her flat. I'd even manhandled one cad who was attempting to take advantage of her distress. Our loyalty to Eleanor was cementing her loyalty to us.

I was not fond of boats, so took the new Agatha Christie novel *Death on the Nile* as a distraction. The mail packet slicing through waves in the English Channel did not have the majesty of a Nile steamer, but the trip from Southampton to Guernsey was swift enough for us to arrive in time to dine at the Royal Hotel with the local BU representative that night. Guernsey was a sunny holiday island, self-governing and conservative with a small c. Residents had little enthusiasm to join the stampede into fascism, our host complained.

The sun rose from behind Sark the following morning, and I faced the nine-mile journey across to the smaller island in a motor launch without joy. Brown cliffs rose slab-like before us, rising and falling as the boat bobbed through the swell. My joy diminished further when it transpired the harbour was round on the French-facing coast of the island, adding fifteen more minutes to count off one by one as we hit patches of rough water and spray showered over our heads. Seagulls mocked my white expression, and Sissy gripped my hand in concern. I was also coughing rather more than usual and regretted tucking into the Royal Hotel's full English breakfast.

Blonde, red-cheeked, flushed with the joy of a new bride, Melissa relished the waves and pointed to one seabird after another. To me, they were just gulls, but no, Melissa knew the names of each species. I couldn't appreciate it at that moment, but she held interests beyond crushing 'inferior' races and purifying the English bloodline.

This Lilliputian radio station better be worth it, I thought more than once. Still, a week free from the tensions of Black House alone would compensate for the misery. Plus, the venture would most likely flop and simply waste Mosley's money and the Party's energy. Stacking an organisation with failures, outcasts, and has-beens came with drawbacks.

Inching closer through the waves, we were at last embraced by the calm of a tiny harbour slotted between cliffs. Gratefully, I staggered onto land, taking the rough hand of a crumple-faced local man. He spoke a few pleasantries in a soft-vowelled accent a little like that of the West Country, a little like a colonial. A horse and cart carried our luggage up a steep dirt track through a cleft in the hillside, and another waited to take the four fascists and me.

I said I'd join the others later, then returned to the harbour, craving peace after all that motion. Viewed now from solid land, the sea was a beautiful deep blue, and ten miles or so across a restless strait the French coast basked under summer sunshine. Ice cream citadels of clouds towering from the horizon could have been painted in oils by one of the Great Masters. It was not a bad place to bring a bride for a honeymoon. Or for smuggling…

No firm ideas had come to me for my third Harry Bretton detective novel since the success of *Bretton's Second Case* and the belated popularity of *Blackshirt Detective* which had followed on its back. I glanced round at the harbour, suddenly awake to its potential. Harry Bretton could investigate smuggling from France to Sark. But smuggling what?

My musing came to an end as I reflected that *Blackshirt Detective* had involved diamond smuggling from Amsterdam. Another smuggling storyline was out of the question.

'Bonjhur musyeur,' a voice from behind me broke into my thoughts.

It was the man who helped me off the boat as If I'd been an invalid.

'You'd be thinking.'

'Yes, I was thinking this would be a good place to land er, spies. In a novel I'm writing.'

'Spies in Sark? There's a title for your book right there, musyeur.'

Harry Bretton and the Spies in Sark. It was a terrible title; it should sell well.

* * *

Our group was welcomed to Stocks Hotel, which had the appearance of a small manor house in grey granite facing a tightly mown lawn. We lunched at the home of the *Seigneur*, which was reached by a ten-minute stroll across the flat top of the island on one of the dusty sunken tracks serving as roads. The Seigneurie was said to have been built over a monastery dating back to the Dark Ages. It hid behind an arched granite gateway and was graced by architectural additions of different ages, including a tower. When a man tired of London, he could find peace in a haven such as this.

Sybill Hathaway, Dame of Sark, had been *Seigneur* of the island since the death of her first husband. Her son had already explained the Radio Plan in detail to her but explained it again over lunch. The bespectacled Dame didn't appear to share great enthusiasm for the fascist cause—this would be purely a business deal. It was chiefly a question of money; how the profits would be split and how much the radio station would pay for renting Sark land and for a cottage to house the technicians.

A company called Air Time would be a party to the contract, and the term would be for thirty years, with twenty-five percent of revenues destined for Sark. A thousand pounds in advance was mentioned for the Dames' son. Funding would come from the New Museum Investment Trust, and I smiled as I glanced over the papers Julian was handing round. My original mission had been to discover where the fascist's money was hidden out of sight of the Security Services, and rather too late now, I had the name of an account at Westminster Bank, Trafalgar Square branch.

Much of the information I'd been seeking these past two years was about money—where it came from and what it was used for. I thought again about that name we'd found in the National Socialist League office and others who could be bankers or financiers. Rich men backing one political horse or another, and some even making two-way bets.

Commerce bored me, but Melissa bored me more. The Dame twitched as Julian's wife expounded Mosley's vision for Britain and the Empire and how glorious it would all be. And was there a Jewish problem in Sark? Of course, there wasn't, and the Dame dismissed the idea. The Jewish population amounted to one chambermaid over from Austria, and she wouldn't be overthrowing anything other than bedsheets.

The five of us walked a loop around the northern part of the dumbbell-shaped island after lunch, occupying us for an hour or so. Melissa switched off her fascist voice once more and became entranced by the ponies in the fields and the fine views. Julian helped her spot birds, which one or the other of them managed to name in turn. Birds looked to be their shared interest, though she'd already mentioned her plans to have lots of children. I smiled, hopeful Julian would be happy in the choice his family had foisted upon him.

Sissy said she was tired and returned with the others to the hotel while I explored more. I spotted a pub but not much by way of a beach; the cliffs fell sheer into the English Channel on all sides. I wasn't sure what holidaymakers visiting Sark did after their first two hours, but to be sure, it was restful. Perhaps visitors simply took the air, sketched, or composed detective novels.

We ate locally caught fish for dinner, a meal marred by Melissa returning to her pet themes, cranking up to full volume after a couple of glasses of wine. 'We have to warn the world about the Jewish menace. I don't see why your radio won't transmit propaganda.'

'No propaganda!' Julian thumped the table, grinning broadly at his triumph in sealing the deal. 'Popular music, sport for the men, fashion tips for the ladies.'

'I know a few men who could use fashion tips,' Sissy said, touching my shin lightly with her toe.

'And women who follow sport,' Eleanor added.

Julian pressed on. 'And we'll have comedians; people like comedians.'

'But they can't make jokes about Hitler,' Melissa said. 'That's important. They can't make fun of the Führer.'

'Of course not, of course not, dear,' Julian said. 'We'll write that into the contracts.'

He was serious, too. Julian never deployed sarcasm or irony—what you heard was what he meant.

'The Leader's speech at the Criterion was right on the nail,' Melissa said. 'At last, he's seeing the light about the Jewish threat.'

'But I've heard him called a kosher fascist,' Sissy said.

'Not anymore.'

I suspected the Leader had shaped his antisemitic speech to please Hitler, given he was falling out of favour with Mussolini, but Melissa was never particularly interested in subtlety.

'Why isn't Department Z doing more about the Jews?' she asked.

'Perhaps we are,' I said, raising my eyebrow.

'I've not seen it.'

'Ah, but you won't see it,' Sissy teased. 'We work undercover, by night, silently.'

'Silently,' Eleanor echoed, before draining the last of her wine.

'You weren't silent at that, what, Norwegian Link office.'

'Nordic League,' Eleanor corrected.

She was less amusing company than she used to be, all the frivolity of the red-headed ex-debutante had gone. At best, Eleanor smiled rather than collapsed in fits of giggles, and each top-up of wine only made her quieter. I wondered if she regretted joining the Party. Was any cause worth the death of a friend, let alone fascism?

'Well, everyone knows about your burglary,' Melissa said after a pause. 'What on earth were you thinking, Hugh?'

One of those annoying coughs came unbidden and provided the perfect prompt for me to escape. 'Please excuse me, ladies. It's time I took some air.'

I wanted to walk on my own and left the table without further apology. I'd go back to the pub we'd passed at the top of the hill that climbed from the harbour. I'd order a pint of whatever beer they served and one for the closest Sark fisherman, and we'd talk the price of bass or whatever subject he wished that did not involve global domination.

A gulp of clear evening air made me cough again. That bullet wound to my right lung would be with me forever, although my breathing was generally improving, so perhaps some repair work was going on deep inside my chest. As the sun set beyond Guernsey, it cast a red glow back on the east coast of France. A stillness came to the air, and seabirds streamed back to find their roosts. For a moment, I felt at peace. I could stay here for a month, read, walk, work on my novel by day, snuggle up to Sissy at night, and to hell with Department Z, MI5, and the lot of them.

Once within the Bel Air Inn, I spotted my friendly helper from the harbour propping up the bar, talking in the oddest language I'd heard since returning from India. At first, it sounded like French, then more like a foreigner speaking French badly.

'Bonjhur, musyeur.' The Sarkee greeted me again, then switched to the king's English for my benefit as he turned to the barman. 'This man writes books, him.'

Posing as a novelist had begun as a useful cover story when I first moved to London, but I truly enjoyed the release of writing. Made-up danger and mystery provided the perfect foil for real-life equivalents.

'A pint for my friend,' I said.

'Cidre, mersi.'

'And one for me.'

The man nodded and moved close, conspiratorially. 'Funny though. You know them spies of you'rn? Got me thinking.'

I tried not to frown. It's the novelist's curse that people are constantly explaining their own plots for books which would sell by the thousand if they were only given time to write them. Worse, they'd allow me to do the work of writing the book, and we'd split the fortune it made. I braced myself for the inevitable.

'My spies?'

'I reckon I've spotted them,' the Sarkee whispered.

I paused in the act of reaching into my pocket for change. 'Where?'

'Harbour, four of 'em. Couple of hours after I sees you.'

'Come outside.'

'Your pardon?'

'Please.' We went out into the evening and stood on the dirt road. 'What spies?'

'It were late afternoon, and I'd finished mending my pot. Three men and a young madame, in a boat, sneaking into the harbour. Come over straight from France by the way they come. Wouldn't take a cart, only a few bags between them.'

'Where are they now?'

'They took a cart in the end because they didn't know the way to the Dixcart Hotel.'

'Where is that? Precisely?'

He offered instructions and a quick way I could reach it, and in moments I knew it was barely a hundred yards beyond the hotel we were staying at. Just above the inn, I turned onto a narrow track just wide enough for a cart that ran parallel to the cliffs until it reached a path somewhat to the east of our own lodgings. Once within a wooded dip I found the Dixcart Hotel, a three-story building with wings, built in an assortment of stonework and doused in ivy.

Dusk lay deep in that hollow, and the spies were not the only ones who could sneak. I was unarmed and had been in holiday mood, but shook myself out of it. *There's always a risk*, Valentine had said. Perhaps it had been a throwaway line, but perhaps he knew more than he was prepared to share.

I crept cautiously into the hotel grounds from the back, peeking into one window, then the next. French windows fronted a long dining room, offering me a view of the few remaining diners. Two men sat at a table close to where I watched from behind a shrub. They didn't have the look of typical English holidaymakers. A woman came to join them, but they barely acknowledged her. No smiles, no effort to stand in respect for the lady. She sat down sullenly and glanced my way just as I ducked back.

I knew that face. She'd dyed her hair—or just as likely had grown out a blonde style from the year before and returned to natural brown. When she volunteered for Department Z she gave the name Ruth, but we had no idea of her real name on the day she betrayed us.

This was too much of a coincidence. The four of them—if there were, in fact, a total of four—must be up to no good. It took only a few minutes for me to move stealthily round the building and find the lane through the trees back to Stocks.

My people were by now gathered in the lounge, commencing a round of brandies. Sissy picked up my mood immediately.

'Hugh, what's wrong?'

'Ruth's here,' I announced.

Every one of them fell silent until Melissa piped up. 'Who's Ruth?'

'Drinks down, arm yourselves, and be outside the front door in five minutes. Melissa, you're staying here.'

'Oh, I always miss the fun.'

'Believe me, this isn't going to be fun. Ruth is here to kill us.'

Chapter Ten

We would be murdered, as would anyone else who got in the assassins' way, then the killers would escape in their boat. It was a simple plan, hatched by someone who knew exactly where we'd be. More precisely, where *I* would be. For once, I didn't have half a dozen heavily armed men held close by in reserve. I was not in my flat with its triple-locked doors and ex-army porter with revolver beneath his desk, or at Black House where agents would spring to my defence. I couldn't leap into my car and hare off at fifty miles per hour or even run for a train. There were no city alleyways to disappear into and no forests to hide in. I was to be the proverbial rat in a barrel.

All of us, bar Melissa, had packed a Walther PPK automatic as a natural precaution, but with only one magazine apiece. A tommy gun would have been handy right now.

Once the four of us were assembled in front of the hotel door, I quickly sketched the situation. It was very likely Ruth and her confederates were biding their time and would arm themselves once it was fully dark. Perhaps they would wait for the small hours, and just perhaps they would carry out a reconnaissance before striking later. I did not trust my life to 'perhaps.' Small bags, the man had said, so the foursome was not planning on a long stay. They would at least wait for full darkness before creeping over to our hotel to reprise the slaughter that had killed Julia and too many others.

'So,' Eleanor said. 'Do we just wait for them here?'

'No,' Julian said. 'If they attack the hotel, everyone will be in danger.'

'Meaning Melissa?' Eleanor said tartly.

Julian was stung in his weak spot. 'Yes Melissa, but everyone else too.'

'We could just leave,' Sissy said.

'How?' Eleanor snapped. 'Swim?'

'There must be a boat.'

'We'd have to find one first,' I said, as calmly as I could. 'There's not a single streetlight between here and the harbour, and we could easily be ambushed in pitch darkness.'

'It's just—' Sissy began.

'You know how these people operate; you've seen it,' I said.

'Yes, they use grenades.' She touched her left cheek. 'Which means we need to get away.'

'What happened to not giving up while one of them is breathing? The men with Ruth are probably the very same who hurt you last year and killed Julia. Terrorists cluster in tight cells.'

Sissy claimed to have shot one of the attackers, but for all we knew, he'd survived to kill another day.

'We have to kill the bastards,' Eleanor said. 'Don't give them a chance, like they didn't give Julia a chance.'

'No, Eleanor, whatever people say about Department Z, we're not killers; we don't decide who lives and who dies. Let's keep some respect for the rule of law. We'll take them by surprise, walk in on their dinner. Department Z, you're under arrest and all that malarkey.'

'We don't have jurisdiction,' Julian objected.

Eleanor raised her pistol. 'Yes, we do.'

'It's the only option,' I said. 'We all know the drill; we've done it before.'

Sissy continued to protest. 'Yes, we've done it before, but we don't have Hills or Walsh—'

'Let's get them before they get us.' Eleanor started down the gravel towards the lane.

Sissy let out a heavy sigh. 'Here we go again.'

Armed with pistols but handicapped by too much wine, we moved into the dark. Thank goodness the brandy was left untouched, and I hadn't downed a pint of cider before my fisherman had spilled the news. With luck, the opposition might have a similar handicap.

Sissy was right about the grenades, so defending our hotel was no option. My first impulse had been to pick a spot on the narrow lane leading from the Dixcart hotel to Stocks and conceal my team behind the hedges to await the enemy approach. But the assassins would be well armed by then and prepared for action, and if bullets started flashing about in the night, who lived and who died would be down to luck. Even if it reinforced my reputation as the world's least secret agent, I had no choice but to show our hand directly.

Anyone paying attention over the past year should know that when Department Z bursts into a room, we mean business. Julian and Eleanor would wait in the bushes at the end of the French windows, and I'd walk boldly into the hotel reception with Sissy checking nobody came up on me from behind. With luck, we'd have surprise on our side.

Reception was unmanned, but we could hear the clatter of crockery out of one doorway. I strode through into the dining area, now deserted apart from our quarry. Two of the men sat at the table, drinking coffee, not wine.

'Department Z, nobody move!' I commanded.

Ruth looked straight into my eyes, then straight into my muzzle. The man with his back to me turned his head slowly. He set down his coffee cup, freeing his right hand.

'Nobody move. *Restez vous monsiuers!* Sissy, there's one missing—watch that staircase.'

The woman we called Ruth was the first to speak. 'Mr Clifton, I—'

'Surprise, surprise. The biter bit, eh Ruth? If I can call you Ruth.'

She glanced at one of the men, then the other. I expected spite or bluster, but she was scared.

Julian was fiddling with the latch on the French windows from the outside. Nobody locked their doors in Sark.

'These Frenchmen,' Ruth stuttered, 'they forced me.'

Was she trying to distract me with a ruse? Now she noticed Julian coming into the room, followed by Eleanor. Too much was happening at once. I could only half-see the man beside Ruth. His hands vanished from sight.

'Stop!' I commanded.

Two simultaneous shots from Julian and Eleanor sent the man crashing onto the table face-first. Ruth shrieked and threw herself onto the floor. The man with his back to me froze, but Eleanor shot him in the leg anyway. He sprawled onto the floor, then his colleague slid off the table and tumbled on top of him in a shower of coffee cups, cutlery, and glassware. A cigarette packet fell last and bounced off his face.

A sudden silence held for a moment. Julian advanced to threaten the prostrate Frenchman, pinned under the body of his comrade. Two roses of blood expanded across the back of the fallen man's jacket.

'Get up, Ruth,' I commanded.

Slowly, she complied.

'You bitch,' Eleanor said.

The slight woman barely out of her teens rose to her feet, hands half-raised. I'd no proof who she really was or where her allegiance lay. A tear came to each of her cold blue eyes.

'Who are they? Your comrades. Quick!'

'Francisme,' she said. 'French fascists. I…I was tricked into helping them.'

'You fucking, fucking bitch,' Eleanor said, moving closer.

'Eleanor,' I raised a hand to calm her.

Ruth's throat exploded in a splash of red as Eleanor's gun fired. Her forehead crumpled at the second shot, and she was thrown back against the wall.

'For Christ's sake!'

'That was for Julia!'

'Eleanor, we needed her. We needed the information.'

'There's still him.' Eleanor waggled her gun towards the live Frenchman.

He'd need luck to still be alive by the end of the evening.

'How's your French?' I asked angrily.

'Pretty damned *bon*.'

A shot barked from the hallway. Then another. Yet again, I'd put Sissy in danger.

'Julian, watch this one. Eleanor, cover that window in case there's more coming round from outside.'

'Am I allowed to shoot them?'

'Don't play stupid.'

Sissy gave a shout, then fired. She pulled herself into cover with her back flat against the wall by the foot of the stairs. Someone fired back, and the bullet ploughed plaster low on the opposite wall.

'Sissy, are you all right?'

'There's one upstairs,' she said.

'It's not a maid or anything?'

'Maids don't bloody well shoot people.'

I noticed a bullet had taken a chunk out of the corner just above where Sissy crouched.

She shouted at someone across the hall to get back. '*That* was a maid,' she said.

From upstairs came yelling, followed by a scream. Sissy crouched to change her position and risked a glance round the corner. 'He's gone.'

'So, we'll wait a few minutes. We can't run around the hotel shooting at shadows. Innocent people will die.'

'What if he's fetching grenades?'

She was right.

'Bloody grenades,' I cursed, pushing past her and nipping up the stairs in the hope a round metal object didn't come bouncing down to meet me.

Another flight of stairs continued upwards, but my quarry had been on the first floor. I suppressed a cough as I edged around the corner with my head at skirting board level.

A flurry of pink nightdress and bare matronly legs rushed towards me. 'A man in my room,' shrieked the woman. 'There's a man in my room!'

I rolled back so she could pass. 'Which room?'

'At the end,' she waved her arm. 'Get out of my way!' She thundered down the stairs towards Sissy, shrieking and yelling warnings.

More room doors opened, and heads peered out.

'Police, get back into your rooms!' I shouted.

The doors slammed closed, and the best I could do was cover the one that remained hanging open. It drifted closed then slammed shut, perhaps because a window had been opened. It was time to be calm. If the fourth man had climbed out of a window or found a fire escape, a chase through the dark offered us nothing. He would be desperate to get away and I was not desperate to lose a friend pursuing him. We were all unhurt, and we had a prisoner. All we had to do was hold the dining room until daylight.

Chapter Eleven

Bona fide Hotel guests tumbled down the stairs, and Sissy ushered them into the Lounge rather than have any flee into the night and its dangers. The hotel manager stood bewildered in the central lobby, and I shouted to him across the hubbub.

'Which rooms are the French in? Three men and one woman.'

He had to fumble through the register to check as I waited impatiently at the turn of the stairs, hand sweating as I gripped my Walther. The Frenchmen had booked at short notice, so were given two rooms on the second floor.

'Pass key!' I ordered, and he threw the bundle up with such bad aim it was heading both wide and short, but Sissy side-stepped and deftly caught it.

'Does the island have a doctor?'

The manager nodded. 'I'll go and fetch him.'

'Quicker to telephone?'

But given an excuse to leave, the man was already on his way.

Satisfied all was quiet upstairs, I moved cautiously along to the pink nightdress woman's room at the end of the first-floor corridor. The final Frenchman had indeed escaped out of a window and was nowhere to be seen. I advanced up to the second floor with Sissy close behind me. The first room we unlocked had clearly been shared by Ruth. Her pathetic small pile of belongings lay barely unpacked—and the Frenchmen hadn't even trusted her with a gun. Perhaps she'd been the victim of manipulation after all. I found both French and British currency and a few documents.

In a second room, whose door was unlocked and hung open, I discovered a revolver and two submachine guns of foreign make still hidden under clothes in the bottom of a small suitcase, together with eight magazines bundled up in a French newspaper. In another case, six grenades were wrapped like apples, and a tobacco tin contained what looked like primers. A couple of hours later the team of assassins would have been fully armed.

Much as I wanted to take up this stockpile and arm myself to the teeth, it was a better strategy to leave all the incriminating evidence for the benefit of the police. Very quickly, I made notes from the identity documents and passports.

Back downstairs again, my team had moved away from the carnage to the less chaotic end of the dining room. Julian's face was even more pallid than usual, and his hands shook as he gripped the pistol that rested on his thigh. Odds-on, he'd fired the shot that killed the first Frenchman. He came into the Party as an accountant, not an assassin, and I'd coaxed him into Section Z3 in the hope of keeping him out of danger.

Guilty perhaps of what he'd become, Julian slapped his gun onto a table as soon as he saw me return and pushed it away from him. 'I need to get back to Melissa and make sure she's safe.'

'I understand,' I said. 'But you'll need to take that.'

He regarded the Walther with loathing.

'And be careful on the way; there's still one on the loose. If the coast is clear and you get back to Melissa, hide your gun somewhere and wait for the police. You were never here.'

'But—'

'You were never here; you're innocent. You were the intended target of communist assassins, but your security detail came across them by accident. Which happens to be true. Blame me for the killings.'

He nodded. 'This will sink the radio project.'

'That's the least of our problems. You'll need to hold the fort and bluff it out. Buy time for us to get away and find out what's going on.'

'Where will you go?'

'Into hiding. It's me they'll be after.'

'How can you be sure?'

My explanation had come quickly, perhaps too quickly.

'So it's all about you, is it?' Eleanor piped up. She was making an attempt to patch up the man she'd shot.

I glared at her, and she turned her attention back to affixing a makeshift bandage. Eleanor could have a point.

'First thing in the morning, Julian, phone Lucy and have her warn everyone—this could be a move against the whole of Z3. Get home as soon as you're allowed and take over running the section. I'll get messages through as and when.'

'So you're going to hide and leave the rest of us to it?'

'No, hiding is the wrong word. Going undercover, putting the secret back into secret police.'

'Jolly good.' He straightened his back.

'If the local police give you a hard time, call Inspector Renton at Scotland Yard, drop my name, and suggest he liaise with the islands over their investigation.'

'But Renton is Special Branch, and this lot aren't communists.'

'No, it's not us versus them anymore; Francisme are fascists.' I directed my heaviest words at Eleanor. 'These killers were sent by our own side.'

Julian set off back to his Melissa. Department Z was compromised by the killings, and we clearly had yet another traitor in our midst, so for the moment, at least, I had to rely on straightforward investigation by the authorities. I imagined the island police to be much more pleasant than Special Branch, but the coming few days would be uncomfortable for Julian and his bride. However, I was the one with the dark reputation, and he was the one with a father in the upper reaches of British Union, so sooner rather than later, he would walk free.

Eleanor had already burned through two of the Frenchman's cigarettes and threatened to stub the second one out on his face. She'd at least applied a tourniquet. The injured man chiefly employed curses and obscenities, and Eleanor's interrogation was curt and laden with threats.

'Has he told you anything?'

'Nothing useful,' she said. 'We need to set Parker on him.'

I didn't employ murderers or torturers, and her attitude made me boil with anger, but I put a lid on it. It wasn't the time for more melodrama.

The island doctor hurried into the room, exclaiming, 'Good Lord, what's all this?'

Eleanor switched from inquisitor to would-be nurse, explaining the injuries and what aid she'd given so far. Whatever the Frenchman called her next sounded very unpleasant, but it was the last we heard him say before he began to gasp, then lost consciousness.

'Will he live?' I asked.

'Go away,' said the doctor.

We left the doctor to his work, hoping the patient would survive to be interviewed by the police. Sark had no resident policemen, I quickly learned, so officers would need to travel across from Guernsey. I doubted even the Dame could brush away two deaths and a bullet-pocked, blood-spattered hotel, so the legal situation was perilous. Perhaps the Party held some sway in the islands, but the likelihood was the local judiciary would exercise a centuries-long tradition of doing things their own way at their own speed. British Union's policy of bribery, bullying, and influence-peddling may not work out here.

It would take time for the Guernsey force to be alerted and assemble enough men. Given the story of the hotel massacre would grow in the telling, perhaps they would even request support from the British garrison, which would buy us even more time to get away.

As soon as the sky started to brighten, Eleanor, Sissy, and I followed the track to the harbour, with a boy from Stocks Hotel helping with our hastily packed bags. The once-sleepy island was alive with people, full of alarms at invaders. I heard someone shouting for the militia to be raised, and I imagined being accosted by men armed with pitchforks and blunderbusses. As I passed the Bel Air, my fisherman spotted me and hurried over.

'Bonjour,' I said.

'Bonjhur—and you with the spies,' he said. 'Were they real?'

'Yes, sadly. Thanks for warning me; they were more dangerous than we thought.'

'They says there was shooting. Did you shoot them all?'

'Not all—has their boat gone?'

'Yes, afore dawn.'

'Do you have a boat of your own?'

'My brother does.'

'A hundred pounds to take us to England.'

His jaw dropped at the sum I was proposing.

'It has to be right now.'

'England is too far. Jersey?'

'How far is that?'

'Twenty mile.' He waved his arm to the south.

At least that would put us ahead of the police and away from any reinforcements the terrorists may send.

'Twenty pounds if you can only get us to Jersey.'

He nodded immediate agreement, then became wary. 'But you're not in trouble with the law, now?'

I took out my Department Z badge. 'We are the law.' He wasn't to know we had no powers out in the islands. 'I have to get back to headquarters in London and warn about those spies.'

'I'll fetch me brother.'

* * *

Those twenty miles felt like fifty, and the small Sark fishing boat pottered along at no more than ten knots. To make things worse, Jersey's harbour was on the south coast, meaning our scenic excursion was even more extended than I first expected. The white-painted wheelhouse was at the back of the little blue boat and the three of us found space among the crab pots and rope in the waist. Eleanor sat sullenly on a side-bench, sea spray drying on her Oxford glasses when she used them to examine her Walther. She put the weapon away, removed her spectacles, and slipped them into her coat pocket. I'd been lying down on the opposite bench, a trick to avoid seasickness my mother taught me as a child, but I slowly raised myself. France bobbed on the horizon behind her, in and out of view.

'What?' she said, meeting my gaze.

'You murdered Ruth.'

'Ruth murdered Julia.'

'An eye for an eye leaves us all blind.'

'Oh, stop it. You haven't complained about me shooting that Frenchman who was going to pull his gun on you. Or that other one.'

Unashamed, she was claiming two kills, three if the injured Frenchman did not survive.

'If you want to carve notches on that gun, I'm sure the boatman has a knife.'

'Stop playing the innocent. You've killed people.'

'He hasn't,' Sissy said wearily, her back against the wheelhouse.

'Everyone knows—'

'No,' Sissy said. 'Remember the communist they found dead in an East End warehouse? I killed him, not Hugh. I shot him three times. God, that feels like years ago now.'

Eleanor cocked her head in surprise. 'And who killed that one in the back street back in thirty-five, the one who murdered those policemen?'

'One of his own side did that,' I said. 'A mercenary called Baxter.'

'And other people accounted for all the other deaths laid at Hugh's door,' Sissy added. 'He's never killed anyone.'

'Ha!' Eleanor exclaimed.

'But it serves our purpose to make people believe otherwise,' I added.

'So it's all lies.'

'To survive in the intelligence world requires a little lying.'

'Quite a lot, at times,' Sissy added pointedly.

There was no profit of making an enemy of Eleanor. She'd killed in the hot blood of the moment, and perhaps her revenge was now complete.

'What's done is done,' I said. 'You mentioned the communist who murdered the policeman back in thirty-five. Well, that man Baxter who killed him was…' I paused, not sure of my own facts. 'He was part of a network of conspirators. It is quite likely the same network was behind what happened to Julia, duped Ruth, and employed those Frenchmen.'

'Communists?'

'No, if only it was that simple. Our enemy is deep inside the British Establishment and playing puppet masters. They've had chances to kill me before but decided letting me live served their purpose.'

'But not anymore? So they came to Sark to kill us because what, it's unfinished business from last year?'

'It can't be. They achieved their mission last year. If anything, eliminating Ruth and her gang was *our* unfinished business.'

'She didn't seem to be part of the gang,' Sissy added.

'No, I think she's an idealist who was fooled last year, then fooled again. She ended up in something deeper than she intended and may not have been working for the people she thought she was.'

'She was still a traitor, and it's still her fault Julia is dead,' Eleanor said. 'And she was leading them to kill us, because she's the one who knows what we look like. Bitch.'

'Yes.'

I'd heard that concentrating on the horizon was another way of avoiding seasickness, so tried that.

'But if they're not finishing old business, then what the hell were they up to?'

'New business. Someone contracted that bunch to kill us, someone we've annoyed, or someone who is afraid of us.'

'It could be the White Knights,' Sissy suggested.

'My money is on the Nordic League,' Eleanor added.

'Or any of the others. The Young Britons are top of my list.'

'You don't like them, do you?' Eleanor mused. 'Didn't they blackball you?'

'More fool them. But they let Julian in and soon had him dancing to their tune. There's a fair chance that everything we saw last year was down to them.'

'Including putting Mosley in power?' Eleanor asked.

'And putting themselves in positions around him.'

She looked towards too-distant Jersey, then back again. 'Are we fighting our own party? Have you got us fighting the Leader?'

'No, and no. Honestly, Eleanor, if you want Mosley to be anything more than a puppet, we need to beat these men. And they're all men.'

'Lead me to them.'

'Patience. We need to calm down and think this through.' I took a deep breath. 'The Guernsey police may want to hang a murder tag on someone, and even if they believe the story Julian is weaving right now those Frenchman had friends who won't sit idly by. And someone back in London betrayed where we would be. *Exactly* where we would be and when. Our lives aren't worth tuppence until we prove who's really behind this.'

And it would take a lot of proving.

'Eleanor, you've got an aunt in Paris?'

'Cousin.'

'Go straight to France from Jersey; there must be a regular steamer. Catch a train to Paris, raid your trust fund, and lay low for a while. Brush up your French, then work your way into the French fascist movement. You're not an antisemite, Eleanor?'

'No, I don't care about the Jews one way or another. They're not killing my friends.'

'So pretend. Peddle all the anti-Jewish nonsense Melissa trots out with the same conviction she has. Resign from the BU, find that group called Francisme, and join them.'

'But why are French fascists after us?'

'No idea. We don't know where their orders are coming from or who is paying them. Discovering that is going to be your job, your penance.'

She shrugged. 'Why the hell not? And where are you two going?'

'We're not telling you.' I lay back on the side bench and put one hand under my head. 'We're not telling anyone.'

Chapter Twelve

We travelled faster than the news, and Julian was clearly making a good fist of playing for time. I telephoned the bakery from Jersey and told Lucy what was happening. She'd already heard from Julian and was alerting all our agents across the country. Male-dominated Black House underestimated Lucy, seeing only a young blonde from Essex with crooked teeth and not her innate skill for bringing order to chaos.

From Southampton, Sissy and I took an awkward and indirect route north by train, requiring an overnight stop in strife-torn Manchester, then a loop back into the West Yorkshire coalfields by a branch line. British Union was strong in the north, but the region was not wholly in the grip of the fascists. Blackshirts were fighting for control of the streets of Manchester, but the ports of Liverpool and Hull remained militantly socialist, as did Sheffield, snuggled against the Pennines. Leeds was firmly in Mosley's grip, and Department Z even had an office there. A Blackshirt stormtrooper garrison at Catterick kept an eye on York, sympathetic areas of the North East and the road to Scotland. The Scots would rather go their own way than Mosley's way.

I telephoned Moat Hall from Clayton station and spoke to Hopkins, my father's butler, and asked him to come and collect us. A taxi driver would be just one more witness who could betray us.

'They can't be everywhere,' I said as we waited for Hopkins. 'If AA Thorne is behind this, I know how few men he has to call on. MI5 has about two dozen officers, and as the Secret Intelligence Service doesn't even officially exist, it must have less. And most of those should be abroad, because there's a gentleman's agreement on who does what.'

'So we outnumber them,' Sissy concluded.

'Better still, they can't watch Black House and the bakery, and my apartment, and yours, then send men up here too. Those Frenchmen were most likely mercenaries, pulled in at short notice by someone who'd used them before.'

'If they're the same mercenaries as last year, it must be the same people paying them…' She paused.

'Therefore?'

'They planned everything that happened.'

'Everything that's brought us to where we are, and I mean everything. Which is troubling because Julian's father was deeply involved in the events of thirty-five. He employed mercenary killers then, admittedly British ones.'

'Julian's father wouldn't have risked his own son's life,' she objected. 'So he can't be the villain this time.'

'Unless the plan was just to kill me.'

'Oh darling, everything is not about you.'

'This time it could be.'

'You're saying that if AA Thorne is behind all this, he went to all these lengths because he hates you as much as you hate him?'

'Because he knows I'm onto him.'

'Well, it would have taken a lot of money to hire those men and get them to Sark. How much has AA got—can he keep doing this?'

'Plenty of the Young Britons have money, but recruiting armed men without attracting attention takes time. Which gives us a chance to stay ahead of them.'

A maroon-painted car pulled up in front of the station, the little Austin 16 employed as the Moat Hall run-around. I'd asked Hopkins specifically not to come in my father's Rolls.

Hopkins took our bags. 'It's very good to see you, Mr Clifton, and Miss Poe too. I'm sorry we were not more prepared. Nobody told me you were coming north.'

'Good,' I said.

'There have been telephone calls for you,' he said over his shoulder as he drove. 'From Black House, from Mr Thring—'

'Junior or Senior?'

'Mr Julian, I believe—I recognised his voice. And a call from a bakery? That was probably a mistake. Two newspaper reporters also called, and your father was rather brusque with them.'

'He told them to bugger off?'

'His words precisely, sir. I read in the newspaper that you thwarted another communist attack.'

'Indeed.'

'And there are three letters waiting for you.'

We swept into the tree-shrouded gravel drive of Moat Hall, and Hopkins pulled up the handbrake with a creak. 'It's getting rather stiff,' he said.

Hopkins carried Sissy's case into the gloom of the hallway, and I followed with my own. Dark wood, suits of armour, and portraits of the previous owner's ancestors set the scene.

'Is my father home?'

'I last saw him in the orangery, sir. Shall I bring tea?'

'Please. And we are ravenous, so anything Daisy can rustle up in short order will be welcome.'

'There's some fine tongue. I'll let her know immediately. Will you be staying? I'll have your rooms made up.'

My father was taking tea with a widow named Mrs Percival, who was perhaps ten years his junior. It took time to work our way through introductions and what passed for an explanation for our sudden arrival.

Mrs Percival's face suddenly brightened. 'Oh, did I read you had been terribly heroic recently?'

'If you read the *Daily Mail*, you read correctly, Ma'am.'

'Oh, call me Angelica.'

'Angelica.'

'Son.' My father indicated the open door, and we stepped out onto the lawn, which was still wet from a recent shower. 'A police inspector telephoned. Something about a murder; two murders, I think, he said. What have you got yourself into now? Is this the same story as the one in the *Mail*, or something new?'

'Same one, just a different perspective. Sissy and I need to lie low for a few days until the truth emerges between the journalistic excitement.'

'You're always welcome here, son. And Miss Poe.'

'Thank you, Father. We had to hot-foot it up here, so if you've any cash to hand, that would come in handy. And I don't suppose you have any nine-millimetre pistol ammunition?'

'Not my cup of tea, lad.'

'If I may intervene, Master Hugh.' Hopkins came up behind us, and the maid followed him, bearing a tray. 'I did notice that on your last stay, you left two boxes of bullets in a drawer beside your bed.'

Of course, I had.

'I left them alone and took the liberty of locking the drawer.'

'Good man.'

My father jerked his thumb towards Hopkins. 'Where do you find staff like that these days?'

If Hopkins and a dozen men like him ran the country, we'd live in an idyll. The social order hadn't been arranged very well.

'I hope you pay him well,' I said.

'I reward them that needs rewarding. And I did what you said and put the miners' wages up. The buggers are working harder for it too. You know nothing about running mines, yet I'm listening to you, and we're making more money than ever.'

The mines and works of R R Clifton Ltd were fully occupied and receiving the best contracts because Julian Thring was nudging the right people. Corruption had run rampant since Mosley's commissions had started to run the country, and it was ironic that the money flowing into my father's coffers helped fund my fight against the fascists. I believe it was Lenin who said the capitalists would sell us the rope with which to hang them.

My post included a picture postcard of Guernsey's Castle Cornet signed by Julian. It said simply *All is well*. Valentine had hand-written a short note ordering me to return to Black House and to telephone him immediately. The third contained just a card of the type often posted in tobacconists' windows with the message *Lonely, Comrade? Hull is the Athens of the north.*

I tapped the card on my hand, thinking immediately of the woman I knew as Verity, sometime MI5 agent, double agent, Moscow stooge, or outlaw idealist. Athens was our personal code, and Hull could indeed mean Kingston-upon-Hull, one of the diehard socialist salients. Calhoun had hinted his men were cracking down hard on the communists, and she was either feeling the pressure or sweating undercover as she secretly helped apply it. I'd place a lonely-hearts advert in the *Daily Worker* and see if she responded. The newspaper had been officially suppressed but still survived underground.

My best course of action was to tick suspects off one by one. The agents of Room Z had collected a great deal of information about fascists, socialists, trade unionists, and politicians of all shades. I had built up a wide network of contacts, and although I trusted very few of them, not many would conspire to kill me. Not all at the same time.

Chapter Thirteen

I decided it was time to phone Valentine, using the telephone box at the edge of the village.

'Where are you?' he demanded.

'Back working undercover,' I said. 'We've another traitor at Black House.'

'Not in Department Z.'

'Our mission to Sark was confidential; not many people knew about it, so we were betrayed from within. Again.'

He was quiet, maybe considering whether I was accusing him of being a traitor in the same way he'd unmasked his predecessor as a Special Branch informer.

'You must tell me where you are.'

'I can't tell anyone. I'm all over the newspapers, so I need to lie low.'

He didn't dispute the point and made no attempt to defend himself against the unspoken suggestion he could be the one who set me up for a fall.

'Mosley is very angry his radio plan has been ruined.'

Of course, Mosley would think this was all about him. It would suit my purpose.

'Am I in his bad books?'

'For not spotting the plot…but you did fight off the attack. Joyce is putting a propaganda spin on the mess,' Valentine said.

'So I've seen; French Communists.'

'Who else?'

It was hard to believe an intellectual like Valentine would believe that cooked-up story, but the nature of authoritarian rule is that lies become so commonplace they are treated as facts by even those who know them to be untrue. Britain was not yet a dictatorship, but Mosley and his gang were carrying out the groundworks.

'I'm setting Z3 to discover the facts. As to who wanted us dead, internal security is your area—'

'Blake's area,' he corrected.

'So set Blake and Z1 to investigate the leak. When our enquiries converge, we should discover who gave the order to attack the Radio Project.'

And by default, the attack in France that left Julia dead and Sissy fighting for her life.

'A good plan,' Valentine said after a moment's silence. Whether he agreed it was a good plan was another question. 'I'll talk to young Thring when he gets back, see who he blabbed to. And that wife of his. How about your mistress, can she be trusted?'

I caught my breath but knew this was what London society thought our love amounted to. 'Sissy knows the score.'

Yes, and she was out to settle it. Valentine didn't mention Eleanor at all, and the fewer people who knew of her involvement, the better. I hadn't seen any reference to a mystery redhead in any of the newspaper stories I'd read.

'Do you have any evidence that there's a link between the incident in Sark and the group who attacked Mrs Simpson's villa last year and killed our agent?' Valentine's question was almost off the cuff. He didn't sound as if he was leading me or testing me.

'I have a hunch.'

If Valentine found the proof, so much the better. If he found cause to disprove it, then he'd rise to the top of my list of suspects.

'And so the attempt to kill the king too?'

'That makes sense.'

He again paused before speaking. 'I suppose you are building a thesis that if your assailants were the same group as last year, they must be acting under the same direction.'

Was he asking me, reading my thoughts, or rehearsing his own?

'And you would then suspect they're using the same inside source of information,' he added.

'I might.'

'Which if all your hunches and suppositions are combined would make whoever is behind all this a very dangerous person. Someone who would stop at nothing to achieve their aims. Stay…wherever you are if you must, but direct your agents to stop harassing those petty political parties and make the hunt for these attackers their priority. This order comes straight from Mosley.'

'Will do.'

'And in the meantime, leave it to us to discover the traitor.'

* * *

In fear for her life, in her last moments Ruth could have been telling the truth. If her confederates were agents of Francisme, they must be the tool of the plotters and not themselves the instigators of the plot. During the crisis of 1936, it had been the last men standing who had won. But if this was the same shadowy group I'd been up against the year before, this latest move was curious. Would they have put such extreme effort into ruining the Radio Plan, which even if it came off was only a money-grubbing exercise? Even if my hunch was right and AA Thorne and his cronies were behind this, I didn't understand their timing, unless having me as that rat in a barrel was too good an opportunity to miss.

As evening drew in, I walked the three-quarter mile to the village with Sissy at my side. Men tended to behave better in the company of a woman, and a woman with an automatic in her purse was an asset I needed on those unlit streets. Five terraces of back-to-back houses in grubby brick had been built by my father and uncle when they expanded into coal mining. The road to the colliery swept past those houses, and a lane one car wide led back to Moat Hall. Anyone trying to reach the hall by the obvious route would need to pass by the village, then know which of several side lanes to take. Unguided, they would easily end up in a farmyard or down one of the colliery access roads or be enjoying a scenic climb up into the Pennines. My father leased the corner shop to the Co-operative Society, which operated it as a grocery and general store. It was the obvious place for motorists to stop to ask for directions.

It was a world apart for Sissy; wide empty streets and the sooted brick of two-up-two-down houses. Each street in the village had been named after a battlefield, and the trade unionist Horley lived at 13 Alma Road. I'd heard the pit siren a couple of hours ago, so he should be home if he worked the day shift. I rapped on the door.

A boy answered. 'Dad, it's a man!' he yelled back into the house.

Horley appeared, in shirtsleeves and braces, barefoot.

'Mr Clifton?'

He looked round me at Sissy. On the only occasion they'd met previously, she'd pointed a gun into his face.

I put my finger to my lips. 'Pop your shoes and jacket on and walk down to the social with me.'

He glanced once more at Sissy, as if expecting to be shot on the spot.

'What's this about?'

'I need your help.'

A few minutes later, we were walking with Sissy a few paces behind. Horley must know she was playing bodyguard, and it kept him on edge.

'The fascists are after me.'

'Ah, but I thought you were one o' them. And aren't you wanted for murder now?'

The good old *Daily Mirror* had no truck with Joyce's stories. He'd surely close it down soon.

'Strictly speaking, I'm wanted for questioning in connection with two deaths abroad. As is my companion.'

'I bet it was her,' he said with a tick of his head.

'French fascists were hired to kill us,' I said.

'But you're a fascist.'

'Not fascist enough these days. And the truth is most people are joining Mosley's party to feather their own nests. My father wouldn't join, so I did. You're working full time because I'm playing at being a fascist, and other men playing at being fascists are giving our mines their business.'

'Don't expect me to thank yer.'

'Well you might consider granting me two favours. I want you to place this advert in the *Daily Worker*. You must know how to reach them.' I passed him a short note and two half-crowns. 'That should cover it.'

'Didn't see you as a *Daily Worker* reader. This one of them secret codes?'

'Of a kind. I've a good friend who is one of the comrades.'

'Wait. You're not—'

'No, I'm not a communist agent. Don't think too much about it, and don't mention this to anyone. People are being killed.'

'I'm not working for the fascists.'

'No, you're working for my father and me. If it helps, I'll give you a fiver.'

'I don't want your money. What's your second favour?'

'This is a small community; everyone knows everyone, and you don't even lock your doors when you go out.'

'Nothin' worth nicking,' he said.

'Keep an eye out, keep an ear out. I want to hear about anyone who doesn't belong here sniffing around. Southerners, foreigners, Blackshirts, men who clearly don't work for a living. Women who don't fit in—don't overlook women.'

He turned to Sissy. 'I wouldn't dare.'

'Make up any excuse you like for keeping the village on its toes. Bailiffs, land-grabbers from the Church after tithe-payers, whatever you like.'

'But why should I, Mr Clifton? Why should any of us bother with the likes of you?'

'Have no doubt. If they get me, they'll pull my father down too. The mine will be nationalised or sold off to one of Mosley's mates who holds no truck with unions. We all fall together.'

'Bloody hell,' he looked off towards the hills.

'I wouldn't ask you if I didn't trust you.'

'Trust?' He again looked round at Sissy.

She smiled and shrugged the shoulders of her coat without removing her hands from her pockets.

'Chances are they'll call in at the corner shop and ask for directions to the hall—road maps of this area are terribly out of date. Find a reliable lad and lend him a bicycle. He's to run a message to the hall if anything happens. I may not be there, but someone will pass your message along.'

'The lad from the shop uses a bike.'

'I'll make it worth his while. And with luck, we'll keep our pits, and you'll keep your jobs and houses.'

Now, he gave a laugh. 'And I thought this was all big city bollocks, Blackshirts and bent coppers and all that. If we see these strangers, do you want 'em, you know, sorted out?'

'It may come to that, but not in the first instance. Let's find out who they are and what they want.'

He looked off towards the distant hills. 'I remember when we was lads and played cowboys and Indians in the woods. You shot me in the back, you bastard.'

'Yes, but then your tribe tied me to a tree and chucked dirt bombs at me. It made us even.'

Horley gave a chuckle. 'If only we'd known.'

'The innocence of childhood. Here, I know you don't want my money but buy the lads down the social a pint on me. But don't say it was me.'

* * *

Horley might betray me, but it would be a brave man who shopped the son of the boss in full knowledge he'd be thrown on the dole and evicted from his house, if not slain by the cold-blooded killer staring from the front page of the newspapers. Two days later, the air was heavy, and distant thunder greeted the arrival of the boy from the village Co-op. He parked his bicycle by the kitchen door and was enjoying a glass of milk by the time Sarah, the kitchen maid, brought me to him.

'Sir, Mr Clifton, sir,' he said, giving me an army salute. 'I was sent to tell yer there's people looking for yer.'

'Right now?'

'Yes, not an hour ago, honest sir. There's a van with a London shop on its side. Asking for here. Me dad sent 'em the wrong way.'

'Was it a baker's van?'

'Yes.'

I gave a laugh. 'Thank you. They're probably harmless, so send them this way if you see them again. But keep your eyes peeled for more southerners.' I gave him a sixpence and he beamed, then glugged the rest of his milk.

'Now scarper!' the maid said. 'What's a tyke like him doing, running errands for you sir?'

'Doing his bit to make Britain a better place. Thank you for giving him the milk.'

'Well, he looks half starved.'

'So you're doing your bit, too.'

Thunder grew louder and more frequent as the threatened storm moved in to soak my messenger before he'd make it home. Splashing through puddles, a green-bodied van with Fulham Bakery painted onto a cream side panel in flowing red script arrived half an hour later. Hopkins pushed a brolly into my hands, and I went out to meet it. Jimmy Walsh was at the wheel, a handsome man in his late twenties who held a dream of becoming a motor racing driver. His natural talent had led him to become my driver of choice, and we'd fought our way through a firefight together, so he was as dependable as a fascist could be.

'Around the side.' I waved my free arm. 'By the stables.'

I followed in the wake of the van over the slippery cobbles of the stable yard, showing Walsh where I wanted him to park. Lucy Parmentier extracted herself wearily from the passenger seat, straightened her skirt, and knocked back a strand of wayward blonde fringe. She gave me a crooked smile as she ducked under the cover of my brolly. Agents of Room Z did not salute.

We hurried into the hall through a side door and through to the library, which had always been my personal retreat. After gratefully accepting tea and a biscuit from Hopkins, Walsh told a tale of woe, of getting lost in lanes and being misdirected by suspicious locals. He'd drifted into the Party after years of short working or employers going bankrupt, blaming the last government for his misfortune. I'd been able to add him to the bakery payroll together with Lucy so neither had to take daytime jobs as many of my people still did.

'I brought this,' Walsh said, opening his coat to reveal the butt of a Webley revolver.

'How about you, Lucy?'

'It's in me handbag.'

She was a terrible shot, tending to close both eyes as she squeezed the trigger, but at least Lucy could send bullets in the general direction of an enemy, which would give them pause for thought. On Women's Section exercises she was usually given charge of the medical bag.

'Right, supper is in an hour. We've had rooms made up, so you've a chance to freshen up. Sorry, Walsh, you're up on the servant's floor.'

'I know my place,' he grinned.

'Socialist!'

'National socialist,' Lucy quipped. 'It's all the rage now. You should read your letters, sir.'

'We'll unpack in the morning when the rain's passed.'

Following my call from Jersey, Lucy and her Chelsea Wives had gathered up all the files relating to the Young Britain Club and its members and everything we had obtained by raiding the offices of the various far-right groups. We had touched a nerve somewhere, unless Valentine was correct, and this was all about Mosley's radio dreams. Once the files had been loaded into a bakery van Lucy and Walsh had driven north and waited in a hotel in Grantham that Sissy and I had made use of before.

My father didn't keep horses, so the stable block was used principally as a garage. The hay loft had been swept clean of hay and remained unused apart from storing furniture turfed out of the house during the latest renovation. In the morning, we quickly converted it to the northern headquarters of Department Z3, and a perfectly decent desk of Victorian vintage thrown out by my father found a new life.

Lucy spread a set of files along a former dining table scratched with age, together with the past three months of reports from our regional agents. Normally, we kept these in a concealed room at the bakery, as many related to BU members and the running of local branches. When I thought it was judicious to do so, I'd pass a report on to Section Z1 to have a corrupt official removed. My preference was to finger the antisemites, the ones with militant views on minorities such as gypsies, the ones who flaunted their association with German Nazis, Italian Fascisti, or Spanish Falangists. The idle and ineffective I deliberately left alone.

'We've had lots of reports about the big move against them communists up here.'

'Operation Dragon North,' I said as I stood by her side.

'Yes. There's recruiting for the stormtroopers and buying lorries, and more rifle training. It's not very secret; the whole country must know.'

'I don't think this is about Dragon North.'

Z3 was not even involved in the operation, so no side in this undeclared war had reason to try to clear us off the pitch.

'Anything more relevant?'

Lucy selected a file. 'Priscilla found this.'

Priscilla was one of the women who made up Lucy's unit of administrators and file compilers. Most of them were older than she was, married and had come into the Party along with their husbands. Others joined simply for something to do.

'It's a note in your writing, if I can read it, which I barely can. Honestly, Mr Clifton, with your education and university and that. Anyway, when you were at the Nordic League office, you found a minute of a meeting between them and the National Socialist League.' She shook her head. 'Confusing, isn't it? These names do get a bit similar.'

'What was in the minute?'

'That's all you wrote—you found a minute.'

I groaned, then gave a little cough. Perhaps it was the lingering smell of hay irritating my lungs.

She wagged a finger like a schoolteacher. 'But we have all those bits of paper you stuffed into your sacks like naughty St Nicholases. Listen to this.

We've found that the Militant Christian Patriots are just the Nordic League people under another name. And so too are the Liberty Restoration League.'

Lucy smiled. 'And they all shared an office with the White Knights, so a lot of them are the same people, too. It's not like lots of parties, it's just one. Like a spider with lots of legs.'

'And an extensive web, no doubt.'

My head hurt with so many petty little organisations interbreeding like some decayed noble family.

'Have you found any reason for any of these tinpot groups to want to kill me?'

'Not yet.'

'Or spoil the secret mission we were on to Sark?'

'The radio thing?'

'So it's not even that secret?'

'Well, we find out things, don't we?'

Lucy collected another selection of files. 'I want you to see these, too. You might sit down; there's a lot of them.'

I sat in an armchair that had seen better days.

Lucy gave me a pile of twelve reports. 'All of these mention the National Socialist League. Now, there's a few posh people who flip and flop between these groups, lords and ladies, generals, MPs, and some of our top nobs. No ordinary people like me and Jimmy.' She held up a finger to instruct me. '*But* lots of our ordinary members are joining the National Socialist League as well as staying with us. And some are even leaving us to join them.'

'Us as in?'

'British Union.'

'And them as in the NSL?'

'This man is the treasurer.'

She passed me a file labelled Peter Wise.

'He's supposed to be one of our propaganda officers,' she said. 'But now he thinks he can be the NSL Treasurer as well.'

We'd had the Propaganda Officer for the North-East followed on one of his trips to London. I always wanted to know what Joyce's placemen were up to, so it had been a fairly routine assignment for two of my younger agents. Wise had slipped their tail easily, as if he was practiced in the art. By taking up this post within the NSL he was adding a second string to his political allegiance but could have even more to hide.

'We need to keep an eye on him,' I said. 'But if you find out anything more, it's for my ears only. Understood?'

I must have sounded curt, as Lucy flinched.

'Yes, fine, sir.' She stood with her hands crossed at her midriff like an errant schoolgirl. 'But can you tell us what's going on? I mean, Mr Thring is away, and we haven't seen Eleanor, and one paper says it's communists, and another has you murdering French tourists. Now you're hiding up here, and so are me and Jimmy. I mean, what's the truth? We have to know, Mr Clifton. If there's Frenchmen coming up here to kill us, we need to know.'

'Someone wants me out of the way,' I said. 'And Dr Valentine wants the whole of Z3 ordered to chase the men who disrupted the Radio Plan.'

She closed her eyes and gave me a shrewd smile. 'But we're not going to do that, are we, sir?'

'Not all of us. We're going to send everyone we can spare to every fringe political meeting they can attend. I have a suspect, but what I'm short of is a motive.'

Chapter Fourteen

I wondered who they would send. Word reached me that a man was loitering at Clayton station, asking for a taxi to Moat Hall and to his frustration being told there was none. The stationmaster was the local informer for Z3. Shortly after I put down the telephone, it rang again.

I did not expect them to send Charles.

'Hugh.'

'Is that Charles?'

'Yes, yes, but there's not a taxi to be had. Are there any up here?'

'I'll send Hopkins to collect you.'

So it was Charles, Viscount Wickersley, my friend I'd served with in India and the man who'd first talked me into the spying game. Soon afterwards, the boy from the village rushed in again to say there was a tall gentleman with a little moustache asking for me at the train station. He won another sixpence and was sent away by Daisy, the cook, with a couple of sandwiches from the tray she was making up for my team.

Everyone was to make themselves scarce, but also make themselves ready. I'd lead Charles for a walk on the lawn, in full sight of the bedroom Sissy had been assigned for the sake of appearances but was not using. I picked up one of the little cast-iron tables from the patio and lugged it a little further out, then came back for two chairs. Sarah, the maid, was watching, so I asked her to reconstruct the sandwich platter as if just for two and ask Hopkins to find some white wine as soon as he returned.

I waited in the open until Charles appeared, led out of the orangery door by Hopkins. Nobody else could eavesdrop on what we said out there. Nobody could sneak up on us unobserved by my friends who watched from the house. It was a good distance to the copse beyond the formal gardens, so we'd have fair warning of anyone approaching from that direction. Charles must by now subscribe to the universal view that I'd have no compunction in drawing my pistol and shooting him dead, or that his back was being watched for any false move. He glanced about himself as he advanced onto the lawn, rather like an opening batsman moving to the crease in front of a silent, expectant crowd.

We shook hands, then I offered him a seat.

'This is very pleasant. I always enjoy coming up here,' he said. 'Though I think you're in for a storm.'

Clouds were gathering once more over the Pennines.

I signalled to the house, and he glanced behind himself.

'Sandwiches,' I said. 'Ham and cheese.'

He relaxed into his chair, although they were far from comfortable. 'You took a little finding.'

'Did you guess I would be here, or were you told?'

'It's an easy guess, though it's the fifth place I've tried.'

'And who sent you?'

'I was just concerned—'

'Who sent you? This is a long way to come on a whim, and it sounds as if you're expending a lot of time looking for me, even for a man of leisure with no need for employment.'

His bright Nordic eyes drilled into me.

'Another shooting, Hugh. You can't continue like this.'

'Who sent you? Calhoun?'

He knew I'd check, or perhaps had already checked.

'I'm sorry I ever drew you into all this,' he said. 'Things have got out of hand.'

'An understatement, Charles. Things have got very out of hand. What was the line you spun me, two and a bit years ago, right here on this lawn; no risk, no danger?'

'Surely you never believed that.'

I touched the thin scar above my right eye. 'This is just the latest souvenir. Friends are dead, people I thought of as friends are dead, others are lucky to be alive. And Mosley…Mosley was not supposed to win an election. I was expressly recruited to help stop him.'

'No, you were recruited to provide information. All this Blackshirt hero nonsense is entirely of your own making, and you've done very well by playing both sides.'

'If you count having friends killed and maimed as doing well. Whose side are you on now, Charles? Are you embracing the new reality, bending with the breeze, or however people excuse their shift in allegiance?'

'Whose side are *you* on now?' he challenged.

I couldn't answer because I had no clear idea. Politics had never interested me; the king was little more than a fascist puppet, the Church had lost my respect, and the dominions of the Empire must surely be handed back to their people one day soon.

'Decency,' I said.

He gave a snort. 'Try selling that to Stalin.'

'You don't work for MI5, do you?' I challenged. 'I originally thought you did, but if so, I'd have seen more of you last year when we needed every man. Have you been working for the Secret Intelligence Service all along? Even when we were in India?'

'If SIS existed, it wouldn't operate on the UK mainland,' he said. 'Or so I'm led to believe.'

'But they could operate in France, or in Sark.'

He looked away. 'Don't put me in the same box as the villains.'

'To be honest, I'm not putting my trust in anybody. Other than Hopkins.'

The butler was making stately progress across the lawn, balancing the tray of sandwiches, two glasses, and a bottle of wine.

'He's a good man,' Charles said, then waited as Hopkins poured white Bordeaux for both of us with a satisfying glug-glug.

'Will there be anything else, sir?'

'Be ready to take Viscount Wickersley back to the station in say, an hour?'

'Very good, sir. It looks like we'll have rain within the hour, so I'll keep the car by the main door.'

I glanced at the clouds and agreed.

'I'm pleased you're contemplating letting me walk away,' Charles said as Hopkins retreated.

'Well, Charles, we are friends. And I don't do away with people I find inconvenient—I'm not a Nazi.'

'Neither am I. But listen Hugh, Europe is heading for war, everyone can feel it. God forbid it's a rematch of 1914, but it could be Italy against Germany, Germany against Russia, Italy and Germany against France.'

'But Italy and Germany have formed—what are they calling it- an axis.'

'Yes, yes, dramatic words, but what are pieces of paper worth? It's anyone's gambit. There are Prussian generals still itching for revenge against us for their humiliation in 1918, and I'm lunching with admirals rubbing their hands at the chance of having another crack at the *Kreigsmarine*. Jutland wasn't the victory it should have been.

'Then the RAF is planning for the defence of the islands against the *Luftwaffe. Planning*, not just talking about it over lunch. You've read about what's happening in Spain, with Hitler's Condor Legion bombing a town to rubble.'

'Guernica.'

'Yes, that's the one. The bombers will always get through, everyone knows that, yet Mosley indulges the RAF with more fighter squadrons.'

'Fighters are cheaper to build than bombers,' I mused. 'So the RAF can quickly create new squadrons, and Mosley can boast about numbers. And building fighters looks less aggressive; it will make Hitler less nervous.'

'Hitler is nervous regardless, and we must avoid a second Great War. The hard truth is we need an alliance with Germany and pull them away from this axis with Italy. That's what we're working for.'

'*We* being the Secret Intelligence Service?'

'It's what we're *all* working for. And you need to play your part.'

In the distance, I heard thunder.

'What you are saying is that if I return to heel, dark forces will stop trying to eliminate me.'

'I imagine it would help. Stop rocking the boat, Hugh. You've won a good position in Department Z, by good luck or good judgment. Keep it, use it, yes, embrace it to use your own words. Bend with that wind.'

I wondered if this had been Charles' agenda all along, but it was pointless to ask him.

'Guernsey have requested that a warrant is issued for your arrest,' he said.

'Yes, but we're not in Guernsey.'

'Scotland Yard will be instructed to serve it.'

'Oh come on, it was self-defence, us or them.'

'Nevertheless.'

'Oh this is a threat isn't it? If I play with a straight bat, a man with a title will speak to another man with a title in the smoking room of their club, and all this will go away.'

'You know the rules of the game by now.'

'But I don't follow those rules. I'm a player, not a gentleman.'

'Be sensible, Hugh. I imagine this legal nonsense is a formality, something than can be cleared up in a few days, but you'll need to come back to London.'

'London is the last place I'm going.'

Charles lowered his voice. 'Honestly, this is not a very clever hiding place. I didn't need a frontier scout to follow your trail here.'

'It's temporary.'

'Once that warrant is issued, there will be a convoy of police heading this way. And they'll be armed because you have a certain reputation.'

'Public enemy?'

I recalled the James Cagney gangster movie and had no intention of dying face-down in the rain.

'Now I'm rumbled. I'll be on my way, rest assured.'

'Give yourself up. Telephone Inspector Renton at Scotland Yard and turn yourself over to him. I know you trust each other.'

'Trust? Have you ever told your SIS masters how you recruited me for Calhoun?'

'No, that arose out of a chance conversation, and I keep it to myself. And would anyone believe me, Commander Clifton, Blackshirt hero, the man who saved the king? Now, I'm famished, and these sandwiches will curl if we leave them any longer.' He glanced at the sky. 'Or we'll both be struck dead by lightning.'

I offered him the plate and he took one.

'I suppose you are more useful to them if they think you're my friend,' I said.

He took a bite, chewed, and considered the gardens before replying.

'To be completely blunt, Hugh, that makes me more useful to you. Especially if they believe I've pulled you around, dissuaded you from the course you are taking. Come back to London, come out into the light where everyone can see you.'

Chapter Fifteen

Beneath Black House is a series of basement rooms. Initially, there had been just one with its floor, walls, door, and ceiling all painted black. The reputation of Room B1 had grown such that it now had two grim brothers, but B1 remained the largest, most well-used, and most infamous.

When Melissa Thring had been invited to Black House to meet with Dr Valentine, she had expected to be having tea in his office, with Julian as company and perhaps with cakes. Now, she shuffled on a hard wooden chair. She'd been led into the basement room by two Blackshirts, who'd closed the door on her, mercifully leaving the light on. Sark had been so very dark at night, and she'd not stopped thinking how quickly a lovely trip had turned to terror. A single lightbulb hung from the ceiling a couple of feet in front of her, so bright it caused spots in front of her eyes when she looked away.

Two men came in, swiftly taking their seats behind a desk at the far end of the room. A Blackshirt pulled the door closed again. Dr Valentine said nothing at first. Light reflecting from round spectacle lenses completely concealed his eyes. Beside him was the sallow, weasel face of Blake, elevated swiftly to become the new head of Section Z1. Julian had told her he'd been some sort of dodgy lawyer with an unsavoury reputation.

Valentine took a little cigar from a crocodile skin case and lit it. The room quickly filled with its pungent, heavy odour. Melissa tried to sniff her nostrils clear as the wall seemed to close in. The room was oppressively dark, blacker than black, cold, and sinister as a dungeon in a gothic novel.

Just like the one Hugh had lent her about a vampire count. This was all Hugh's fault, the whole thing, this wasn't how national socialist Britain should be at all.

At last, Valentine spoke. 'Forgive us, Woman Section Leader Thring, but we have to interview you formally.'

'I don't know why; I wasn't even there when those people were killed.'

'Who did you tell about the radio project?'

'Nobody. I mean, I—'

'So you did.'

'It was to be our honeymoon. Naturally, I told a few people about going to Sark. It sounded exciting—'

'Who?' asked Blake, his pencil poised. His voice had a rat-like squeak to it.

'My mother, er, friends.'

'What friends?' Valentine's glassy substitutes for eyes glared straight at her. 'That was rather foolish, considering the importance of what your husband does for the Party.'

'Mother has done nothing wrong. It's Hugh Clifton. He drags poor Julian from one bloodbath to the next. I told Julian he didn't need to take a gun to Sark, but Hugh says take a gun and so he did. Without that, there wouldn't have been all the shooting.'

'Or you would all have been murdered by communist assassins,' Valentine said.

'That's what Hugh says—but we don't know it for a fact.'

'What do you know?'

'I know you should be spending your time hunting communists and throwing the Jews out, not locking me in here. I'm a loyal member, I'm a section leader, I run a riding school for cadets. I carried the standard of the women's section at the Battle of Cable Street. I helped bring the Women's Institute over to us. I was spying on my friends for the party.'

Her plea made no impact.

'Apart from your mother, the Women's Institute, and your favourite horse, who else knew you were going to Sark?'

Melissa made an effort to look as if she was thinking hard. She must help them, help the Party, show she was dedicated and true.

'Hugh can't have told people because he doesn't have any friends, apart from us. There's Sissy, but she's as loyal as me. Have you seen what they did to her face? These very same Frenchmen.'

'You're saying that the very same Frenchmen attacked the Sark hotel as attacked the villa last year where Section Leader Poe was injured?'

'Yes.'

'Would you confirm you know *that* for a fact? Did you see them?'

'Julian said they were the same.'

'Had he seen them before?'

'No, but Sissy said. Or Hugh said they were the same.'

'Julian said that Sissy said that Julian said…so you do not know, beyond any doubt, the same men were involved in both attacks.'

'Well, no.'

'Back to who you told about the radio project.'

'Nobody.'

'Very well. Who you told about travelling to Sark?'

'What about Eleanor Fitzherbert?' Melissa blurted. 'She's a silly, frothy thing. Gets drunk and giggly. She could have told any of her boyfriends or barmen or anyone.'

Valentine barely gave her time to stop speaking. 'Tell us more about Eleanor Fitzherbert's role. Was she involved in the shooting?'

'Yes, yes, she went off with the rest on their hunting trip. All squiffy and carrying their German guns.'

'But she didn't come back?'

'She ran off with Hugh and Sissy.'

'To where?'

'I don't know.' She shrugged deliberately heavily.

Blake leaned in and spoke quietly to Valentine. 'Fitzherbert is walking out with a section leader of the First Division. We can quickly find out if she's come back.' He paused, then added. 'Her flatmate was killed in the attack in France last year. Fitzherbert found an excuse not to be on that mission.'

'Yet was keen to be on this one,' Valentine said. 'Is she a red-haired, rather well-bred young lady? Who uses those fashionable pocket spectacles.'

'That's her,' said Melissa.

'And according to the file, she speaks French,' Blake added.

Valentine mulled the idea. 'Clifton said the same thing. It was his excuse for taking her.'

'See, Hugh's idea again,' Melissa threw in. 'She's the one you need to talk to, not me.'

The men conferred in whispers, nodded, made hand gestures before Valentine spoke again to Melissa.

'I have a lot of respect for your husband, Mrs Thring,' Valentine said.

'My father-in-law is very important in the Party.'

'I'm aware of that, and I assure you Commissioner Thring has been kept fully informed of developments. Your father-in-law is very influential, and of course, we are taking note of that, but nobody is beyond the reach of Department Z. Your husband is being very honest with us, or at least makes a good appearance of being honest. However, you strike me as the sort of person who would sell her soul to buy her way out of this room.'

'That's not fair! My so-called honeymoon was ruined. We spent a week stuck in flipping Guernsey while Julian was questioned. And me, in a cell like this. Well, not like this, but a cell. A police station room. Now it's all over the newspapers—and, of course, the story is all about Hugh Clifton. No mention of Julian putting his life in danger for the Leader, or for the king.'

'Clifton…' Valentine shook his head. 'He's a distraction; the newspapers either love him or hate him. Your husband's interests are best served by keeping his face off the front pages.'

Melissa fell silent.

'Do you know where they are? Hugh Clifton, Sissy Poe-Maundy, Eleanor Fitzherbert– your dinner companions, your holiday companions. Your husband's closest friends.'

'No.'

'If you think you are being treated unfairly, you should be sure there's a room just down the corridor where people are treated even less fairly. And one beyond—well, you can imagine. Now, you're going to sit here and have a think while we talk to your husband again; he's waiting in that room.'

'You mustn't hurt Julian! You mustn't torture him or anything.'

'Have you ever considered what role Department Z plays in this new Britain?'

She fell quiet.

'Have you ever given thought to *how* we carry out our work? You wouldn't mind if it were a communist along in room B3. Or a Jew.'

'No, I suppose.'

'Enemies of the Party are enemies of the state.'

Valentine stood up, nodding to Blake, who collected his notepad. Valentine rapped on the door, which opened at his command.

'We'll be back in an hour. Or so. You have time to think.'

Both left the room, and a key turned in the lock. Then they switched off the light.

Chapter Sixteen

Our northern base had no sooner been established but by then it was time to leave. My father's Austin 16 was the vehicle I'd learned to drive in. He maintained it in addition to his Rolls, chiefly for Hopkins or the chauffeur-mechanic to run errands. I instructed Walsh and Lucy to pack up the baker's van and drive it down to Highwood, Baroness Rockwell's place in Kent. Sissy could, at some point, go to stay there with her mother, and it could make a handy hiding place for me too. Our enemies had already guessed we might make for Highwood and Charles had shown up unannounced the day before he made the longer journey to Yorkshire. They may not have the energy to search it twice, particularly if they knew for certain I'd gone elsewhere.

Not spending another night at Moat Hall, we quickly packed then I drove Sissy across the county to York. It took little more than an hour, and I parked in front of a guest house off Walmgate where a card in the window advertised vacancies. We might be expected to find the grandest hotel in the city, but circumstance demanded we did what was least expected. I also wanted to stay some distance from the station so as not to bunch both our escape routes together. We ate in cheap restaurants, and I began to grow a moustache and let stubble darken my cheeks.

Sissy scraped her knuckles across my stubble as we lay in the small bed in the small room with the low ceiling.

'We can't do this for very long,' she said. 'I'll go mad living like this. I need to go back to London.'

'No, that's what they want us to do, we can't go to London.'

'I didn't say *we*, I said *I*. Hiding is not for me, pretending to be Mrs Outhwaite from Halifax. I ask you, darling, do I sound like I come from Halifax?'

I admitted she did not.

'Little places like this, rough clothes. I know it's all for the good, but we can't find out anything by hiding.'

'That could be why they want us to hide.'

'So don't bloody well oblige them. Well, you can, but I'm not. You think this is all about you, that it's you they want to kill. So, we'll test that idea. You keep running, and I'll stop.'

I noticed a spider in one corner of the ceiling, waiting.

'Of course, if your theory is wrong, your experiment might end in them killing you. It's one hell of a proof, Sissy. Why don't we leave the country, as I've suggested before?'

'Running even further? They hired Frenchmen to kill us when we were in France and in Sark. That man Baxter you were squabbling with when I first met you, he's an explorer. They could hire him to find us up the Amazon if we ran that far.'

'Oh, Sissy.'

'You do what you need to do up here, and I'll go back to the Section. Then, if they're coming for all of us, at least I'll have plenty of good people by my side.'

Good people; fascist secret police? I suppose in this topsy-turvy world, I'd skimmed the cream from a pail turning sour, and Sissy would be safer away from me. Her plan rested on my next gamble coming off.

* * *

The following morning, I walked to the York railway station. I hadn't shaved, was wearing a pair of workmen's overalls, a flat cap and gripped an unlit pipe between my teeth. It was well known among my associates that I didn't smoke and was often remarked upon. I kept my cap peak low as I loitered in the cavernous space of the station, right hand in my pocket, left resting on a broom I'd bought from a market stall along the way. Too many uniforms polluted the streets of the city. Two of Commandant Allen's Women's Auxiliary Police were strolling through the market, and a dozen grey-shirted BU cadets were streaming out of the station, being led on some cultural tour by an older Blackshirt. We were not far from Clifford's Tower, where a couple of hundred Jews were burned alive in the Middle Ages, and that would surely be on the itinerary.

Above me, the vast station roof curved to match the bend of the track, and its girders stretched away like the ribs of an extinct sea monster. Locomotives hissed, and the air was thick with steam and the smell of coaldust. Down one platform, a section of stormtroopers with slung rifles and kitbags by their side were waiting for a local train as if departing for war.

The train from London arrived precisely on time and disgorged its passengers as I watched from the southern end of the platform. Detective Inspector Renton of Special Branch was conspicuous by the absence of a suitcase or briefcase of any description in his hands and by the manner he stepped from first-class cautiously. He looked about himself as he walked sedately towards the footbridge with none of the rush and excitement of his fellow travellers, and not expecting me to be positioned well behind him rather than ahead. Two men who stepped off from third class behaved in the same manner, keeping perhaps thirty yards behind Renton.

I took my time before slinging the broom over my shoulder and crossing the bridge after them, but ensured I kept my eyes on the last two detectives. Once over the tracks, they split down staircases to left and right and took positions either side of the entrance to the ticket hall. A pair of Fascist Police strolled onto the platform, with chests puffed out as if they were the new proprietors. Britain was becoming crowded by men in black casting their shadows over ordinary lives.

Both detectives looked away, as if to avoid arousing suspicion and becoming embroiled in a spat about jurisdiction with the FP men. I seized my moment to saunter through into the ticket hall, quietly and tunelessly whistling *Cheek to Cheek*. Renton was standing in the dead centre of the hall, where he could best be seen. I walked swiftly up to him and didn't pause as I passed. 'Send your men for a cup of tea,' I said.

He made after me towards the road exit, clearly irritated he hadn't seen through my disguise. 'And what of your men?'

'They've just had theirs.'

'Wait here,' he said.

'No, I'll see you in the Cholera Burial Ground. It's across the road.'

It also gave me a long view back towards the station and a hundred-yard head start if Renton emerged with his officers or they chose to creep out afterwards. A short sprint would take me to the arch where the road pierced the city walls, and beyond it, York offered plenty of narrow alleyways to vanish down. Sissy kept a distant watch, but nobody else would come to my aid. Department Z had an outstation in Leeds, but I didn't know any of the agents well enough to put my liberty in their hands. I lay the broom aside once it was no longer needed as an impromptu weapon and went across the road to wait by the grassy rampart at the base of the city wall.

'The man of many disguises,' Renton said as he strolled up to me, blowing away a cloud of smoke. 'And a man on the run. Nobody is above the law, you know. Not even Department Z.'

My right hand remained in my pocket, and he should know why.

'Hugh Randall Clifton, I hold a warrant for your arrest.'

'Are you planning to serve it?' I challenged.

His expression said it all. Duty dictated he should, intelligence suggested he might hold it back.

'Let's walk towards the river,' I said, knowing this put his men even further away.

He assented and started to walk beside me, on my left. 'I've never been to Guernsey. Is it as nice as they say?'

'When people aren't shooting at you.'

'Their police have you down for two murders, an attempted murder and string of other offences down to not settling a hotel bill. They've requested our assistance in bringing you to book, and Mr Julian Thring gave them my name. Which means my involvement was your idea.'

'Yes.'

'Before I arrest you, I have a question. Is the fact I still have a job down to you? Most of the brass in the Met have been cleared out and replaced by Mosley's lackeys, and half the officers at my rank have been sacked or told to retire. But not me.'

'I put in a good word,' I said. 'You've an excellent record hunting down communists.'

'That doesn't put me in your pocket.'

'Nor I into yours. But our needs often converge.'

'How do they *converge* this time?'

'The same people were behind the incident in Sark, the mayhem last December, and the shooting of those two policemen back in thirty-five. The day you arrested me the first time.'

'Can you prove that?'

'I will, but it should be your case too.'

'Should it? My orders are to serve this warrant, take you back to the Yard, and interview you formally.'

'And will you?'

'I'll keep it for a better time.'

I relaxed a little. We had reached the river, just upstream of the Ouse bridge, with its medieval turrets at each end. Sissy took station by one of the bridge turrets, but I couldn't see Renton's men anywhere.

'Meeting here to talk was your idea, so talk,' Renton said. 'All Guernsey have are statements from Mr and Mrs Thring, who say they didn't witness the incident, and an injured Frenchman who clings to his consul. He claims a whole gang of you burst in while he and his two colleagues were having dinner and started shooting.'

'He had three colleagues in total, and we were hardly a gang,' I said. 'And it was self-defence.'

'Shooting a man armed with a coffee cup, and a completely unarmed woman is hardly self-defence. Even in—where is it—Sark.'

'One of the men was carrying a pistol.'

'Which he didn't fire.'

'Guernsey police surely found the machine guns and hand grenades in their rooms? And they were not the Thompsons we use and not good old British Mills bombs, so don't say we planted them.'

A bench offered a view across the ruddy brown water to a park and gardens, then to the towers and gables of the ancient city beyond.

'I can't call it a formal interview, but sit down, and I'll make believe you're telling me something like the truth.'

'You sit, I'll remain standing.'

'Sit down, Clifton. If I wanted to nick you, I'd have the area ringed with uniforms.'

I complied, and he sat next to me, taking out a notepad. The story I told included my helpful fisherman, Ruth the traitor, and my attempt to keep the situation calm before the soon-to-be-dead Frenchman reached for his gun. I omitted Eleanor and Julian's part in the shooting, letting Renton believe I'd darted round the room exercising my legendary skills with a pistol.

'John Wayne could learn a thing or two from you.'

'Honestly, inspector, they were the most terrifying moments of my life.'

'Since the bodies piled up last December.'

'Yes, since then.'

'And where was Lady Poe-Mundy when all this was happening?'

'She's not *Lady*, merely the *Honourable*.'

'Not honourable enough for you to marry her.'

'Sissy was behind me, holding off the fourth Frenchman, who escaped to his boat in the dark. The hotel must have confirmed there were three men and a woman in the French party?'

'The witness statements were very confused. There were six of you, there were four of you, two of you. The Frenchman in custody said a red-haired woman tortured him.'

'Oh, oh, there was a red-haired hotel guest. She may have been a nurse, tried to help with his wound. He was swearing a lot. I know that much French.'

'And this woman you called Ruth had French papers in which she was named Hilary Devon.'

'Another made-up name,' I said. 'She claimed to be the sister of the young chap your men shot in the back the last time you arrested me. Neither were what they claimed to be.'

'Both now conveniently dead.' His face betrayed he believed less than half of what he was hearing.

Renton glanced at his notes. 'You maintain that this Ruth and the Frenchmen were sent to Sark to finish the job they started last December?'

'No, they finished that job, so far as it achieved its objectives. This was a new one, commissioned by the same people.'

'But your Department Z can't prove it. I see why you want proper detectives to investigate the case.'

'The more the merrier.'

'I can turn a blind eye today, but you're a wanted man, and I can't call off the hunt. Guernsey plan to charge you with murder, and at your trial you can plead self-defence. If you don't appear in court over there, it's going to be hard for them to press charges against the Frenchman. He's claiming those weapons were planted in his room, and you were sent out as a fascist murder squad.'

'Fingerprints?'

'I don't know if they've an expert over there, but we can send one if they make a request.'

'Suggest it.'

He raised his eyebrows. 'In the meantime, the warrant stands, and if I don't arrest you, there are plenty of officers who will. Even those pumped-up Fascist Police will have a go, though they don't know their arses from their elbows. And those bloody suffragettes in uniform.'

'Women's Auxiliary Police,' I said.

'Yes, them. In the end it will be up to those people up high.' He pointed to the sky. 'Will they find some legal flannel to let you walk away, or will they just watch you go down?'

I nodded.

'One day, this is all going to be over, you know: Mosley, Blackshirts, Department Z. You'll be plain Mr Clifton, facing a long charge sheet. On the bright side, they don't hang people in Guernsey anymore.'

'No, Victor Hugo campaigned against it,' I said.

'Who?'

'French writer, believed in the strength of the human spirit in adversity.'

Renton lit up another cigarette and blew away my attempt to bring philosophy into the conversation. 'If I'm going to save your neck, I need to interview your honourable lady friend too. Is that her up on the bridge behind us?'

'She's nearby, but if we change places you won't try to arrest her, will you?'

'What would be the point? One of you will shoot me if I try, or your lady friend will get her mother—or the king—to pull strings for her. This is a fine country you and your fascist friends are building; I hope you're pleased with it.'

'They're not pulling strings for us at the moment.'

'No.' He looked pleased, as if he'd just come across a key clue or I'd hoisted myself by exposing a gap in my statement. 'You've hit the real reason I'm not arresting you. Not so long ago you were the golden boy. Shooting terrorists, well, that's what Hugh Clifton does. So, what have you done to upset Mosley? Why are the Baroness and her friends at the palace being so quiet? And why are all those British Union lawyers who used to talk you out of custody just sitting on their hands?'

'I've been wondering, too.'

'I bet you have.'

'Stay here, and I'll send Sissy along. Please be nice to her.'

'I'm always nice,' Renton growled.

Chapter Seventeen

As soon as the express train departed carrying Renton and his men back to London, Sissy bought a ticket for the next. She had plenty of places to stay in the capital and would move from one to the other, following my logic that our enemies couldn't be everywhere at once.

After driving her to the station and helping her onto the train, I took the Austin and drove around the southern sector of medieval walls and out of the far side of the city. The only road open into Kingston-upon-Hull led from Beverley, the others being closed at one end by Blackshirts and by socialist volunteers at the other. On a fine summer's day, the Austin rattled along the near-straight road that led south-east of York. The old car struggled as it climbed into the Wolds and was happier coasting down the east side. As the cathedral of Beverley came into sight, so did military camps to both sides of the road.

I ate a good lunch of roast beef in a half-timbered public house and engaged in conversation without betraying my purpose. Beverley had become a frontier town, with black shirts heavily in evidence. The regular army was being kept away in case they made their own decision on which side to take if the situation blew up. One road to Hull was kept open in the interest of trade, and to maintain the fiction the port was still under control of Mosley's government. A custom post a mile south of the town exploded the fiction.

Mine was the only vehicle on the road as I drew up to a halt at the command of a customs man. I wound down my window.

'Purpose of your visit to Hull?' The man asked, omitting the *sir* I'd have expected.

I showed my Department Z badge without a word.

'Very good, sir.'

That was better. I drove on for perhaps another six miles, seeing no other vehicles until a clutch of military lorries came into sight. A chicane of sandbags had been built at what looked like a chosen defensive position. To right and left was an encampment where lorries and cars were parked, some painted black and emblazoned with the white flash-in-circle emblem of British Union. A six-wheeled Lanchester armoured car carried this new livery, setting it apart from British army greens and browns. Stormtroopers lolled against it, wearing side caps and a black-dyed version of army battledress.

I may be a wanted man, but now was the time to discover whether I was wanted so badly that a nineteen-year-old corporal of the Fascist Police would have my name and photograph to hand. He held up his right hand to stop my car. His left arm wore a brassard embroidered with the red lettering FP, and his peaked cap carried a red band. A handful of FP men with pistols at their hips were backed up by stormtroopers wearing the badge of the newly raised Third Division on their collars. Other men manned a watch post, and I could see heads bobbing from entrenchments.

'I've gotta ask why you're going to Hull.'

'I import timber. Through Hull.'

He glanced into the back of my car.

'Step out. We're searching your car.'

I reached into my jacket pocket, and immediately two Blackshirts levelled rifles at me.

'We're looking for contraband. Weapons, money, socialist propaganda. You're a businessman—are you Jewish?'

'No, but I can drop my trousers if you want me to prove it.'

His features gave a tic.

'Or, if you'll let me reach in my pocket.'

'You're not bribing me, Jew.'

'I want to show you something.'

I was allowed to bring out the Department Z badge.

'Whoa, not seen one of them before.' The youth began signalling to the watch post.

'I'm ordered to go to Hull,' I said as calmly as I could. 'The timber business is just my cover.'

The next FP man to come over wore the badge of a Sub-company Leader and puffy cavalry-style trousers to stress his importance.

'What's this?'

'Department Z, he says,' said the youth.

The officer nodded, checked the badge, then leaned in to speak through my open window. 'You don't want to be waving that about in Hull, sir. They'll skin you alive.'

Now I was sir again. What dark magic a piece of brass could weave.

'No, please keep it safe for me.' I handed over the brass badge on its little leather fob and asked for the officer's name.

'Can I have your name too, sir, for the records?'

'I've many names, which one would you like?'

'I see. Well, we'll hold this here until you get back, sir. If you get back.'

The officer stood to full height and gave the Roman salute, his young comrade copying him. I offered such a half-hearted response as can be managed sitting in a car, then drove away unsure of what I was driving into. British citizens were banned from travelling to Spain to fight in the civil war that had been raging for a year with increasing brutality. Mosley didn't want his men dying for Franco's Falangists, and though he'd care little if British socialists died out there, he'd rather they not gain weapon skills and return battle-hardened. Franco was probably going to win now he had the bombers of Germany's Condor Legion on his side, but the butcher's bill was becoming horrific. It must not happen here.

Just beyond rifle range of the fascist barricade, I came to a second near-identical chicane of sandbags, advertised by red flags hanging limp in the airless afternoon. The men and women who manned it wore red armbands in lieu of a uniform, and two at least carried rifles. Mosley probably had the authority to launch an armed assault on the city, and if the regular army played to his tune, it would be a quick victory, but a victory, which would stain his name with blood that history would never erase. He repeated constantly that he was not a man of violence, and he knew that to send troops to wrest control of an English city from its inhabitants would be an admission of weakness. The message it would send to the world would be terrible and paint him in the same shade as Franco. Yet he'd recently approved the use of mortars against 'terrorists and subversives.' Battle may yet come to the streets of East Yorkshire.

I pulled the Austin to a halt beside a poorly painted sign reading Free Hull.

A militiawoman leaned in to question me. 'Why are you coming into Hull, comrade?'

'To purchase timber for mines in West Yorkshire.'

I offered her the name of the company my father used to import pit-props from Norway, when he couldn't get Canadian ones, and offered my assumed identity. Fortunately, Britain didn't yet demand that its citizens carry continental-style identity papers, and a gentleman's word was still his bond. I had a few old invoices to offer as confirmation of my occupation and my identity as Clive Outhwaite.

She walked around the Austin, looking mostly at the tyres. 'You won't fit much timber in the back of this.'

'I only do the paperwork. I just hope the Blackshirts let the lorries through after the ship comes in.'

'They will if you pay them. And you need to donate to the cause before you enter Hull. A pound.' She'd been sizing the Austin up to judge my worth.

'May I reach for my wallet?'

'If that's where your money is.'

The socialists were far less suspicious than the fascists. It could be their undoing.

'For the cause,' I said, handing over a pound note.

'The fascists will skin you for more on the way back.'

'I don't doubt it.'

She filled out a yellow piece of paper printed with a red star and a few lines of basic information about my identity as I shared the made-up details. Once satisfied, she handed me my papers. 'Drive on, comrade.'

I was never so happy as to be inside a ring of militant socialists. It put me out of reach of the fascists, and when the story of the badge worked its way back to London, they would know I was out of reach. Everyone must believe I'd fled.

Chapter Eighteen

Unit Leader Danny Hills was not very interested in the finer details of fascism. He'd read a few pamphlets and been to plenty of meetings and had enjoyed donning a uniform once again when invited into the Blackshirts. He enjoyed being part of Department Z even more. The Metropolitan Police would never have allowed him to be a detective, let alone a detective leading a ten-man unit working undercover. As a working-class Londoner whose face told a story of a tough life, it had been easy for him to join the National Socialist League. At first, he'd muddled it up with the Nordic League, but that was for the upper class, and the new party was aimed squarely at the workers.

Hills was not the only BU member attending the meeting in the church-like Ealing town hall. He spotted familiar faces in the audience, committed their names to memory but concluded they could be attending only through curiosity or had simply made a mistake. The meeting was not explicitly billed as being for the NSL and from the posters could have been a regular British Union event.

The first man on the podium, sitting to one side, was one on the watch list: Peter Wise. He was supposed to be a BU propaganda officer, so what he was doing beside the NSL banner was a mystery. More of a surprise was the man who marched up to the lectern. It was William Joyce, Mosley's closest man, dressed in a dark suit of cheap make. Hills had heard Joyce many times before and settled down to enjoy the speech. He didn't always follow the thread of the arguments or remember all that was said as Joyce spoke so quickly and ran his thoughts together. It was always inspiring though, as though he was *meant* to understand and *meant* to agree with the rhetoric.

'We are not Marxists!' William Joyce asserted. 'The workers of Britain reject the shackles of Marxism…the orders of Moscow.'

The speaker's sentences ran on breathlessly, ideas piled one on the other, and as usual, Hills struggled to keep track. It sounded impressive, though. The audience applauded when Joyce paused at last to take in oxygen—or paused in expectation of applause. Hills wondered if Joyce was even allowed to speak at a rally for another party, or whether his plan was to win the NSL recruits over to the BU, yet it wasn't his place to question the men at the top.

'But we must cast off sordid materialism, the slavery of capitalism, without falling into the trap of being communists!' Joyce boomed.

More applause.

'We are building national socialism on a British model, not copying the Italian fascists, or even German national socialists.'

He spoke very well, and Joyce was entrancing. Except when he started going on about the Jews, because it didn't add up that the rich Jews and poor Jews were working together. In Hills's experience, rich and poor wouldn't give each other the time of day. Employers exploited their workers, and landlords bled their tenants dry no matter what their creed.

'They will say we are Hitler's puppets, but we are not and never shall be,' Joyce continued, 'but if Hitler calls on us to help him repel the oriental hordes, then white British manhood should stand at his side.'

So under the NSL we would be Hitler's puppets, Hills thought.

People were clapping, making jolly-good-show noises. Hills had stopped trying to remember names of people he'd spotted, there were too many. And dare he even make a report on Joyce? Lucy would be discreet in typing up his reports, but she wasn't in the office this week, and the Wives might not all be so trustworthy. Some were married to important men in the Party.

Hills worked his way out of the hall amid the crowd. Life had been simpler when he'd been arresting pickpockets in Brixton or turning a blind eye to the street girls' trade. But turning that blind eye had been his undoing. Still, he had his respect back and a fiver a week in his pocket, so the girls smiled at him once more. He could look the world in the eye.

Of course, he should make a report on Joyce. On all of them. Nobody was beyond the reach of Department Z.

'Hills? Sergeant Hills? Danny Hills!'

A face from his past emerged from the crowd outside.

'Remember me? Eric.'

He'd fought beside the man in the early months of Mosley's movement; trading blows with socialists in the East end.

'Eric, how are you doing?'

'Oh, out of work again. But didn't I hear you was with Department Z now?'

Hills tried to laugh it off. 'If I was, I couldn't tell you.'

'No, no, you are. I've heard you are. Do you think you could get me in?'

'Aren't you one of these national socialists now?'

He shrugged. 'I can be both.'

'Well, Dr Valentine's the man in charge. He's very particular who he has in Z.'

'And that Clifton bloke.' Bill's eyes widened. 'The communist killer.' He mimed a machine gun.

'Yes,' said Hills.

'It said in the paper he was wanted by the police. Shot the wrong men or something. And a woman.'

'Just be careful what you say about him.'

Eric glanced to one side. 'Are you here tonight spying for Z—'

In a moment, Hills grabbed Eric's jacket collar with both hands and pinned him against the stonework. He was a big man and used to taking down men who were even bigger.

'You spying for the communists, Eric?'

'No, course not. Lemme go.'

'What if I tell them stewards that you are? They'll beat the shit out of you, then kick you black and blue, then report you to Z if you're still breathing. We'll have you down the basement of Black House, and you don't want to find yourself down there, chum.'

'Sorry, didn't mean anything, Danny, honest. Leggo, mate.'

Hills relaxed his grip. 'Don't joke about Z. You never know who's listening.'

Chapter Nineteen

'The name is Philomena, Mina to my friends,' she said.

I'd first known her as Verity, and I'd also heard her called Georgina.

'Nice moustache,' she said. 'A brilliant disguise, nobody would recognise you.'

She put her lower lip behind her upper teeth as her face creased with mirth.

The pub was panelled in dingy brown wood, reeking of smoke and spilled beer. A row of spirit lights above the bar were mostly empty and drinks prices were more on par with Mayfair than the back streets of Hull. Few customers now had the money or the heart to fill the vacant tables.

'So what brings you to Hull?' I asked.

'It's quiet,' the woman said. 'No Special Branch, no MI5—and no Department Z.'

'There was once a young Canadian named Lucille McKenna working as a volunteer typist in the headquarters of the Manchester Communist party,' I said. 'She seems to have vanished in mid-1935. Just gone from the records; well, the records we seized when we knocked their office over. I wonder where she is now?'

'I wonder,' said Verity from behind a cloud of blue smoke. She had no distinctive accent, or purposefully concealed her accent, but over our several meetings, I'd gained the impression she must have been born on the far side of the Atlantic.

'Recruited by MI5 to infiltrate the Blackshirts,' I said.

'I've heard they do that,' she said. 'From time to time.'

I coughed. 'You smoke more than ever.'

'Tobacco addiction is a capitalist trick to enslave the workers,' she said slowly, then shifted her tone and gave a laugh. 'Or some such plot.'

'Does it help with the pain?'

'That's my excuse. It's only my leg, now.'

She suffered from a pronounced limp, which was hard to disguise. I recalled a photograph Julian once owned in which Sissy posed beside a serious-faced but highly attractive brunette. Crow's feet now clustered around her eyes, and her forehead creased as she spoke. Verity looked older than her years, older than me, even though our files suggested she was younger. Or had been younger the day Department Z marked her down as being dead.

'Are you any closer to vengeance for how Parker hurt you?' I asked.

'Up here, no. Things are very tense in London; we can hardly breathe.'

She lit another cigarette from the butt of the last to emphasise the point.

'He's going full tilt at the Jews now.'

'I know,' she said. 'I've missed my chance for now.'

'He's been ordered up here for Dragon North.'

'For which I'll not be hanging around. And, honestly, if we kill Parker someone else will just take his place. Someone worse. That Blake is a real bastard; he was in Belfast fitting up IRA members.'

I'd not had much opportunity to get acquainted with Valentine's new man, but his very quietness suggested something cold and slimy lurked beneath the surface.

'How about AA Thorne?' I asked.

She thought for a moment. 'Foreign Office?'

'Once upon a time, but now Secret Intelligence Service,' I said. 'Head of.'

'Oh.' Verity gave the merest hint of being impressed.

'I thought that might be a useful tip you can pass to Moscow.'

'As if I talk to Moscow.'

'He's one of the Young Britons. I need to take him off the field.'

I slurped rather too much beer at once and had to wipe froth from my new moustache.

'You want him killed?'

'Retired hurt, leg before wicket, I don't care. I just need him out of my way.'

'Hugh, I don't have the power. We're hunted, just like you are. Simply staying alive is the challenge. Free Hull gives us a refuge, but how long will it be before Mosley sends in the tanks?'

'A few weeks at most. Will the socialists fight if he does?'

'Not against tanks and machine guns. Throwing rocks at the police and giving Blackshirts a taste of their own medicine is one thing, but there's no army here. It's not Spain; there's no mountains where guerrillas can hold out, no great arsenal the workers can seize. Hull isn't Barcelona.'

'Or Guernica.'

'No, it can't become Guernica.'

'Nobody wants that.'

'Not even Mosley, to set an example?'

'He's a man of peace,' I said with deliberate irony.

'Ho, ho, ho. And you believe that, after you've seen what he's planning here. Department Z must be in on the detail of this Dragon North. I mean dragon, fire-breathing, death, and destruction.'

'The name's just there to add drama. You know what the military wing is like.'

'You have to tell me everything you know. Lives depend on it, and if I'm going to keep you safe here, you need to give me something in return.'

I sipped more beer and wiped away more froth. 'Well, Dragon North is the country's worst-kept secret. The third stormtrooper division is deployed between here and Beverley, but they're just boys. And it's called a division but that's just fascist pomp, it's more battalion strength at the moment. It will take more than what I've seen to storm a city.'

'What about the army?'

'Perpetually locked in spats with Francis-Hawkins and the Blackshirt commanders, so not to be trusted to launch an attack on their own people. And the Territorials have been stripped out by men joining the stormtrooper units. So you're safe for at least a couple of weeks.'

She knocked back the cheap whisky, for which I'd paid the price I'd expect for a single malt.

'And so is Parker, for now.' She slammed down the glass. 'One day, he'll meet justice, but this Thorne is yours. Another drink?'

'Why not?'

'Are you still dallying with Sissy?'

'Yes.'

She nodded. 'Pity; you're a handsome chap.'

'Verity, I can't—'

She waved me away. 'Sorry, not enough to do around here. Buy me another drink. I can't imagine why you've latched onto Sissy, though. Don't you see through her?'

'She was your friend once.'

'I made her my friend—it was a mission. She's a dedicated fascist and daughter of a fascist, and I won't bore you with what I think of the aristocracy, but you can guess. Yes she's pretty and she's got money and connections and all that jazz, but Sissy will bring you down, she'll betray you. She's your weak link, Hugh.'

'Sissy—' I began, then stopped. Asserting Sissy was seeing the light and, therefore no longer a through-and-through fascist could throw her into a whole new pit of danger.

'Or are you just stringing her along because she's useful?'

'You can assume what you like about Sissy, and about me. There's no absolute truth in our world.'

'So here's a truth. Those Frenchmen you killed were not communists,' Verity said.

'Perhaps not, but somebody wants me out of the way. They failed to kill me but have ensured I'm a wanted man, which may be enough for their purpose, whatever that is. Meanwhile, your communist friends have been very quiet of late; they're clearly up to something.'

And Calhoun knew they were up to something. His men were engaged in an operation that had nothing to do with Dragon North.

'This is what we're up to,' she said, indicating the pub around her. 'We're under siege.'

'Your siege distracts a lot of attention,' I said. 'And it would be convenient if Department Z was also blind to whatever it was you were really up to. One less security organisation to worry about.'

'You always over-estimate Moscow,' she said. 'What if Mosley's people are behind this? They suspect your loyalty or fear you're becoming just too powerful. Big bold Hugh Clifton, the man of action. Just think how jealous those Whitehall office clerks must get, just shining the seats of their pants while you grab the headlines. Perhaps they just don't like you. Remember how the Nazis rewarded Ernst Röhm for building up the brownshirts.'

'They threw him in a cell and shot him.'

'So, drink while you are still alive.' She waggled her glass.

'I'll buy you another, but then I need to make a telephone call.'

'There's a phone box down the street,' she waved a hand, then cranked it right to indicate a corner. 'But it doesn't look like a normal one.'

I bought her another overpriced whisky then went outside to where I'd seen a public telephone box. By some quirk of history, the Hull Telephone Department was still independent and painted its phone boxes cream rather than Post Office red. Telephone lines to Hull hadn't been cut, superficially to maintain the illusion the government was still in control, but also reflecting the likelihood the port was riddled with fascist sympathisers and informers. There was no guarantee one side or another was not listening into the calls. Valentine had recently set up Room W for exactly that purpose.

All calls had to go through an operator, which increased my wariness. I needed to be cautious in everything I said once I'd recited the number for Fulham Bakery. Asking for one of the numbers at Black House would be too obvious.

The operator sounded tired, and her Yorkshire accent slipped through any training in elocution. She put my call through, and I expected to hear the ring tone and, after a few rings, the alert voice of one of the Wives. The tone I heard was not the one expected.

'I'm sorry, caller, but that number is not available.'

Chapter Twenty

Sissy stood before the smouldering ruin of Fulham Bakery. Firemen were still at work dousing the last flames as Hills came up beside her.

'Sad sight, Miss Poe. The boss said this would happen one day.'

'It only takes one communist with a petrol bomb,' she recited.

'Black House would have been safer all along—I said it to the boss time and again. We're moving everything there we can find.'

It was more good foresight than good fortune that Lucy and Walsh were wandering the country with the pick of the current files. Sissy was one of few who knew Hugh had also created a second copy of every important document and had it driven to a safe store somewhere in the north. All was not lost, but the duplicate archive was just a collection of boxes, not indexed or filed in any way, and it would take months to bring order to it. For the short term, Lucy's roving filing system would be invaluable.

'You know Eleanor Fitzherbert has deserted?' Hills added. 'Sent in her notice, says she's had enough of politics and is going travelling. All right for them who has money.'

'Can I see the letter?'

Hills pointed to the ruin of the bakery. 'In there.'

'I see. What did we save?'

'The vans are all fine, and Lucy and Walsh are still away wherever the boss sent them. The fire didn't reach the flour store.'

'So the guns are safe.'

'The guns are safe. Shall we all get over to Black House then, move into the top floor? Mr Thring is running Room Z until the boss comes back.'

'I'm staying away,' Sissy said. 'Until we find out more about who tried to kill us. And now this.'

'We don't know where to start on that French thing. And all our lot are still busy chasing those little groups and clubs the boss had us join.'

'Are you discovering anything useful?'

'More names. Mrs Vectis-Hunt got into a meeting of the League of Loyalists, and Jenkins went along and stood guard outside to make sure she was safe. When everyone left, he said he saw some of the same faces as when he watched kicking-out time at a meeting of British Array. More toffs and army officers, that lot. And one of the names Mrs V-H wrote down was a geezer I saw at a National Socialist League meeting. Same people in different beds, if you get my meaning.'

'It sounds futile. Why don't they just stick with the Party? I'll speak to Julian...Mr Thring about setting our agents on the new task.'

'But where do we start?'

'I don't know. But this fire tells us what our secret enemy was after. Closing us down, stopping us looking into things they don't want us to find.'

He surveyed the ruin again. 'Lucy's a sharp girl. She'll have taken all the juicy stuff.'

'Let's hope she has.'

* * *

Eleanor's Chelsea flat was only three streets away from Sissy's own. The living area was smartly decorated and hung with a couple of pieces of abstract art the Nazis would call decadent.

One bedroom stood empty now Julia was gone, and Eleanor hadn't yet the heart to find a replacement flat mate. Thankfully, Julia's belongings had been cleared out and sent back to her parents, who'd refused to allow any fascist flags, uniforms, or regalia at her funeral. Reputedly, they had thrown away the letter of sympathy signed by Mosley in person and the medal that accompanied it. No speeches or salutes were given over Julia's grave.

Julia's old bedroom was a bald place to sleep in. Sissy habitually partied into the small hours and rose slowly in consequence, but she would not risk restarting the social whirl. She needed to carefully pick up the threads while keeping moving between places of safety.

A hammering on her door brought her round from sleep.

'Eleanor Fitzherbert!' called a high-pitched but male voice.

Police was her first thought. But Renton had sounded satisfied when she'd spoken to him on that bench in York. The clock showed it was just before seven. Her next thought was to reach for her Walther.

'Sissy Poe-Maundy!'

More hammering.

'Just a minute.'

An emerald-green silk kimono was the most modest garment in reach.

'Open the door!'

Pulling the belt of the kimono tight about her waist, she glanced out of the window. The car parked along the street offered no clue. It was black, but not one of those Wolseleys Special Branch often used.

'Open the door, or we'll break it in!' The voice was far from the gruff policeman's bellow.

'I'm armed, I'm warning you.'

'Put it away, for your own good.'

'Who are you?'

'Commander Blake, Department Z.'

Yes, she might have recognised his squeaky voice, but she'd not met him on more than a couple of occasions.

'You better not be armed either.'

'We just want to talk. Is Fitzherbert there?'

'No,' she said.

'Hugh Clifton?'

'No, I'm on my own. I've put my gun down, and I'm unlocking the door. And I'm not decent, so keep your eyes to yourself.'

Sissy unlocked the door, then stepped back smartly as she could. One of Blake's men came into the room first, gingerly, as if expecting to be shot several times. Blake edged around his back.

'Get dressed. You're coming to Black House.'

The men from Z1 at least had the decency to wait out in the hall. For a moment, she considered making an escape from one of the windows, but she'd probably break a leg or twist an ankle or be shot in the back for her daring. Quite deliberately, she donned her uniform, lightning-in-circle brassard and all. She straightened her beret in the mirror. Ignoring calls of 'hurry up' she applied enough foundation to conceal her scarred cheeks, then enough lipstick to reinforce that feminine charm few hot-blooded men could ignore. Lipstick was not supposed to be worn with the uniform, but it matched the red of the brassard.

Blake's blood was likely as cold as a lizard's. He said nothing on the short car journey, sitting beside Sissy and keeping his eyes front. Once parked behind Black House, he led the way inside, with his man following close behind Sissy. She'd seen this routine before and knew where it ended.

'B1,' said Blake.

Two Blackshirts escorted her down the staircase. Julian and Melissa had both endured an uncomfortable couple of hours down there, and now it was Sissy's turn.

* * *

'The Thring couple have been down here, telling me a story which sounds rehearsed,' Valentine said. 'Melissa Thring more or less admitted as much in the end.'

'She was very upset by what you did.'

'Upset? Good. We won't hold power if we're afraid to upset people. I'm sorry if that doesn't accord with outmoded upper-class ideals of politeness and etiquette. Now, Woman Section Leader Poe—you've dropped your husband's name?'

'For professional reasons. A married woman doesn't own her own surname.'

'Very modern.'

'And we don't use the woman prefix in our rank titles anymore. It's far too much of a mouthful.'

'So, *Section Leader Poe*, I've heard two nearly identical Boy's Own stories in which Hugh Clifton single-handedly fought off four communist terrorists. It makes exciting reading in the cheaper newspapers, and makes very good copy for *the Blackshirt*, but I know that's not how it happened. Do not insult my intellect by telling me the story is true.'

'We prepared that story for the police. If anyone was going to be arrested and charged, it would be Hugh.'

'Very noble of him.'

'It keeps the rest of us in the game.'

'So you were all involved?'

Sissy saw little purpose in lying to Valentine. She'd be questioned again and again, then they'd perform the lights-off trick. A man might be threatened with torture, but a woman could be threatened with so much more. It was too much to hope that Z1 hadn't sunk so low.

'Melissa stayed back, but yes, four of us were there.'

'Including Eleanor Fitzherbert? Where is she now?'

'We had a letter saying she'd resigned and gone travelling. It's all been too much for her, losing her friend Julia and now this. It's not funny being in a shooting match; it's not like in a cowboy film at all.'

'If she gets in touch again, or you find out where she is, we need to know. Immediately. And the same applies to Hugh Clifton. Is he back in London too?'

'I last saw him in York.'

'Close to his father's house?'

'No, that's an hour or two away. Yorkshire is bigger than one would imagine. We stayed a few days with his father, but it was an obvious place to hide, so we moved on.'

'You came here, but where did he go?'

It was part of the game to play the loyal agent and part of the game to let Valentine know Hugh was beyond his reach.

'Kingston upon Hull.'

'Hull, excellent.'

Valentine clearly already knew or wanted to give the impression of being all-knowing.

'Has he defected to the socialists? Was he a socialist plant all along?'

'No, and no. He's confusing the trail. And I came back to find out what is happening.'

'On his orders?'

'No, but he agreed because he wants to keep me safe from whoever is trying to kill him.'

'Kill him? Not you, just him? It raises the key question of whether you were attacked because of the Radio Project, because you were Department Z or is all the drama just about Hugh Clifton? Is he a problem the leadership must worry about?'

'No, he's your star agent. The very best.' Sissy swallowed the hypocrisy. 'And the bakery has been destroyed, so this is not just about Hugh.'

'I never liked your little nest down there, but I understand it had its value. So if Department Z was the target, why was the bakery attacked and not Black House?'

'Well, Black House is guarded. There's always at least a dozen Blackshirts here, agents working onto the night and then the listening section in Room W, and the barracks is more or less next door. We can't just be firebombed here.'

'Hmm. You know this can't continue. You and Clifton running your own little spy network, arresting who you please. Shooting who you please.'

'No, it won't.' She looked from one to the other. 'Hugh has even talked about retiring, not from the Party, but from all this. It's very dangerous what we do.'

'Is he losing his nerve?'

'No, he worries about me.' She tapped her cheek.

'You look very smart, I must say. Dressing to impress.'

'Dr Valentine, I need to ask you a question, if I may.'

He opened his hands. 'We're all friends here.'

'Are you a member of the Young Britain Club?'

'No. Are you, Blake?'

'Not on your life,' he said. 'I don't have a title or a nice country house.'

Valentine pushed his spectacles marginally further up his nose. 'And let's be honest, Section Leader, you know I'm not a member because on Christmas Eve, somebody burgled the Young Britain Club and ransacked their office. The burglars took the membership lists, committee minutes, and all, which looks very thorough. As was painting communist slogans on the walls, which was pure camouflage. It bears the hallmarks of either B Division of the Security Service or your Section Z3. And I know where I'd stake my money.'

'I wasn't involved.'

'No, but your lover doesn't share everything with you, does he?'

No, he doesn't. 'He wants to protect me.'

'From the truth. Rather like the argument used by an errant husband when his wife discovers what he's been up to with an actress—I only lied to protect you.'

'If I don't know, I can't tell the police, or MI5, or—'

'Me.'

'Or communists if they capture me and lock me away like this.'

'You're not locked away.'

'May I leave?'

'Will you continue working with Z3, if you're finding it dangerous and your lover is worried about your safety?'

He read her dilemma as correctly as if he'd been reading her personal diary—which she did not keep. 'I sometimes think I should stop pretending, stop being an investigator, and go back to being an ordinary party member. I've been in Z for two years now, and it's tiring, it's worrying. And I've had to kill people. There, I said it.'

'Be a little more careful the next time you knock on her door, Blake.'

'Who have you killed?' Blake asked.

'I don't even know the names.'

'The best way.'

'But if you think Hugh is causing problems for the Party,' she said hurriedly, 'then perhaps he should retire.'

Valentine nodded rhythmically. 'It might come to that.'

Chapter Twenty-One

I drove around the western districts of Hull looking for a card advertising vacancies. It was an area of newly built houses favoured by the prosperous middle class, so my car would not look out of place, and I might at least be given a decent breakfast. Politically, residents were less likely to favour the socialists, so I might face less searching questions. A widow named Mrs Whittam took me in as a temporary lodger. The man who occupied my room previously had been a junior bank clerk who deserted the socialist enclave to seek his fortune in cities where there were still fortunes to be made.

Mrs Whittam also had a telephone in her hall, where I was allowed to take calls in emergency. I expected emergencies. One of those cream telephone boxes also stood just a street away, so I made sure I had a plentiful supply of copper pennies. From a stationery shop, I bought two notebooks and a half a ream of paper and used the dressing table in my room as a desk. Somehow, I must connect the information being gleaned by my agents across the country with that already held in Lucy's files. *Why now?* I'd asked myself. At first, I'd thought the Sark attack was a simple attempt to take me off the board, the Young Britons simply tidying up, or A A Thorne being especially vindictive. Following the burning of the bakery, it was clear that Z3 as a whole presented a threat. The dogs hadn't been called off my scent, meaning enough men near the top of BU were willing to be convinced by whatever agenda was being pursued.

One of our raids must have triggered this—most likely that on the White Knights or Nordic League. I was sure the Imperial Fascist League didn't possess the clout, and even Joyce wanted them gone. Curiously, he was blatantly consorting with other far right groups, and I wondered who he was deceiving. Perhaps we should have knocked over the National Socialist League, too.

My pencil paused over the sheet of paper. I could instruct Hills to put together a raid on the NSL to get to the bottom of how deeply Joyce and other BU men was involved. But that may be exactly what our enemies wanted; a chance to catch Z3 in the act, ambush us, shoot down the best of us, and ensure the survivors were killed trying to escape or simply make them vanish. Calhoun had been right when he'd repeatedly accused me of not being subtle enough.

Peeking around Mrs Whittam's curtains, I watched socialist militia moving along the street from house to house. I counted eight men and young women, of whom only one was armed with a shotgun, and none of the others sported pistol holsters. The armed man and three more remained in the road while a pair worked each side of the street, knocking on every door in turn. I gripped my Walther as I heard Mrs Whittam answering a knock. Edging open the door to my room, I heard them asking if she'd seen anything suspicious, any strangers, any fascist infiltrators. Of course Mrs Whittam had seen nothing, she minded her own business. And would she make a donation to the cause? Ten shillings would be welcome.

Mrs Whittam called me down to dinner and retold the story of the socialist militia and their rapacious demands. I repaid her the ten shillings, for which she was grateful. I suggested she put an empty jam jar by the telephone, and each time I made a call, I'd drop sixpence in.

I needed to speak to Bruno, but a long call to the German Embassy was out of the question, and if MI5 were worth their pay, they should have the telephone to his flat monitored and his post discreetly read. Charles, Viscount Wickersley, had been animated by the prospect of an alliance with Germany. If this was the agenda of the Young Britons, or SIS, or a faction with the fascist movement, it must have a partner at the German end. Quite possibly, it was Bruno himself. If so, it was up to him to convince me to come on board.

After some passing of messages, I managed to have a telephone conversation with Lucy. She and Walsh had moved into a Women's Section training hut on Baroness Rockwell's estate almost a mile from the house, and it had no telephone of its own. A reliable young woman named Jenny had been sent down from London at Lucy's request to help carry the burden and run messages from house to huts. I urged the little team to go through the papers we'd retrieved again, tag every person of interest so we could make them the targets of new enquiries.

Sissy had been rattled by an interview with Valentine, but she claimed to be holding up well. She'd volunteered to be the canary in the coal mine, and I'd agreed with some reluctance. It was a toss-up whether she was in more danger staying with me or taking her chances in London; separated, we could at least work at the problem from two ends, and one stood a chance of hauling the other out of a hole.

Between his clipped words of reassurance, it was clear Julian did not come away from room B1 with happy memories. He told me that rather than diluting his enthusiasm for the party, the experience had stiffened his resolve to crack this case. I knew Sissy frequently had moments where memories of squeezing a trigger three times and ending life unsettled her, but other than the boastful types, chaps rarely talk about such things. Julian offered no clues about how he truly felt about shooting those Frenchmen—or the vague shadows in the dark he'd helped bring down during our scrape in December.

My landlady noticed how often I was on the telephone or had to walk out to the box at the end of the street. My mother was ill, I said, so my sisters were anxious, and my business partner was struggling with the workload while I was away. She asked me more about my sisters, and as I already knew them like family was able to oblige. Behind the fibs, I knew Sissy was setting tasks for the women of her section, while Lucy was keeping the files safe, reading and re-reading, and copying down the details agents sent through to her. And my business partner Julian was in charge. Even dispersed, Z3 could fight back.

Chapter Twenty-Two

Sissy had decided there was little profit in staying in Julia's room as the subterfuge had been so easily uncovered. She resolved to remove her things and stay at a series of hotels. In the daytime, she might be found at Black House, but at least at night, she should be safe. Before it grew completely dark, she walked back towards the flat Julia had shared with Eleanor with the intention of clearing it swiftly.

She passed a café-bar the Blackshirts boycotted as its owner was an Italian Jew. From the corner of her eye, she saw the flash of glass as the door opened behind her, and a figure darted out. Sissy's hand was in the pocket of her black leather coat in an instant, and she spun round.

'Bon soir.'

The young redhead wore a woollen travelling coat in a striking leaf-green, and a matching feathered hat which would have suited a pantomime Robin Hood.

'Eleanor?'

'Surprise!'

'You're supposed to be in Paris.'

'Yes, isn't this excellent?'

'But Hugh ordered you to go to Paris and stay there. You had a mission.'

'That's what everyone thinks.' Eleanor took Sissy's arm and began to propel her down the pavement the way she'd been heading. 'Hugh is all over the papers; on the run, the bakery is burned down. So my proper place is here. At your side.'

'It was an order. And you resigned, and I told Valentine that—'

'Excellent, don't you see how cunning this is? Everyone thinks I'm in Paris. It's basic secret agent stuff, Sissy, straight out of one of Hugh's books. They won't see me coming.'

Eleanor's eyes sparkled at the prospect.

'You'd better hide and keep out of the way.'

'Don't be cross; you need me. What if Hugh doesn't come back from wherever he's hiding? Suppose they get him—who's going to rescue him if not you and me?'

'Eleanor, just…just slow down. It's become very complicated.'

'Let's un-complicate it.'

Sissy stopped walking and threw off the arm. 'Fine, you're back. And I hate to say it, but we need every single agent we have.'

'So give me a new order,' Eleanor said with a wiggle of her head. 'Section Leader.'

'Have you been drinking?'

'Of course—I've been sitting in that bar for hours waiting for you.'

'Don't return to your flat—get a hotel room.'

'Got one. I'm at the Grosvenor.'

'Have you seen your Beau?'

'Not yet.'

'Do you trust him not to blab?'

Eleanor crooked a finger. 'I wind him around and around.'

'Be careful.' Sissy sighed. 'I'm going to set you following people—you're good at that. Choose a less *haute couture* coat, though.'

'Paris, brand new. What do you think?'

Eleanor stepped back to display the coat.

'It's fine, Eleanor, you clearly didn't waste that one day in Paris or however long you were there. But you need to calm down, I mean honestly, you're bounding about like a cat.'

'I have to,' she said. 'Don't you see?'

Tears glinted beneath the shadow of the Robin Hood hat.

'I killed Ruth,' she said, then glanced away. 'I just can't get it out of my mind. I was so angry with her. And the Frenchman too, well, that was just fear, wasn't it? If I didn't get him, he'd get me. That's the logic of our world, isn't it? Kill them, or they kill us.'

Sissy hugged Eleanor close.

'I murdered Ruth.'

After breathing heavily for a moment or two, Eleanor stepped back and gripped Sissy at the top of both arms. 'Have you read what they say about us? In the little newspapers, in the French newspapers. Department Z are, well, these evil murderers. Like the Spanish Inquisition, or whatever is going on in Spain right now. But that's not us, is it? We're making Britain a better place.'

'We are.'

'Else, what's it all for? Julia, Ruth—whatever she was really called. Hugh on the run...'

'You can walk away. You've sent in your letter.'

'No, no, don't you see? I enjoy it. I bloody well enjoy it. There, I said it.'

'Eleanor—'

'My father would just marry me off, and my mother wants a dozen grandchildren to coo over. I'm supposed to snag a man with a title and spend the rest of my life in his country house making small talk about horses with boring people like Melissa Thring. But instead, I'm doing something, I'm making Britain a better place, I'm keeping that philandering cad Mosley in power.'

She gripped hard. 'I'm back, Sissy, and I really want to do this.'

A drunk ally was still an ally. A murderous ally was still an ally.

'Fine. There's a meeting of the National Socialist League tomorrow in Bethnal Green,' Sissy said. 'If there's a man on the platform called Peter Wise, Hugh wants him followed. We need to find out where he stays when he's in London, so Hills and Rinker can pay a visit one night. I was going to send one of the Wives, but I'd much rather you did it—you know what to do, and he's thrown off a tail before.'

'Super.'

'But dress dowdy,' Sissy said. 'No make-up—and hide your hair.'

'Yes, ma'am.'

'Hills will be with you.'

'Not so super. He's…well, he thinks I'm just a girl. Walk with me to my flat, would you, so I can collect some things, and a few dowdy disguises too.'

Sissy was immediately wary. 'Blake came for me there.'

'Well, he won't come again, will he?'

After a moment, she admitted this was true. 'I need to collect my things, too.'

Arm in arm once more, the two women walked along King's Road as if they had no care in the world beyond what they'd just bought in the shops or where they'd dine that evening.

Sissy slipped her hand into the right pocket of her coat as Eleanor unlocked the front door.

'I know what you're doing,' Eleanor said. 'And don't worry, I'm not about to do a Ruth.'

'Worrying keeps us alive.'

Eleanor led into the hallway with Sissy a couple of paces behind. Far enough back to be able to pull her Walther and shoot without it being snatched from her hand. Perhaps she'd react fast enough, but perhaps not. Sissy drew the weapon just in case and let it hang by her side.

Eleanor paused with a foot on the bottom step of the staircase. 'Shall I draw mine too?'

'No.'

With a shrug of her shoulders, Eleanor led the way up to the first floor and unlocked her flat. For a moment, she paused, then nudged the door open with her toe, keeping her right hand free. She snapped on the light.

'Perfectly safe,' she announced.

Sissy followed Eleanor into her bedroom, just to be certain. Her heart went cold at what lay on the bed.

'What's that?'

A well-loved teddy bear missing an ear lay where Eleanor might sleep.

Eleanor was considering her wardrobe and gave barely a glance back. 'That's Gubbins, he was Julia's lucky mascot. I couldn't bear to post him back. Sorry, that was a bad pun; *couldn't bear*.'

Her eyes followed Sissy's outstretched pistol. 'Oh.'

A dagger had been plunged through the breast of the toy and pinned him to the bed.

'Get your things quickly,' Sissy said. 'I'll get mine, then let's go.'

* * *

The National Socialist League held their meeting in the baroque town hall on Patriot Square, Bethnal Green. The venue had at one time held communist congresses, and in the years before Mosley took power his party had been banned from using it by the council. Its leaders would not dare ban fascists now, those who'd survived electoral defeat and hadn't been arrested under broad interpretations of the Public Order Act.

Peter Wise shared a platform with John Beckett, one of those wordy thinkers trying to mould the philosophy of fascism into some shape. There was no fascist Karl Marx to hang policies on and no Trotsky to lend it a global vision.

Eleanor once flirted with becoming a Trotskyite, expounding the need for revolution chiefly to annoy her parents. But permanent revolution was such a grim idea, setting the Department Z's of the world in a continuous hunt for spies and counterrevolutionaries to put against a wall. And the risk, of course, was that one day, she would be denounced when they'd run out of genuine enemies, and it would be her back against a wall.

Beckett led the meeting. Once the rhetoric and the repetition was filtered out, she found his ideas clever, less crude than Joyce's speeches, which dragged the Jews into every problem, and with more substance than Mosley's long rallying monologues. Beckett had been a Labour MP and wanted to pull the masses behind national socialism by using the same techniques as the communists employed to promote their revolutionary goals.

'Don't you find him boring?' Hills whispered during the closing applause.

'No. He makes me think. The common people must be behind the movement.'

'You mean people like me?'

CHAPTER TWENTY-TWO

'Yes, people like you.'

As the follow-up act, Peter Wise merely rammed home and repeated Beckett's points, adding little original thought of his own.

'He's supposed to be working for us,' Hills said in a whisper.

'I know that.'

The meeting closed to scattered applause rather than the orchestrated din normal at the end of a BU event, and no patriotic music accompanied the speakers leaving the stage. As the audience filed out, a pair of young women stood either side of the door, asking people for their names, cash contributions.

'Excuse me, madam. Would you like to join the National Socialist League?'

'No, thank you,' Eleanor said sweetly.

'Already a member,' growled Hills.

'Are you?' Eleanor asked once they were outside.

'It's only a shilling,' he said. 'And I claimed that back from Thring.'

'I bet you did.'

'We weren't all born with a silver spoon in our mouth. Thought you was supposed to be hiding?'

'I am,' she said.

'I was told to check if you were armed.'

'I am.'

'Bloody hell—sorry—Section Leader Poe said you weren't to come armed.'

'Danny, evil people are trying to kill us.'

'Unit Leader Hills,' he corrected.

'No ranks, no uniforms, no saluting,' she said. 'So tonight, you're Danny.'

'You stay here, then, *Eleanor*. I'm going over there.'

Peter Wise emerged even before the last of the audience had departed and struck a quick pace around the corner to where a car was parked. Then he waited, presumably for a driver. Eleanor signalled to Hills, who immediately grasped her meaning and vanished to fetch their own vehicle. It was the powder blue Alvis tourer belonging to the boss, but he wasn't needing it and would understand.

Hills picked Eleanor up from the kerb and pulled away before she'd fully closed the door.

'They went south,' she said. 'The car's a reddish colour—Humber I think. Silver tyre hub on the back.'

'I see it.'

'There it is, turning right.'

'He's turning right.'

'I said that.'

The evening Traffic in north London was light, but not so light the Alvis would be easily spotted. Its colour was not subtle, but black could scream police or British Union. The driver of the car in front was heading for the city centre, but a sharp left took him out of sight. Eleanor only just noticed him take an immediate right, setting him back on the central London route once more.

'Trying to throw us,' Hills said. 'Or he just knows his route well.'

'The file says Wise is from Middlesbrough,' Eleanor said. 'So I bet he's going to a hotel.'

'Not everyone can afford smart hotels,' Hills said. 'And all these little parties are skint. He'll stay with another NSL traitor.'

'Counterrevolutionaries,' Eleanor mused. 'Put them against a wall.'

'You what? Have you been drinking?'

'Not nearly enough.'

'You posh girls think you can get away with murder.'

'That's not funny Hills.'

'Damn it. King's Cross—he's going home.'

'Well, I'll follow him.'

'All the way to bloody Middlesborough?'

'Just stop the car.'

Wise looked about himself once his driver had left him by the kerb. Hills and Eleanor were still arguing at that point, so he'd set off towards the entrance before having a chance to notice a young woman step out of that Alvis. Eleanor was wearing the dullest brown second-hand coat she could buy, with her hair bound up inside a knitted cap of faded pink.

He'd vanished. Wise should be headed for the ticket hall. No, he was going down the stairs to the underground. Peter Wise was indeed wise, throwing off a possible tail or even deceiving the NSL's driver in the way he appeared to be deceiving British Union. He could be on the right side, after all.

She popped smartly down the stairs in his wake, pausing to see her target pressing coins into a ticket machine. Eleanor turned her back to him, reaching for her purse and pretending to hunt for change. One advantage of being a female agent was so many men disregarded any threat they might pose. Wise was off towards the Northern Line. Once his head had vanished down the escalator, Eleanor breezed past the ticket collector.

'Miss—'

She flashed her Department Z badge without even looking him in the eye and darted to the top of the escalator, taking the steps at speed. There was Wise, waiting on the northbound platform. She hung back in the access tunnel until the train had clattered to a halt then walked briskly to the nearest carriage, just ahead of the one Wise had taken. Her pulse was up. Plenty of hotels to suit all pockets clustered around King's Cross, so Wise had either a friend or relative somewhere in north London he could stay with. Or even a lover. She smiled, as dirty secrets were the best secrets to uncover.

Eleanor removed that rather nasty and quite distinctive cap and shook her hair free. Surely, nobody could have missed a redhead following them. For good measure, she slipped on her gold-framed Oxford glasses, blurring her long-distance vision, but the very design allowed her to pop them on and off at will.

Wise got off at Highgate, and Eleanor followed behind three other passengers, making no attempt to hide. She hung back at the ticket barrier until Wise reached the street, then she quickly flashed her badge.

'Miss!' called the ticket collector.

She turned haughtily. 'What?'

He offered a half-hearted Roman salute as she turned away to resume hunting her quarry. Wise was walking at a relaxed pace now, crossing the road, choosing a certain street, then another. This area reeked of new money. At last, her quarry was welcomed into a fine Georgian house, only now glancing Eleanor's way, and only now pausing just for a moment to notice the redhead in an old coat walking with purpose along the far side of the street. Then the door closed. She had an address.

Chapter Twenty-Three

German shipping interests in the port of Hull had to be protected, so providing an excuse whereby Bruno Vogel, German Cultural Attache, might come north. I met him by the waterfront. The harbour was quiet, suffocated by the blockade. Even the fishing boats were being harassed, stopped and searched by the navy.

He asked after my health and I his. Beyond the pier, where a ferry was tied up and silent, the Humber stretched wide and brown, with the southern bank just visible as a dark line. Long, sleek, and threatening, a Royal Navy destroyer lay at anchor half a mile out into the estuary, and at least three other grey vessels formed a blockade line reaching both inland and out to sea. From the low silhouette and prominent large gun turret, one appeared to be a monitor, designed for shore bombardment.

'It was not easy to get in,' Bruno said. 'The *kozi* think every German is a Nazi.'

'An easy mistake to make.'

'So I came with your friend Philby and played cameraman. I brought my Welta.'

He plucked the strap of the case that dangled from his neck. Bruno had dressed down into the part, not choosing the black leather coat which had inspired Sissy to buy me one and set the fashion trend for Department Z.

'I said I'm Polish. Accent is accent, *ja?*' He spread his arms. 'And I don't look like a character from a Lili Riefenstahl film.'

He was slight, dark-haired, with a sallow complexion.

'Have you seen *Triumph des Willens?*'

'Yes, it's impressive, scarily so. Bruno, look, I know it has been a long journey for you—and for Philby—but there are things that cannot be said on a telephone.'

'I'm pleased to come. There are Germans here, worried for their business, worried they'll be rounded up by socialists. Shot also, like the socialists do with businessmen in Spain.'

'The Falangists shoot people too.'

'Only socialists. Have you become a socialist, Hugh?'

'No, but someone wants to shoot me anyway. I'm on a death list.'

'Not ours,' Bruno said immediately. 'You see, I brought a camera, not a pistol.' He plucked the strap again. 'Then Germany has no spies in Britain, so it would be hard for us to even plan...such a thing.'

'You're still holding to that line?'

'Britain is our friend, so why should we spy?'

'How about in France? You must have agents in France—and links with French fascists.'

'*Ach*, you think Germany was responsible for what happened in *die Kanelinseln?*'

'And therefore also behind last year's assassination in Cannes.'

'That was very *gros*, ah crude, amateur.'

'But the outcome served Germany's interests, given, as a result, we have a fascist government and a fascist king. When there's a conspiracy, the best question to ask is "who wins?".'

Bruno watched a swooping seagull for some time.

'It is not in Germany's interests to have you killed,' he said at length. 'Berlin believes what I tell them, and I tell them you are valuable. To me, so to Germany. Von Ribbentrop was asking for you; he did not speak you at the coronation party. Come out of your hiding, show your face again. Come to London, come to dinner at the Embassy. I'll guarantee your safety.'

Returning to the capital would be like walking into a lion's den smeared with an appetising sauce.

'Everyone wants me back in London, but I'm staying here.'

'With your permission, then, I will invite Sissy.'

'You don't need my permission, Bruno, and neither does she. What is the Nordic League to Germany?'

'Useful,' he replied.

'Not a front organisation for the Nazi party, or the Abwehr?'

'If it was, I wouldn't tell you.'

'They're in contact with Von Ribbentrop.'

'He's a busy man; he has many contacts.'

'How about The Link, Admiral Donbas?'

'Your admiral was dismissed because he was too close to Germany.'

'Which for the head of Naval Intelligence isn't a bright idea. So you do talk to him.'

'He called his organisation *The Link*. That's not hard to understand, is it, Hugh? He's not even hiding what he is linking.'

Bruno reached for his camera as if it were a weapon and lowered his voice. 'There's a woman watching us.'

'A friend of mine.'

Verity was gone from sight again, perhaps deliberately revealing herself for Bruno's benefit before slinking into the shadows once more.

'One of your Department Z?'

'We have agents everywhere.'

'Just like the Gestapo,' he said. 'Or just like what the Gestapo wishes everyone to think. You've done very well, Hugh, with your British Gestapo.'

It was not an accolade I'd ever wanted.

'The *kozi* sent a man to watch us. I lost him back over there. I think *auch* he went to follow Philby. But I should take photos.'

He unclipped his camera case, removed his Welta camera, and unfolded it. 'Royal Navy,' he said, focussing his interest on the destroyer. 'Britannia rules…the brown river. As a friend you need to tell me everything you know about the plan for attack on this city. We trade information, this is my trade.'

I told him what I knew. From a certain perspective, this was treasonous, but Dragon North was a plan which deserved to fail and for the world to know it had failed.

'Quickly then, Bruno, I need to know what else is happening beyond

Dragon North. Some plot is underway, and my enemies want me dead or arrested or in hiding so I don't spoil it.'

'I'm not aware of a plot.'

'Something to do with an alliance between Britain and Germany? Is that a realistic prospect?'

Bruno raised his attention from the camera. 'Der Führer is nervous about Britain,'

'Britain is nervous about your Führer,' I replied.

'We should never be enemies; we do not threaten each other. You can't sail your navy to Berlin, and our army could never put a single boot on your island.'

'So if not enemies, is mutual distrust a good basis for an alliance?'

'Mosley is weak. I'm sorry if that offends you, but he is weak and vain. Pleasure-seeking.'

'I don't know him well enough,' I said. 'And if you think Mosley is weak, then it would make him a good partner for Hitler, because we know who'd wield the whip.'

'Hitler's specific criticism is that national socialism was born in the alleys of Berlin, not the drawing rooms of Gordon Square. Your Mr Joyce is far more popular in Germany; he's a street fighter, Mosley is an aristocrat.'

'But Hitler was a witness at Mosley's wedding.'

'And Mussolini is very, very angry for that. He doesn't want England allied to Germany. Also Stalin. He'd like to see the two great Anglo-Saxon nations fighting each other. And that would be such a tragedy for all of us, for all of Europe.'

'So we keep things as they are, and everyone is happy.'

'No, no, that's not how the minds of the men up high work.' He jerked his head upward. 'On our side—and on your side too. It is about power. That warship out there, you have perhaps two hundred; more, even. Britain has the most powerful navy in the world and the greatest empire in history; who wouldn't want to be its ally? Germany will protect Europe by land, Britain by sea.'

He slowed his words, almost mocking what he was saying. 'It will be a perfect partnership.'

I picked up Bruno's tone. 'You don't like the idea.'

He admitted nothing. 'The Soviets and the Italians will work against any alliance being formed. And Japan, they don't want a stronger Britain.'

'But we haven't picked up a shred of evidence that any of them are fomenting plots.'

'Ah, but the best plots are very secret,' he said mischievously. 'But think, Hugh. Why would Britain *want* to be allied to Germany? You've never had ambitions on the continent of Europe, and Germany cannot help defending your empire.'

'But Germany wants *our* help?'

'To balance the French. To contain the Italians in the *Mittelsee*—the Mediterranean. And to help Hitler's war against the Slavs. You have read *Mein Kampf?*'

'I'm afraid I rather skated over it after the first hundred pages.'

'*Lebensraum,*' Bruno rumbled the word like distant thunder. 'In *Mein Kampf* war in the east is inevitable. Poland, Russia, the little countries in between. Will Mosley send troops to support Germany's armies?'

'He won't even allow volunteers to go to Spain. Mosley says he wants peace.'

'All leaders say they want peace,' Bruno said. 'But your Royal Air Force grows, and your Royal Navy builds new ships…*aber* you have more than you will ever need already.' He flung a hand towards the destroyer. 'I'm reminded of the Battleship race before the *Weltkrieg*, and the *Weltkreig* was started by alliances. Friends make leaders confident.'

'Too confident?'

He answered with silence.

'People on our side are working to make this alliance happen; you said it yourself.'

'And you know who they are,' he said. 'If you are truly Britain's Gestapo.'

If I'd voiced names, he would not have confirmed them, but this is why he'd come north, to drop one heavy hint which could never be traced back to him.

'Don't look behind, Bruno, but I think your man has found you.'

'*Ach*, a short man all in brown?'

'That's the one.'

The brown man wore a red armband on his left sleeve and was not even trying to hide.

'Here, stop. I had better take your photo. Step back, put your hand on the rail. Yes, smile. Peace makes us smile.'

Chapter Twenty-Four

Room Y looked inwards towards the quadrangle of Black House. It had been claimed by Sissy for her section and had accommodated extra filing cabinets once Room U was full. Julian was sitting behind the desk as Sissy came back into Room Z with a document retrieved from yet another room. He frowned—he could tell she was worried.

Sissy slapped down the latest file. 'Daniel Cooperman. Board of Deputies of British Jews.'

'Are you sure?'

'Eleanor's got the address right; Hills posted one of his men in the morning, and he reports that Wise came out by the same door he went in by.'

'So Wise is Jewish?'

'We don't have definite proof.'

Sissy pointed to a file already on the desk, which came from Valentine's internal security filing cabinets. 'His personnel record says Wise has no registered faith.'

Julian opened the new file and glanced at the single form it contained. Department Z held very little information on Daniel Cooperman, other than noting his connection with the local synagogue.

'This isn't one of our files, it's Parker's. We don't bother with the so-called Jewish problem.'

'On Hugh's orders,' Julian said. 'But it looks as though we ought to start bothering,'

She scowled.

'You said that in Lucy's file—so many bloody files, why don't we just have one system—Lucy's recorded him as propaganda officer for the north-east. And Valentine's file says the same.'

'So he works for Joyce.' Sissy asserted. 'It could explain how he's been roped into this National Socialist League. I mean, it's all Joyce and Beckett, so far as our agents have reported. And Lucy says Wise is the NSL treasurer, not just a hanger-on. But Board of Deputies?'

'He's a spy,' Julian said.

'For who? Is he spying on us for the Jews, or the Jews for us? Or on both of us for the NSL?' Sissy shook her head. 'Hills needs to grab him, bring him down to the basement—'

'Not the basement,' Julian said sharply. 'If everyone is spying on everyone else, we need to keep this away from home.'

'But we grab him?'

'No. I need to talk to Hugh first.'

'But you're in charge, Section Leader Thring!' She couldn't hide her frustration. 'Give the order.'

'I am. And Eleanor is supposed to be in Paris,' he retorted, 'yet she's returned against orders. Have you told Hugh she's back?'

'I daren't, he'd explode. And you mustn't tell Valentine. Someone left a rather ugly calling card in her apartment, and Blake's the only one we know who's been there. So, this Peter Wise, what are we going to do?'

Julian drummed his fingers on the desk. 'I've a meeting downstairs now. Let's not do anything hasty. But if Eleanor is back, Hugh wants to know more about Dragon North. Tell her to set up a dinner date with that stormtrooper boyfriend of hers. He's in the First Division, isn't he?'

'A section leader.'

He nodded. 'I'd better present myself downstairs.'

* * *

It became a heated meeting. British Union kept its darkest activities separate from government business, so despite the King's Party now having the run of Whitehall, the Club Room at Black House was still used for the most arcane plotting. Julian represented Z3, but Mosley was not there, always keen to distance himself from decisions which could bounce back to bite him. The Leader did not always lead.

Dressed in full uniform, Operations Director Neil Francis-Hawkins and his aides were setting out the plan for Dragon North using an array of maps and two blackboards. Parker had also donned his uniform and oozed excitement about his appointed role, boasting he could bring close to a hundred agents north. Wearing a smart civilian three-piece suit by way of contrast, Valentine remained quiet in that studied way which always unnerved Julian. Loud people were the easiest to understand: market traders who bawled out the price of their produce, salesmen with their bargains, street girls who coo-cooed to attract. Gathered in the Club Room were F-H with his military bluster, Joyce with his tub-thumping arguments, Parker with his enthusiasm for beating down the weak, but Valentine stayed quiet.

'Hull first,' F-H concluded. 'Then Sheffield from the south-east, here.' He swept his hand across a map. 'It can't be defended from the south-east. With a diversion here towards the steelworks.' His hand now arrowed in from the north-east. 'We already control Rotherham, so we spring from there.' His hand moved to a third map. 'Last, Liverpool; we tighten the blockade by sea and squeeze it from the land. By that time, the reds will know resistance is futile.'

Joyce chose his moment to speak. 'Why use crude force? We can win the battle from the inside, from the hearts of the workers. Use propaganda, get the people to rise up for us.'

'They're rising up for the socialists, so they'll be crushed!'

'The Leader doesn't want violence.'

F-H snorted. 'Don't talk rot. And you're pretending to toe Mosley's line after what you say about him in private? I hear you call him the *Bleeder*.'

'That's slander.'

'You're the one quick with the slander. You can talk propaganda all you like, Joyce, but I have twenty thousand stormtroopers and a hundred thousand Blackshirt volunteers behind them.' F-H banged a blackboard listing units and formations. 'That's how we win.'

'We're not a military dictatorship; we are a popular movement,' Joyce retorted. 'Hearts, Hawkins, use your brain and win their hearts. Get the people behind us, not under the tracks of your fucking tanks.'

'Sir, sirs,' Julian interrupted.

'Oh, be quiet, Thring,' F-H snapped.

'But we have intelligence reports from Hull.'

'You still have men in Hull?' Joyce asked.

'Agents,' Julian said.

'Well, go on,' F-H said. 'Tell us what your spies say.'

'The blockade is wearing them down. Food is short, prices are high, they're running out of coal, the banks have no money. All we have to do is wait.'

'See?' Joyce folded his arms and glared at F-H, daring him to ignore the intelligence.

Valentine now spoke. 'But your agent in Hull is Hugh Clifton.'

'Yes, as it happens, but—'

'Who, for all we know, has gone over to the communists and is feeding you false information.'

'That's not the case!'

'Open your eyes, Thring, before I replace you too.'

'I can get men into Hull and sort Clifton,' Parker offered.

'They'll be dead men,' Julian said. 'Don't even try.'

'No, we can't fight our own.' Valentine waved the idea away. 'If Clifton's with the communists, we'll deal with him in due course. And if he comes out of hiding, he gets his day in court to plead his case.'

'You mean his day in room B1?'

'Don't be clever, Thring, sarcasm doesn't suit you. Keep talking to Clifton to retain his trust, but don't believe a word of what he's telling you. We need him back here, not on the loose. Leave the meeting, we'll have a conversation later.'

'Sir.' Julian stood and saluted, with irony in every motion.

He retreated, the naughty schoolboy who had dared speak up in class. As he reached the door, F-H thumped the blackboard again.

'Right, that's the intelligence bollocks out of the way. We're not waiting—

waiting doesn't send a message. I want to give the order on Monday the twelfth of July at the latest. The Glorious Twelfth, one month early.'

***

Once back on the top floor of Black House, Julian put on his uniform to bolster his confidence and stood with slumped shoulders, gazing down at King's Road from the window of Room Z. The only thing he could think to do was work, try to bury the humiliation. He'd overstepped the mark in the way Hugh did routinely, but Hugh seemed to get away with it. Looking round for things to do, he sat at his desk, picked up a pencil, and began reviewing his notes on how to bring order back into Z3 after the chaos of losing the bakery. He missed Lucy's efficiency in the office, Sissy was no substitute when it came to organising the work of the Wives. And as for Eleanor…

He threw down his pencil, moved to the easy chair by the window, and picked up *The Times*. Its reporters were well acquainted with Dragon North, so who did F-H think he was surprising with his mass attack? Joyce was right—and the Leader was right if he was also opposed to the plan. *If.* Following form, Mosely would be the proud parent of the assault if it succeeded but cast it off as an orphan if it was a bloody fiasco.

A small item on the inner pages of *The Times* caught Julian's attention. He read it, re-read it, chewed over the possibilities. He immediately formed a plan—then several alternative plans. In only moments, he knew the potential of each and saw the way he used that snippet would challenge loyalties, friendships and decide his own future in the party. His hand trembled as a knock sounded on the door.

A young Welshman wearing the fencing-jacket style uniform of an ordinary Blackshirt manned the outer office and acted as Julian's aide, answered the telephone, and ran messages through the building. Now he rapped on the door still marked with a Z from the days the building was a teacher training college.

'What is it?'

The door opened a crack. 'Sir, it's Dr Valentine to see you.'

Valentine eased past the Welshman, pushed open the door, then closed it behind himself.

'Dr Valentine—I'd have come down.'

'No, I wanted to see you in your roost. Very cosy.' Valentine took the other easy chair. 'I'm surprised to suddenly see you in uniform.'

'Yes, well, as my loyalty has been questioned.'

'Not your loyalty, Thring. Hugh Clifton's loyalty.'

'We were betrayed in Sark,' Julian said. 'But nobody believes us, and the Party isn't standing beside us. What happened to solidarity?'

'You trust too much,' Valentine said. 'If it was not for your father, you wouldn't even be up here. It's your friendship with Hugh Clifton that's turned you into this…well, what do you see yourself as, Section Leader Thring? A spymaster, a stooge for a spymaster, an office clerk who tidies up Clifton's mess? It's time to choose.'

'Choose what?'

'Sides. You're in contact with Hugh Clifton on a regular basis, by telephone, I assume?'

Julian knew there was no profit in lying. 'Yes.'

'And he's still in Hull?'

'As far as I know, but a phone box is a phone box. He could be anywhere, I suppose.'

'If he wasn't in Hull, he'd be lying to you.'

'He wouldn't do that.'

'I don't think any of us know what he would do. Still, in a fortnight or so, the stormtroopers will take Hull, and he'll be collared with the rest of the traitors. Or killed; you know what they're like. If Clifton escapes before then, the Fascist Police and Auxiliary Police have his picture, and they're both beyond our reach, so goodness knows what they'll do if they find him. You know they're led by Frederick Douglas—'

'Dougie, I know him.'

'And he's a member of the very same club that Clifton has a vendetta against, so there will be no love lost. And, frankly, I'd rather none of those scenarios developed, I'd rather the matter stayed under the control of the Department. We tidy our own house. What you must do is find a reason to draw him back to London.'

'Draw him, as into a trap?'

'It's for your good as well as his. We need him here, not hiding in Yorkshire or wherever he runs next. And we certainly don't want him captured by the communists. Or those morons in the FP.'

'The easiest course would be for our people at the top to speak to the authorities in Guernsey and have those charges dropped.'

'If only it was as simple as that.'

'But it is as simple as that. Sir, you need to explain—'

'No, I don't need to explain anything. You need to make sure Clifton comes back to London—that's an order. And it comes from the top, from the very top.'

Julian glanced down at a small article which had drawn his attention. A renowned explorer who'd once intrigued with his father had returned to England and would be speaking to the Royal Geographical Society early in July. If he wanted bait to bring Hugh back to London, this was it.

Chapter Twenty-Five

Bruno was staying at the Royal Station Hotel with Kim Philby, almost the only guests in an establishment robbed of its trade. It was a typical railway hotel, built in that brash Victorian style but now glancing back at more optimistic days. A socialist minder sat in the lobby, bored, eking out the last of his cigarette ration, reading a blurry copy of the *Daily Worker*.

I walked straight up to him, making good use of my relic Yorkshire accent. 'Good morning, comrade. Where's t' desk staff?'

'And who are you?'

'Clive Outhwaite, from Halifax.' I proffered my yellow paper. 'I wonder if this establishment has a room free?'

'A whole hotel of them, comrade.'

'Only for day or two, I'm delayed, you see? It's bloody annoying.'

'The manager's out the back somewhere.'

I took this as leave to walk past the minder, amble around, find a staircase, and nip upstairs. Bruno had given me their room numbers. I tapped on Philby's door.

'H-Hugh,' he said, displaying the stammer which came and went with his mood. 'Come in. You managed to slip past the commissar on the door?'

Philby was in his mid-twenties and hadn't long graduated from Cambridge when I'd first met him. On past meetings, we'd shared college anecdotes together, though I'd graduated before he went up so didn't have a great deal in common. He'd been more interested in politics while I'd either had my head down in the library or been charging around the rugger field.

'I'd offer a drink, but it's too early,' he said. 'And sadly, there's no booze to speak of, just a pot of tea; it's a bit stewed, I'm afraid.'

He took the room's sole easy chair, so I needed to perch on the hard affair by the dressing table.

'I'll skip the tea; I mustn't stay long. How was Spain?'

'Very unp-pleasant. The Falangists are coming out on top, but there's killing everywhere. The communists murder priests, Franco's men murder trade unionists. And intellectuals, well, we've no chance—both sides are killing intellectuals. The International Brigade is suffering horrible losses, German and Italian interventionists have the upper hand. It won't be over quickly, though, so I'm headed back to gather more horror stories for genteel *Times* readers to gasp at over their toast and marmalade.'

'Are you enjoying the life of the war correspondent?'

'Enjoy isn't the right word. But I'm where history is happening, the great battle of our time—right against left. The worst of it is that it's dashed hard to get either side to trust me.'

'You don't worry that one or the other might think you're a spy and put a gun to your head?'

He didn't flinch, or even respond.

'Did you hear about AA Thorne's new post? I saw you talking at the Embassy party.'

'Thorne—oh yes.'

'Careful with him, Kim. He runs the Secret Intelligence Service.'

'Does he?'

'He's not asked you to work for him?'

'Don't be p-preposterous.' Philby almost leapt from his chair and went to stand by the window.

'Thorne uses people and discards them. I've stepped over the bodies. Have you been invited to join the Young Britain Club?'

'No, as it happens. I can't afford to join London clubs on my wages. And don't start bandying about ideas that I'm a spy, certainly not in front of Bruno.'

'Half the men at his Embassy reception were probably spies. And a few of the women, too.'

'Not me, I'm a r-reporter. I'm a reporter!'

'Have it your way, Kim, but things are becoming very hairy. What you're seeing in Spain mustn't happen here.'

'No.'

'But there are people acting like they want it to. We were perilously close to civil war last Christmas and even closer now.'

'I'm hearing it's only a week or two before the Blackshirts attack,' he said, 'but you must know more.'

'No, I'm afraid I don't.'

'C-come on Hugh. I've come all this way, nursemaiding Bruno. At least give me a story. You have the inside word, Department Z—'

'Britain's Gestapo, yes, I know. Sometimes, we over-egg it. In fact, all the time. The British fascist movement is splintered, it doesn't work together, secrets are not shared.'

'Can I quote you?'

'Only if you want a knock on your door in the middle of the night.'

He laughed, and I made a joke of it too.

'I say, do you have a copy of yesterday's paper?'

'*The Times*, no. I don't think there's a national newspaper for sale anywhere in the town.'

'Pity, there's an article I want to see.'

Julian had shared news that gave me a feeling the pieces were starting to move on the board of whatever game was being played.

'I'm curious as to why you came with Bruno.'

'He needed cover, and I'm a reporter.'

'A war correspondent.'

'It's nearly a war, as you said. And you might have a story to tell, murderer on the run.'

'Only half a story,' I said. 'A few clues, plenty of red herrings but no denouement. So I'm afraid on that count I must disappoint you.'

'Ah well, at least Bruno owes me a favour now.'

'I imagine you reporters trade in favours, so let's trade. What I need is intelligence from outside the country.'

Philby put his hands in his jacket pockets and feigned interest in the view of the railway station. 'We're friends, Hugh, but I'm not working for Department Z.'

'No, no, and let's go along with the idea you don't work for SIS either. But I need to understand the connection behind the plot we thwarted in Sark and the one last year which tipped the course of history. One assassination attempt failed, another succeeded, and the choreography was perfectly timed to flick the domino that set all the others tumbling. Link it to a series of other actions coinciding with pivotal political moments over the last two years and you can understand why I'm concerned. The plots are joined at the top like a bunch of bananas.'

'And you've found more bananas?'

'We cleaned up a British militant organisation called Christians Against Fascists last year, but strangely they turn out to be connected to a French fascist grouping called Francisme. What do you know about them?'

Philby half-turned towards me. 'Now it's my turn to trade favours. What date will Dragon North start, and where?'

His question came with a hard edge.

'Hull is the first target,' I said, dry-mouthed. 'And the week beginning the twelfth of July, and I hope this news will only be used so that you are on the spot to scoop the story.'

'That's f-fair,' he said.

'Francisme?'

'Francisme has links to a violent right-wing group known as *Les Cagouls*—I think it means overcoats. In turn, they have links to the *Deuxième Bureau*, the French equivalent of the Security Service, MI5.'

'Not SIS?'

'I imagine they talk to each other,' he said, deadpan.

'SIS are perfectly placed to link British and French extremist groups and the various other players I've come across in this game. An explorer named JEB Baxter, for example.'

'I've heard of him, but n-never met him.'

'He was recruited to carry out dirty tricks in advance of the 1935 election, which would paint the socialists in a bad light. It may have tipped the result.'

'In your favour?' Philby asked. 'The British Union did win seats.'

'Interfering, manipulating, and they're still doing it. Keep your ears to the ground, Kim, please. I know you have a conscience, and Litzi is halfway to being a socialist from what she says in her cups.'

'Careful!'

'I am being careful. But know who you are trading favours with, Philby, and make sure you're on the right side when all this falls out.'

Chapter Twenty-Six

At least Hull had a decent public library, and the socialists made sure it stayed open. I read novels and made a point of reading the *Daily Worker*, which was no longer daily but *ad hoc*. Copies were smuggled in, and the library was the place the proletariat had a chance to read it. National newspapers arrived sporadically, but any seen as mouthpieces of the government were confiscated by the socialists. The latest copy of *The Times* was only two days old, but censors had snipped out two articles, thereby randomly chopping away whatever had been on the reverse. The piece Julian had told me about had survived.

Explorer JEB Baxter was back in England after over a year in South America and would be speaking at the Royal Geographical Society in July. If Baxter was back, there was a fair chance he was up to no good. The risk of simply remaining in the north while Baxter embarked on a new round of intrigue started to outweigh the risks inherent in returning south, and if Julians' information about Dragon North was correct, I had a little over two weeks to find a new bolthole.

Posters and decrees from the People's Committee adorned the vestibule, and I studied each one to gauge the direction the wind was blowing. An old but familiar photograph caught my eye. It was from 1935 when Joyce had me pose for the official photographer in full uniform and wearing a peaked cap. My chin was thrust forward in the manner of Mussolini, and I looked the very model of a modern fascist. Fortunately, it didn't look much like me in real life, yet it had been plastered over the front page of the *Daily Mail* and reproduced umpteen times for distribution to British Union branches. I frequently used the quip that communists probably pinned it to their dartboards.

But here was that photograph of the Blackshirt hero, along with my name and a warning that Department Z had sent spies into Hull. Patriotic citizens were urged to come forward with information. All that was missing was the ten-thousand-dollar reward, and part of me was disappointed. The FBI had offered as much for the gangster John Dillinger.

Subconsciously I stuck my chin forward to mirror the pose, then immediately thought better of it. Checking I was not being observed, I took the poster down. Hull was no longer safe—if it ever had been.

* * *

'You're going back to London?' Verity asked as we sheltered from summer rain in the doorway of a silent warehouse.

'Or somewhere close by.'

She folded up the wanted poster and passed it back to me. 'Are you going to risk returning to Black House?'

'No, no, it's time to be a secret agent for real. How about you? Once the collective fails, there will be a witch hunt. People will inform on their neighbours to get into the good books of the fascists, and everyone who's ever held a grudge against a trades unionist will point fingers. Parker's men will be going door to door and arresting anyone who can even spell socialist.'

'How did the country come to this?' she muttered. 'Ah, well, Hugh. Even if the big attack is all just fascist fantasy, I need to get away from here before winter; I don't think the collective will hold together once the weather starts getting cold. Mosley's not allowing coal or fuel through, he doesn't need to send in the armoured cars.'

'They won't wait until winter, and the attack is no fantasy. Word is the assault will take place in the next fifteen to twenty days. My guess is Monday the twelfth of July.'

'That's a pretty accurate guess—do you know the plan?' she asked urgently. 'The actual plan for Dragon North?'

'Hull will be first. Francis-Hawkins and his Blackshirt commanders are amateurs, but General Fuller will demand a rapid concentration of troops, then a lightning strike on a narrow front using maximum force,' I said. 'Straight down that road from Beverley, pinning your militia against the river, while blocking escape routes to the west.'

'So you are guessing—you don't know the actual plan.'

'I've read Fuller's books, intelligence is about putting the clues together. Francis-Hawkins will want to use the First Division to lead the attack, because they're his baby, and they are the most committed.' I held up a finger. 'But my agents know for certain they're still in the south, with no orders to mobilise yet. And when they do it will take several days. Furthermore, Mosley won't want his crack bodyguard away from the capital for too long. So, they'll need to use trains. There won't be enough motor transport to get them all here quickly, then back south again as soon as the dust settles.'

'We could arrange a train strike. The unions still have power.'

'I thought you'd suggest that. It would slow them up for a day or two and force them to show their hand. Possibly, the plan will go off half-cocked and buy time for more sensible counsels to prevail. There are still some moderate voices in the government, and people who will speak out— including William Joyce, for God's sake. It's not often he says something I agree with. If circumstances were different, I could perhaps negotiate a peaceful transition.'

'You mean if you were not on the run from the Blackshirts?'

'I'm not on the run from the Blackshirts, but from the people who are manipulating them.'

She checked we were still alone. 'And with all your agents, you're no closer to destroying the Young Britons?'

'We've nibbled at them, but only stirred them up.'

'I see why you need to get out before this attack; even if my comrades don't find the smirking fascist in the wanted poster before then, you'll be rounded up by your friend Parker.'

'You know he's not my friend.'

'But I like to test you.'

'Tease me more like. How about we take a boat across the estuary at night?'

'To where? If we could slip past the warships without being caught in a searchlight and not be pulled out to sea by the current, we'll still need a contact on the far side with a car. Someone we can trust not to sell us out, someone who won't get picked up by patrols. We'd need enough moon to be able to see where we're going, but not so much we'd be spotted.'

We were just past the full moon, but there would be none that night if the rain persisted.

'Then there's the tide,' she added. 'Have you seen it up here? The river just vanishes at low tide. We'd have to catch it right, or we'd be just slopping around in mud.'

'Yes, yes—I've never got the hang of boats and tides. Where's the nearest functioning train station?'

'Since the blockade started, trains don't come any closer than Beverley to the north and Brough to the west. But the fascists only let people through on the road leading to Beverley, the way you came in.'

'I can't drive back out that way, they must know my car make and registration number by now. I made a point of letting the Fascist Police find out I was coming here so they knew they couldn't reach me.'

'Well, there's a motor bus to Beverley that runs once a day, apart from Sundays, but your buddies in the Fascist Police make everyone get off so they can search for communist spies. And get their bribe. Even then, they'll tip suitcases out onto the road and haul people off to a cell for no reason. If they don't arrest a few communists every day, they're not doing their job.'

Men who took bribes were often blind to their duty. It offered hope.

'We could sneak out by night, along country lanes,' she suggested, 'but I don't know them, so we'd need to go with one of our smuggling groups and offer them a convincing reason why you needed to leave. And we could still be jumped by a Blackshirt patrol expecting an invasion of Russian Jews.'

I gazed out at the rain striking the cobbles of the dockside. 'So the best of a bunch of bad options is to take the bus and brazen it out?'

'People leave every day, mostly the middle class tired of the siege.'

'That's what we'll do then. You can play middle-class, can't you? I've read your file. We could travel together, pose as man and wife.'

'Oh, that will be fun.' She furrowed her brow.

'We'll be a middle-class couple getting away from those awful socialists. Buy whatever you need to dress the part, that is if the shops have anything left. And smoke a little less in public; it's not ladylike.'

She threw away a smouldering stub. 'Snob.'

'Yes, let's play at being snobs.

* * *

Verity and I would pose as man and wife. Hammond's department store on Paragon Square was suffering as middle-class women were staying away from the town centre, and the staff cheerfully fussed around Verity as she replenished her wardrobe at my expense. I also bought a suit of middling quality and a new snap-brim hat, so I'd appear to be dressing my best. A car dealer was anxious to buy the Austin as his stock was running low. Even if the Fascist Police hadn't made a note of its registration plate, given how little traffic there was on the road there was a high risk some bright spark would remember the little Austin driven by the Department Z officer.

And I needed the money too. I couldn't remember the last time I'd been in this position; being poor was something I'd only observed at a distance.

On Monday morning, we boarded the single-deck motor coach, paying handsomely for the journey. My Walther was left behind, as if rumbled at a checkpoint, we stood little chance of shooting our way out of trouble. Young stormtroopers were itching to use their rifles against socialists, and the revolvers carried by fascist policemen and women of the Auxiliary Police were not just for show. Reports indicated that firearms training was minimal, and most recruits were poor shots, but enough bullets would come our way to create a mathematical probability some would find a target.

Every seat on the coach was occupied, with most of our companions over-dressed for summer and weighed down by suitcases and bags. Cabin trunks filled the luggage pannier. Socialist militiamen allowed us through their roadblock with poor grace; we were the rats leaving before the city sank.

At least we represented three dozen fewer mouths to feed.

As the coach traversed the mile or so of no-man's land, I experienced fear I'd never known in my own country. It was as if HG Wells' invaders from Mars had taken over.

...slowly and surely drew plans against us.

Fascist Police halted the coach and ordered everyone to disembark.

Standing beside the road, Verity's hands twitched by her new handbag, which she desperately wanted to open to find her cigarettes. For all the FP knew, she had pistol in there, so she kept if firmly closed. An FP man's bulldog glare challenged me to be anything other than polite and compliant. We gave our assumed names and offered up faked letters by way of confirmation.

'Don't you have a driving licence to show?'

'No, but I have this.' I offered one of the yellow passes issued by the Hull Collective and stamped with a red star. 'I know it's worthless.'

He barely glanced at it. 'Where are you going?'

'Leeds, at first,' I said. 'Via York. We can't stay in Hull.'

'It's getting terrible in there,' Verity added in her snootiest voice.

'I'll handle this, dear,' I held up my hand as the most patronising of husbands might.

Verity responded with a nervous laugh but narrowed her eyes. If I'd been with Sissy, this was a sure sign I was in serious trouble.

'What's in the bags?'

'Only what we could carry.'

'Entry tax is five shillings each.'

'Quite erm, quite reasonable. Here you are, my good man.'

'Don't come poncy with me.'

'Sorry.' I handed over a ten-shilling note, and he immediately lost interest in us.

'You!' The FP man accosted a man in an old tweed jacket. 'Five shillings.'

'Oh, come on, mate,' he said. 'That's half a day's wages. You can't just rob decent working people.'

'Five shillings or you go back.'

Another FP man grabbed the traveller's small suitcase and tipped the contents onto the ground.

'Aw, stop it! Thought you were the police—you can't do that.'

'I bet he's a Jew,' the younger FP man said. 'They'd rather die than pay sixpence.'

'Here,' I said, digging into my pocket for two half-crowns.

The man in tweed stared at me, as did the FP men.

'I can't have my wife standing out in the road all day, man,' I said to the traveller in my most cross-officer voice. 'I'll pay the money if you just keep quiet and get back on the bus.'

The FP man took my money. 'He a friend of yours?'

'No—we just want to be on our way. We've had enough of troublemakers.'

For added effect, I glared at the man I'd saved. He couldn't be so stupid to think he could prevail upon the good nature of FP men as they didn't have good natures. They were recruited from the worst of the worst; Blackshirts who couldn't be bothered to march, policemen who found honest policing too much of a fag, jaded army veterans who missed the uniform and the shouting. The FP made Z3 look like saints.

'Back on the bus!' yelled the thug in charge.

Gratefully back in our seats, we motored the last miles into Beverley.

'Troublemaker?' the man said under his breath.

'Tell them what they want to hear; pay them what they want to be paid,' I said.

'But it's not right.'

'Welcome to Mosley's Britain.'

Chapter Twenty-Seven

Catching a local train in Beverley proved to be straightforward, with one change required to reach York. Standing on an open platform where all eyes could see us, I tried hard not to look anxious. A Walther nestling in my pocket had become a crutch, and the Department Z badge another. Lacking both, I was back to where I'd begun, unarmed and without authority, attempting to go unobserved by forces beyond my power to fight. We stayed overnight at York's Royal Station Hotel, taking two rooms as Verity had become my sister by this point. In due course, all this had to be explained to Sissy with enough voracity to avoid a slapped cheek and fingernail scars.

I was not going to warn anyone I was headed to London, and I was not going to loiter in York any longer than required to catch a fast train south. Vulgar brassards seemed to be everywhere these days. I wouldn't put it past the Party to pull men off the dole and push them into uniform simply so they could crow about reducing the number of unemployed. Another pair of FP men were hanging around the ticket hall of York station the next morning, and we hurried past as if late.

We caught the express on its way down from Edinburgh, seated in a third-class compartment to both save money and be less conspicuous. A married couple sat opposite us, and the wife tried to engage Verity in small talk.

'Terrible weather we're having.'

'Let's hope July is better,' Verity said.

She played the game for a while, lying most inventively about the imagined life we led, feigning modesty when pressed for detail. She sat by the window and I by the door, so we could maintain we were travelling together or travelling apart as the opportunity demanded.

Opposite me, the husband had been reading *The Daily Telegraph* but put it aside to search for tickets when the door slid open.

'Tickets, please.'

A man accompanied the ticket inspector. His black leather coat, as good as advertised he was a Z3 man, one I'd never met, one of my recruits' recruits. The young agent must know me by repute, if not actually having that *Daily Mail* front-page photograph of the inspiring Blackshirt hero framed on his mantelpiece.

'Department Z,' he announced curtly.

'I'm not familiar with Department Z,' Verity piped up.

'Don't worry, dear,' I said. 'They're here to watch out for communists.'

'Oh, my.'

'Did you get on at York, sir?'

'We did.'

The Z-man took a second glance at me, as if I reminded him of an old acquaintance who had never grown so close as to become a friend. I gave him the slightest of nods, and he responded in kind.

'Don't worry, you don't look like a communist, sir,' the Z-man said. 'Or you, ma'am. I trust you'll enjoy a safe journey.'

At least I recruited polite secret policemen. As I eased back into my seat and tried to concentrate on eastern England's flat landscape, my world felt very small. I was riding a train with no chance of getting off. Z3 was my creation, but unless I turned it into a force for good, it would grow into Britain's Gestapo, as Bruno had predicted. The public clearly feared us, or at least found us an inconvenience, but the very fact I had a man on this train proved how widespread the network had become. Power was at my disposal, and I could use it to turn the tables.

The husband leaned forward, speaking in a low voice. 'This Department Z, it's a bit over the top, don't you think?' He tapped the newspaper. 'But see how well the economy is doing! Unemployment falling, businesses growing at last. At least Mosley is doing something right.'

At any other time, in any other situation, Verity might have launched into a tirade, but she simply smiled when the wife asked what she thought of Mosley, then the king.

'And it was such a shame about Mrs Simpson,' said the wife.

'She would have made the perfect queen,' Verity said, without any irony as to her, the perfect queen would be one who brought monarchy into disrepute and hastened its demise.

We were only just leaving Doncaster when the door slid open once again. Black silhouettes blocked the light. Two men, one bulky, one slight, wore the peaked cap of the Fascist Police with its distinctive red band. Brassards on their left arms only underlined who they were for anyone who remained in doubt. The bulky one stepped into the compartment, nodding at one of our faces after another. I wished I hadn't put my hat on the rack. In his hand the FP man bore a photograph and checked it, looked up at me, checked it again, then his hand slipped to his holster and unclipped it.

'You two, out,' he ordered our travelling companions.

Immediately, the man rose to his feet. 'What, we've done nothing wrong!'

'We're not communists,' the woman pleaded.

'Out.'

The man turned to collect a case from the rack.

'Leave that!'

The FP men stepped back to allow the couple to exit.

'You too, miss,' he said to Verity.

She nodded gratefully and followed the couple. For a moment, I assumed the Z-man had sent the FP here, but he should have known I was travelling with Verity as, on reflex, I'd passed over both our tickets. I cursed the stupid error. Hope remained if the two fascist branches were not cooperating.

'You, move over there,' he commanded.

I started to stand up.

'Stay sat—just shift along.'

I shuffled along until I was sat where Verity had been, and only then did the younger FP man come into the compartment, closing the door behind him. He squeezed past his colleague and sat opposite me, grinning while the one with the photograph turned to show it to me.

'Hugh Clifton?'

'I don't know who you mean.' I tried to reach into my pocket to retrieve the worthless socialist identification papers, but in a trice, an ugly Luger automatic was in his hand. 'Don't move. And keep your hands where I can see them. Stand up.'

'Do I stand up or not move?'

'Stand up, smart arse.'

I did.

'Search his pockets.'

The second FP man patted my breast pocket, then drew out my wallet and the yellow identification paper.

'Hull?'

'We simply had to get away.'

'You're not getting away this time.' The bulky one showed me my own photograph again.

I deployed an irked upper-class officer voice. 'Don't you know who I am?'

'Commander Clifton, Department Z, and wanted for murder.' His smile betrayed a broken front tooth. 'Your fancy title means nothing to me.'

'Or me,' echoed the younger man, who broke into a grin.

Verity's face reappeared at the compartment window. I caught her eye long enough for her to know I'd seen her. The FP man allowed his Luger to loll towards the floor while his comrade searched me.

I fidgeted during the pat-down, so that my back was to the outer door, and the man checking my pockets was between me and the pistol. My chance of surviving a leap from that door would be slim, even if a bullet didn't catch me before I struck the track, but Verity was not going to give me the option. As she slid open the compartment door, I brought my fist into a ball and delivered a sharp uppercut to the younger man's chin. My victim grunted in pain; then his colleague shot him in the kidneys. I threw him aside. Verity was grappling with the gun hand of the armed FP man, and he cried out in pain. She'd stabbed him in the back. I lunged towards them, also grabbing for the gun and throwing my other arm round his neck. With two against one, he was instantly disarmed. I pulled him around, trying to keep a choke hold with the crook of my left arm. Verity stabbed him in the stomach, and he yelled out, then sagged. I had a full grip on him now and clamped a hand across his mouth to stifle the scream as she stabbed him a third time. She aimed the thrust straight at the heart, and he collapsed in a bloody mess.

'Close that door!'

She shut the door, then gazed at the carnage. The man shot in the kidneys was half-curled on the seats opposite, moaning. He arched his back and tried to stand.

'No, you don't!' Verity stepped across to him.

'Verity—'

She drew her blade across his throat, and he fell back onto the seat, eyes staring. The image of Lady Macbeth stood over the second corpse.

'Oh, for God's sake.'

'Wake up, Hugh Clifton, I just saved your life.'

'I'd have talked my way out of it. I've done it before.'

'Your friends in high places don't like you anymore. You've chosen a side now, Hugh Clifton. Welcome to the revolution.'

My head was in a whirr and my heartbeat must be audible in the next carriage. *Grief, the people next door!*

Surprisingly little blood had spattered onto my jacket, but I slipped it off. 'I'm going to find that man from Z.'

'Are you mad?'

'We need help with this.'

Out in the corridor, the male part of the married couple was coming out of the compartment the FP men had ushered them into. 'What on Earth was that racket?'

'My case fell off the rack when the FP men were searching it. I'm a whisky salesman.'

'You said you were in timber.'

'My wife thinks what I do is vulgar, so I say timber. Look, I'm sorry but there's broken bottles all over the floor in there, it's a real mess.'

'Where are those, those fascist police?'

'Waiting for their bribe. It's all they want.'

'But they had a photograph of you.'

'No, they had a photograph of some actor. They probably try this trick ten times a day. I'd sit back down in that compartment if I were you, and I'll bring your things through in a minute.'

'They've not got whisky all over them?'

'No, it's on the floor…and the seats.'

'Has it ruined my newspaper?'

'Sorry, but yes. The FP men are pretty narked.'

'It's a bloody disgrace.' He moved as if to try to pass me.

'Do you want to tell them that? They'll sting you for a pound too, and another for your wife and punch you in the gut for your trouble.'

I rubbed my stomach for effect.

'Just go back in there, and I'll bring your case round in a moment.'

Only partly convinced, he did as I suggested. I moved along the corridor until I caught up with the conductor and the young Department Z agent two carriages further forward.

'Could I have a word.'

The Z-man nodded and followed me to the back of the car.

'Sir?' he asked.

'You recognised me just now?'

'I thought you could be Commander Clifton. You came to talk to us once, and your picture has been in the newspapers.'

I put my finger to my lips. 'I'm travelling in plain clothes with another of our agents.'

'I don't believe what they're saying about you, sir.'

'Read different papers. What's your name?'

'Drysdale.'

'And you're with Z3?'

'Leeds office.'

'Why are you on the train, Drysdale?'

'We're looking out for socialists trying to break out of the north.'

'Are there any FP men on board?'

'Two, they're a carriage or so behind us, doing the same job.'

His reply was straight and honest.

'Come with me.'

Drysdale obeyed orders without question as the best fascists should do.

'I need you to stand guard out here and whatever happens don't open the door. We've some unpleasant business to attend to.'

I couldn't stop him looking through into the compartment.

'Oh.'

'Enemy agents…former enemy agents, dressed as FP men. Block the view as best you can. I'll pass you a suitcase to take to the man in the next compartment.'

He stood guard outside the compartment door, but whatever he was imagining I was up to couldn't match the horrible reality. I took the Luger 9mm, which had shot that poor man in the kidneys, while Verity relieved the victim's body of a Smith and Wesson revolver. We pushed down the window in the external door, threw out two pistol belts, and then skimmed two hats into the slipstream. Next, we pulled off the bloody jackets and removed all identification documents, throwing away the bloodied ones. Verity brandished an FP warrant card at me. 'I'm taking this.'

We folded both jackets into balls and flung them out at a minute's interval. Evidence would be scattered along ten miles of track. The final operation was the most gruesome and most difficult. We propped the closest body in a sitting position against the external door, then I worked the handle, concentrating on not following the corpse tumbling down the embankment. The train had travelled another mile or two by the time the second FP man was ready for his exit. Boots-high he fell outwards. I dearly hoped the people in the carriage behind us were stuck into their knitting, crosswords, or detective novels. If not, I was relying on Drysdale's ability to be officious or menacing as the need demanded.

'We can't get off before London,' I said, surveying the sticky red mess. 'Someone will find this and raise the alarm.'

'Passengers will get on at the next stop.'

'Yes.'

I thought rapidly. I'd paid little attention to the timetable, and we might be stopping several more times. 'Hang out the window as we come into each station. Tell people you've been sick.'

She pulled a face.

'Hold that expression, it will do perfectly.'

In turns, we managed to slip back to the toilet cubicle and clean the blood off our hands. Drysdale fidgeted, pale and unhappy, until he caught my eye and stiffened up. I thanked him to boost his courage. More than once, he deflected the ticket collector and boarding passengers. Verity and I hung our coats on the end of the racks to help obscure the view into the carriage.

The train began to slow as we approached King's Cross, and I opened the compartment door a few inches. 'Drysdale, you need to leave the train with us. Use the door at the end.'

Verity and I left the compartment smartly and made our way swiftly along the platform. Drysdale had to run to catch us.

'Can you tell me what is going on, sir?' he said.

'You've read the papers.'

'Communists trying to kill you…but they were FP men.'

'They were dressed as FP men. How long have you been in Department Z?'

'Five months.'

'That's longer than most of the FP. They're all new, and the officers don't care who they recruit. Absolutely anyone can be in their ranks.'

'But why did you have to kill them?'

We were out in the ticket hall now.

'Killing is a last resort, Drysdale, but something big is underway, and our enemies want to stop Z3 before we unmask their plot.'

His mouth formed an O.

'I've got another job for you.'

'I should be straight back on the next train.'

'Drysdale, there are going to be questions. Fascist Police and real police will be all over that train as we speak; you don't want to go back in there. Do you have family up north?'

'Yes, I live with my Mum and Dad—'

'No wife, children?'

'Not yet.'

'Do you want to join us here, in London?'

'At Black House?' he panted. 'Gosh, yes. I've dreamed of that.'

'So go straight to Black House, King's Road Chelsea. Take a taxi.' I slowed my pace to fish in my wallet. 'Here's five pounds to get yourself lodgings while we sort out a post for you. Show your identification to the Blackshirts at the front door and ask for Room Z. They'll send you up to the second floor, where you'll ask to speak to Julian or Sissy. Use their first names; nobody but me does that. Tell them my first dog's name was Major, to prove you've met me. Tell them the story of the train but tell nobody else; nobody from Z1 or Z2 and certainly not any flavour of police.'

'I could take a letter from you.'

'No, you might be stopped.'

He nodded, his face a mixture of awe and funk.

'Be aware you might not even make it as far as Black House, Drysdale, so keep your wits about you.'

Two more FP men were strutting across the front of the station, took one glance our way, perhaps took note of Drysdale's black leather coat, then deliberately ignored us. I looked round for Verity, but she'd already performed one of her vanishing acts. I hoped she wasn't headed for that safe house the Security Service had its eyes on.

'Your arrival at Black House may attract attention of the kind we don't want, but we don't have many options. Z3 is under attack—our outstation at Fulham Bakery has been burned down.'

'I heard the communists did it.'

'It wasn't communists, whatever the newspapers say, and it wasn't communists who I had a gun battle with down in the Channel Islands. We're on the trail of a dangerous enemy, and they're fighting back. Still want to be part of the fight?'

'Of course.'

'Welcome to the real Department Z.'

Chapter Twenty-Eight

Julian occupied the chair behind his desk in Room Z, while Sissy took one of the comfy leather armchairs and young Drysdale the other. The black-shirted Welsh aide brought tea and ginger biscuits.

'So Hugh killed two FP men?' Julian asked at the conclusion of the story.

Drysdale nodded. 'Then pushed them out of the door. I saw blood on his clothes and on the woman he was with.'

Sissy had already gobbled two biscuits, which she put down to nerves. 'Describe this woman. Was she pretty?'

'Ah, well spoken. A little older than you and about the same height. Blonde hair, and I suppose she was pretty.'

Sissy frowned.

'She's one of our agents,' he said.

'And they were travelling as man and wife?'

'I think it was a cover story.'

'Wait.'

Sissy left the room, and when she returned after a few minutes was carrying a file marked 'Laytham, V. D.'

'Was this her?'

'Ah, possibly. But she was blonde. And older.'

'It's an old photograph.'

'Yes, it could have been her.'

'Verity?' Julian asked, incredulous.

'It's a long and complicated story,' Sissy said.

'But she was—'

'Whatever she was, whatever she is, Hugh finds her useful. For all we know it was her who killed the FP men.'

'Hugh—' Drysdale began, then corrected himself. 'Commander Clifton said he did it.'

'Well, he's gallant like that,' Sissy said. 'Did he say anything more about this invisible enemy?'

'No, but the FP men must have been working for them, or they were enemy agents dressed up as FP.'

'There's a canteen downstairs,' Julian said suddenly. 'Go and have some food.'

Drysdale began a salute, then thought better of it. Once he'd gone, Julian and Sissy sat in silence, contemplating the view, the walls, and each other.

'Verity is dead,' Julian asserted. 'My father told me. At first, I thought she'd just dumped me, then, Father said he'd investigate the facts, find out where she'd gone. And, well, after a few weeks, he confirmed she was dead. Dammit, even the file says she's dead!'

'Everyone wants to make believe she is.' Sissy was regretting eating those biscuits so fast and pressed a hand against her chest. 'Sorry.' She swallowed hard. 'It's not in any of the files, but Parker tried to kill her back in thirty-four after she saw something she shouldn't.'

'Parker?'

'On your father's orders, I think. Verity took out his eye, then he shot her and left her for dead. Have you ever noticed how Parker never talks about how he lost his eye, or never twigged it happened about the same time as Verity disappeared? Everyone else downstairs with scars brags about how he got them fighting this communist or that Jew, but not Parker.'

Julian's mouth fell open. 'And Hugh's known all this time? And told you...and you both kept it from me?'

'Sorry, Jules, but we had to. Hugh didn't want to open old wounds and didn't want Parker to go hunting for Verity so he could finish the job. I don't know how it came about, but she and Hugh work together. Sometimes.'

'But she was a communist spy.' Julian paused. 'Or a spy for MI5...or Special Branch.'

'Or all of them,' Sissy added. 'Even Hugh doesn't know.'

'I'm going to see Valentine,' Julian declared, pushing back his chair and standing to full height.

'Can we trust him, when everyone is out to kill Hugh?'

'Valentine doesn't have to kill him; he just has to sack him. And then me, and then you and put Parker in charge up here. He can close Z3 down if he doesn't like what we do or how we do it, but he hasn't done so yet.'

'No. It does make me wonder,' Sissy said.

'And Valentine doesn't command the FP, so he can't be the enemy.'

'But the FP *are* commanded by that Young Britons chum of yours.'

'Dougie, Yes.' Julian went over to the window and looked down on King's Road. 'F-H put him in charge of the FP because he'd been at the Home Office and knew about policing.'

'Or because the Young Britons put him forward and nudged the right people at the top of the party—we know how they work. Your Dougie is on the list of people Hugh wants removing.'

'Well, perhaps Hugh isn't always right.'

'Dougie did make an ass of you last year, slipping you that titbit of information knowing you'd take it straight to Mosley, leading to all kinds of trouble.' She touched her damaged cheek. 'Including this.'

'Yes, true.'

'Whoever leads them, the FP are still part of Operations, so under F-H's command. Is he the one who is behind all this?'

Julian shook his head.

She tipped her head back and mused aloud. 'F-H and Joyce hate each other. Joyce thinks we're his pets, so F-H must think that too.'

'So you're saying if F-H weakens Z, he weakens Joyce?'

'Well, it's an idea. Other than just blaming the Britons for everything, which is what Hugh would do if he were here. He might be giving them more credit than they are due. He loves detective stories, so he's looking for a villain and a nice clear-cut solution.'

'But it's not clear cut, is it?' Julian said. 'We need to make sure the rest of Z are on our side: Valentine, Blake, even Parker.'

'Absolutely,' Sissy said. 'Shall we go downstairs?'

'No, no, leave this to me.'

'Leave it to the men?'

'That's not what I mean. Valentine thinks I'm just Hugh's glove puppet, and if you come, it will just reinforce the idea. Everyone knows where you stand.'

'My loyalty is to the Party first, not Hugh Clifton. Even Valentine knows that.'

'No he doesn't, he suspects everyone is a traitor. Or could be a traitor. So we need him firmly on our side, and I need to get my father onto our team, too.'

'Now you know how he lied to you about Verity? I mean, Jules, your father might have been the one who ordered her killed.'

'I only have your word about all this; you only have Hugh's word, and he's getting the story from Verity. Or a woman who pretended her name was Verity and is working for who knows who.'

'True—but do be careful. I don't want to end up in the basement again, or someone ordering Parker to kill *me*. Or you.'

Groaning, Julian closed his eyes. After a moment, his determination returned. 'I'm going to tell Valentine what happened on the train, but you need to go somewhere safe in case this all backfires. And as regards this Drysdale chap, introduce him to Hills, but don't trust him. We've made that mistake before.'

* * *

Valentine summarised the evidence Julian had offered for the best part of an hour. 'So Clifton is running around the country being chased by the Fascist Police, which he says are working on the orders of the committee of the Young Britain Club.'

'Yes.'

'And hunted overseas by a French right-wing death squad?'

'Yes.'

'Will he come in?'

'No.'

'And I suppose it would be pointless trying to hunt him, because the first two agents I send will end up as dead as the FP men on the train and the French terrorists?'

'I'd advise against it.'

'Yes, yes, he's the most dangerous man in the country, which was fine so long as he was *our* man.'

'He still is our man.'

'I admire your loyalty. But I'm not sure who you are loyal to—'

'Allow Clifton the freedom to investigate.'

'Freedom? We're not about freedom, Thring, we are about order. Order. And while you're here you can tell me what this is all about.'

Valentine proffered the report Lucy had typed up.

'We have evidence Party membership is fracturing.'

'Joyce's name keeps coming up in these reports.'

'He's riding this wave of national socialist support.'

'Riding it or making it?' Valentine rocked back in his chair. 'These are dangerous suggestions, Thring, very dangerous. Remember what I said about order.'

'I believe in order, too, but these reports suggest trouble is brewing. What is Z1 finding?'

Valentine allowed himself a moment before replying. 'The Jews have at least one agent in a senior position in the Party, but we don't know who he is. Or she. Feeding information back to the Board of Deputies and perhaps making this...' he waved a hand, 'trouble.'

Julian thought better off reinforcing Valantine's hunch with solid evidence. Such evidence could get a man tortured and murdered.

'It's not the Jews we're fighting,' he asserted. 'If I can say that.'

'You can say it but be careful in what company. This obsession Clifton has with the national socialists, where's it leading?'

Julian was at a loss. Hugh didn't always share his thoughts.

'Internally, we know that a lot of our members have been joining the

National Socialist League,' Valentine said. 'Some are in both parties, but some are deserting us. It *is* all down to the Jewish question—these other parties are taking a stronger line. The Leader knows it's a problem and Joyce is urging him to sharpen his rhetoric. Parker wants a free hand to round the Jews up, close their businesses, deport them, but Clifton shows no fear in saying he isn't worried by the Jewish threat.'

'Could that be it?' Julian suggested. 'The reason people at the top want him out of the way? If they didn't, they would be helping clear his name.'

Valentine went quiet. Possibly, he shared the same thought.

'I need to see your information on the members who are switching parties,' Julian said. 'To compare with ours.'

'Very well, I'll give you the authority. All this is a distraction, though; Dragon North is imminent. All the stormtrooper battalions will be engaged, and Parker's men will be with them. Once the stormtroopers have established control of the streets, Parker will hunt down the communists.'

'Fascist Police too?'

'No,' Valentine said. 'Joyce suggested the job go to Parker. The FP are needed to keep control over the rest of the country while all eyes are on the north.'

'Is that wise, knowing how they're chasing one of our own?'

'Is Hugh Clifton one of our own? Because we're chasing him too, Thring. There are just too many unusual things about your friend, and you ought to open your eyes to them. I'm stripping him of rank and position. You are now leading Z3, officially, permanently. Your first mission is to find Clifton and bring him in, by whatever means you find necessary.'

'But what about Sissy?'

'Good old Sissy. She's his Achilles heel, so leave her alone, and she'll lead us to Clifton. Then we'll see where her loyalty truly lies.'

'With the Party,' Julian asserted.

'And not with her wealthy and famously handsome lover? If you believe that you're a fool, Thring.' Valentine's glass-shrouded eyes bore into Julian. 'A fool, or another traitor.'

Julian's pride was wounded, but he felt the walls closing in.

'I specifically ordered you to reel Clifton in. And have you?'
'I have,' Julian blurted. 'I persuaded him to return to London,'.
'*You* persuaded him?' Valentine's piggy eyes widened. 'How?'

171

Chapter Twenty-Nine

We hugged.

'Missed you,' Sissy said. 'Why on earth did you come back down here? Everyone's looking for you, and you're all over the papers. Again!'

Our rendezvous was at the south end of London Bridge. 'Walk,' I said.

She took my arm, and we moved away as just two more bodies in the rush hour crowd.

'Were you followed?'

'If I had been, I wouldn't be doing this!' She pecked me on the cheek.

'Did Drysdale find you?'

'Oh God, yes. Did you actually kill the FP men on the train?'

'No, that was Verity. She killed them both with a knife, quicker than it takes to explain.'

'But you're claiming the kills, like a bloody fighter pilot.'

'You're right, it was bloody. And if everyone thinks it was me, it lets Verity get away clean and it makes the next set of comedians think twice about getting in my way.'

'Oh Hugh, I don't know whether that's gallant or arrogant. And I don't like you and Verity playing man and wife, how realistic did you make your charade?'

'Oh stop it. I'm in enough trouble romancing a fascist without adding a Trotskyite to the mix. Verity helped me get away, and I helped her. She shielded me from the socialist militia in Hull too.'

'Well, you're now a murderer officially and on the front page of all the newspapers, even the ones that support us. So why come back?'

'If Dragon North comes off, Hull won't be safe. And once Julian gave me the news about Baxter being back in London, I had no choice. I thought I'd slip back quietly while everyone still thinks I'm up there, but it just took two stupid FP men to ruin that plan.'

'You know the FP are run by one of the Young Britons? One of Julian's cronies called Douglas.'

We took a turn into a side-street.

'So if the Britons are the ones telling him to have the FP hunt you down, and they're the ones sending killers to Sark, what are we going to do? They're everywhere, and they're snagging the top jobs.'

'And Mosley is letting them.'

'Don't make this about Mosley. You'll be telling me they're controlling him next, winding him up like a clockwork soldier.'

'Well, it's possible. The Britons made sure the king stayed on the throne, and to boot made sure he didn't have an unsuitable queen. A king who everyone says is lazy and too weak to do anything but what Mosley tells him to do.'

'That's even more contrived.'

'Yes, and they contrived it. The Britons now have men in control of the FP, the Metropolitan Police, and the Secret Intelligence Service.'

'But Valentine isn't one of them, so they've not got Department Z.'

'As far as we know.'

'What about…your old masters; who is running them now?'

I stopped by a plain door whose black paint was peeling to reveal another layer of black, then green beneath.

'This is how far I've fallen.'

Up two flights of stairs was the shabbiest, cheapest rented room I could find in a hurry. The Jewish landlord asked no questions and wasn't likely to have active fascists as lodgers. Sissy surveyed the veneer of squalor, no doubt expecting actual squalor.

'Oh Hugh.'

I sat on the faded pink chenille bedspread, and she checked for dust before sitting gingerly beside me on a bed barely large enough for one.

'I used to work for MI5,' I admitted for the first time. 'I get the idea there's no love lost between them and SIS, or Special Branch for that matter. They all plough their own furrow.'

'MI5.' She puffed out heavily. 'Very well.'

'I daren't make contact in case they're bending with the wind too. If AA Thorne is behind all this, he'll be collecting all the aces.'

'Inspector Renton despises the Party,' Sissy said. 'But he didn't arrest us when he had the chance—you were testing him in York, weren't you?'

'Yes.'

'Well, your friend Renton won't last long, talking like he does, but if the Party is being manipulated as you say it is, he could be an ally. Couldn't he—while he still has a job? And MI5 is now led by…' she trawled her mind for the name. 'Commodore Marcus Calhoun. You must know him.'

'I compiled his file. But he was on the candidate list for the Young Britons, and if they've snagged him too, we're sunk.'

'You mean you're sunk. Because he knows you used to work for MI5?'

'It's a gun he can hold against my head.'

'Is there a gun you can hold against his head?'

'Yes, but I don't want to use it. Even if forced.'

'What? Tell me, I need to know. I might need to get you out of a scrape one day.'

'He's a navy man,' I said. 'He's thirty-eight, never been married, and I've seen his heckles rise at jibes concerning homosexuals.'

'Ah,' she said. 'Can you prove—'

'If I wanted to, I'm sure I could. But as for blackmailing a man due to bigoted Victorian laws—I don't want to become that person.'

'Hint,' she said.

'I have,' I said. 'Just once, a shot across the bows. And he knows I've got enough on him besides to sink his career—we'd both go down on the same ship.'

'Do you have any tea?'

'I don't even have a kettle.'

'I must go soon anyway. But…' She paused. 'There's something I have to tell you; Eleanor is back.'

I mouthed a silent imprecation.

'Yes, I know you told her to stay in France, but we need her, honestly we do. We had her tail Peter Wise, and guess what? He could be the Jewish spy Valentine has been looking for.'

Her news only added to my worries.

'But you're not sharing what you know with Valentine?'

'No, we all know what would happen to Wise. They were horrid to Melissa, and I got away lightly, but if he's a spy—'

'He's a very brave man.'

She hugged me tight. 'Oh, but that was you, wasn't it? Hiding in the party, every night and every day knowing you could be dragged down to the basement, or worse.'

'It still is. I'm never going to be on Mosley's side, I'm never going to be that man everyone thinks I am. Or I deceived you into thinking I was.'

'I forgive you, but nobody else will.'

After her hug relaxed, we kissed.

'And I put you in danger when I follow Mosley's orders, and also when I go against them.'

'You're doing what you think is right. And so am I, and we're not so far apart anymore. We're converging.'

I stood up and went to stand by my single window, looking out at the nondescript side street through spider webs and grime.

'What's happening on Dragon North?' I asked.

'Well, Eleanor is being useful there too. Her beau is a stormtrooper in the First Division, and he tells her everything they're up to. He's just waiting for the order to move.'

'Still the twelfth of July?'

'That's what we are hearing, but it's all been stop and start. First this week then next.'

'So the stormtroopers will be concentrated in the north for at least the second half of July, possibly the whole summer. Parker and Z2 will be up there too, beating up socialists and throwing them in jail. Meanwhile, the bakery is destroyed, and I'm being chased around to keep Z3 out of the game. Valentine doesn't command many agents outside Black House, and it sounds like he's wasting those looking for me. The Russians are playing their own games and keeping out of sight. We're spinning a roulette wheel, and at some point, that little white ball lands in a slot. Who wins?'

'We win,' Sissy said. 'The communists are driven out, and the country settles down.'

'Who wins if all these facts are connected? We've learned how the Young Britons operate; a little plot here, little plot there, then it all comes together like a great sprawling Dickens novel so packed with characters you can't tell who is important and who isn't. If the five of us had been killed in Sark, no one would even be asking these questions.'

'Julian thinks Valentine hasn't gone over to the Young Britons.'

'But still, Valentine has given Julian my job.'

'Yes, for now.'

'And Julian is a member of the Young Britons.'

'Oh, come on, Hugh, Jules is one of us.'

'Valentine hasn't stripped your rank either.'

'Stop it, come here!' she commanded.

After a moment, I joined her on the bed again, and she kissed me. 'Don't go suspecting your friends, or you'll turn into Valentine. He lets me run free because he sees me as Clifton bait.'

'Well, you've hooked me.' I kissed her on the lips and kissed her again.

I moved a hand to her knee, but she pushed it away.

'Darling, we can't...not here.'

I retreated my hand. 'Sorry, it's not the bridal suite at the Savoy.'

She tensed at my touch. 'No, it's not just that. Oh Hugh, let's get through all this nonsense first.'

'Very well, we'd better hurry through it then. If Julian is truly still one of us, he needs to stop Valentine being distracted by a Clifton-hunt. We need his eyes back on the ball. And we need to go and visit Lucy.'

* * *

The mobile archive of Z3 had come to rest in the boathouse below Baroness Rockwell's house at Highwood in the Medway Valley. Sissy drove me out there in her yellow T-Type. I'd paid for the repairs needed since it shielded me from a hail of bullets the previous December, and Sissy reciprocated by paying for the lesser damage she'd inflicted on my Alvis. The T-Type was not a subtle vehicle, and its arrival would be noticed by anyone watching Highwood or informers planted among the staff, but any rumours I'd taken refuge in Kent would just add further confusion to my pursuers. We entered by the north gate and parked under a lean-to by the women's section training huts, then walked a mile through parkland to the lake.

Lucy and Walsh waited under the low-beamed roof of the boathouse. Lucy rushed forward as we came into the gloom and hugged me.

'Lucy!'

'You've been sacked, so I don't have to salute you anymore or call you sir. You're just a mate now.'

'Glad to see you safe, *sir*,' Walsh said, then winked at Lucy.

'Aw, leave off, Jimmy,' she said. 'We're undercover. We're like a bunch of old friends.'

I had to smile. Nobody could beat her spirit down.

'We don't have long, *friends*,' I said. 'Let's see what you have.'

In previous years the boathouse had been used for training the women's section run by Melissa Thring, but it was Sissy's women who'd used it more recently. Lucy had taken the latest reports received by Room Z and collated these together with those she'd saved from the bakery. A row of cardboard files lay along one of the workbenches, which ran into the low-roofed building. Sissy and I sat on two of the mismatched wooden chairs.

'Tell him about that bloke,' Walsh said.

'Oh yes, your old friend JEB Baxter,' Lucy said, presenting the file. 'He's back in Britain, and he's giving a talk at the Royal Society a week from today.'

She showed me the clipping. At last, I had a time and a date.

'Baxter's trouble, in't he? It's why his file is all flagged up.'

'Remember what I said about so much happening at once?' I said to Sissy. 'It could be just coincidence.'

'I don't like coincidences. If Baxter's back in play, it means things are coming to a head.'

I re-read the short newspaper clipping.

'That's next Thursday's social engagements fixed.'

Sissy gave a sigh. 'And the dress code includes pistols I suppose?'

'Sadly, yes. And if we're going up against JEB Baxter, we need every man we can find.'

'And women?' Lucy asked brightly.

'Not you. Once we're done today, pack all this into the van and move base again. Try Ashford. Find a little pub to stay in, park the van round the back. We've a couple of good agents based in Ashford, Lucy. Make contact, see how many they can muster at short notice. Then I need you back in London by Monday at the latest, Walsh.'

'I need to show you what we've found, first,' Lucy said. 'And Jimmy will make tea.'

'We're a bit low on milk,' Walsh said, but went off to find the kettle.

'You wanted to see what we had on Peter Wise?' Lucy said. 'You said follow him, so we followed him. He's our propaganda officer, the NSL's treasurer, and something with the Jews as well. What's his game?'

Secret policemen are tempted to play god. In January I'd successfully tipped off a couple of Labour politicians on the slate to be arrested just before the elections, but a couple more either ignored my warning or acted too late and were rounded up. Willful ignorance was often required when I reviewed the information my agents collected.

'Be careful with this file,' I said.

'I wanted to arrest him,' Sissy said. 'But Julian wouldn't make the decision.'

'For which I'm grateful,' I said.

'But is it safe for him to be still running free?' Lucy asked.

'Do you have a problem with Jews, Lucy?'

'No! And you must've asked us all twenty times over. It's not about him being a Jew, Mr Clifton, it's just that he could be spying on us.'

CHAPTER TWENTY-NINE

'Or spying *for* us,' I corrected.

'Yes, yes I s'pose, so we've not arrested him. And we haven't arrested Mr Joyce either, as it happens. Just look at these reports on what he's been up to.' Lucy took up another pile. 'He keeps talking to meetings of these silly little parties. And John Beckett too.'

'Beckett is boring, though.' Walsh delivered almost-black teas to the three of us.

'In some of these 'ere reports people say Joyce is a better speaker than Mosley.'

'Arguably he is.'

'But even if people think it, they shouldn't *say* it,' Lucy chided me.

'We should allow some freedom of speech.'

'Oh, that's dangerous,' she said. 'You showed me that piece Dr Valentine wrote in *Fascist Quarterly*; Follow the Leader.'

'If people don't say what they think, then how are *we* going to find out what they are thinking?'

'Oh that's a good point,' Lucy said. 'A bit sneaky, though.'

'Lucy we are sneaky.'

She smiled her crooked smile. 'I know, just teasing. Gotta have a laugh, else it all gets so serious.'

At times, I was convinced Lucy would greet the final downfall of British freedoms with little more than a cheerful shrug.

'Anyway, some people are even saying that Joyce would make a better leader.'

Including Adolf Hitler, by Bruno's account.

'I've got a list of names,' Lucy continued. 'Now Mr Thring could have *them* arrested without upsetting anyone.'

Walsh was resting against the long bench. 'Some of the old soldiers in the stormtroopers want Francis-Hawkins to lead us. They want an end to the kid-glove treatment of the unions, and they want the troops sent into Liverpool and Hull to sort out the socialists. I'm not much for office work, but I can read. She's had me reading all this.'

Lucy smiled at him. They had been travelling the road together for a month, and I could see a bond had formed.

'And then the sailors want Admiral Domville,' Walsh added. 'Well, the ones who don't want Churchill.'

'Right mix-up, in't it?' Lucy said.

'Perhaps we should have an election,' I said.

Lucy gave a laugh. 'That's not going to happen, is it? Our Mosley's in power, that's it, mate.'

'But his grip on power isn't absolute,' I said. 'I wasn't joking about an election. Mosley must know about all this.' I tapped the bench spread with files. 'Valentine isn't stupid, and internal security is his area. He reports directly to Mosley, so he must know he has rivals.'

'What's he going to do, get rid of 'em?' Lucy asked.

'You've got lists, Valentine has lists,' I mused aloud. 'And someone who can write will be giving the FP lists too. Remember when Hitler purged the Brownshirts? They called it the Night of the Long Knives. It could happen here you know; we could be seeing it happen, right here, right now.'

'Well, it will be good riddance—'

'Wake up, Lucy! Once they start on the round-ups, who's next? Me, you? The whole of Department Z if they think we've become too powerful or too inconvenient or we know too much.'

'But if it's us that's doing the arresting, and it's the traitors we're putting behind bars—'

'They won't be behind bars, Lucy, they'll be stood against a wall. Do you want to be the one giving the order to shoot?'

'I just type,' she retorted.

'That's how it starts.'

Chapter Thirty

The Young Britain Club was located just off Pall Mall. Julian had rarely visited it all year, having learned the truth about the committee's meddling in affairs of state and suspecting they knew how deep his knowledge ran. Only the gullible believed it had been communists who burgled the building at Christmas and stole the records.

He'd accepted the dinner invitation with caution, and as he came into the oak-panelled side room, he found a table set for four with just one empty seat.

'Thring, welcome.' AA Thorne stood and waved him towards the empty chair.

'Of course, you know Dougie.'

Frederic Douglas would soon need to visit his tailor for a new suit to accommodate his expanding waist. He raised a sherry glass.

The other man was older, balding, but also with a spreading waist.

'And may I introduce Marcus Calhoun, who is—'

'Head of the Security Service.' Julian completed the line. 'MI5.'

Calhoun gave just the hint of a nod.

'Have a seat.'

One of the servants appeared by invisible summons and took an order for drinks.

'Do you have a 1920 Bordeaux?' Calhoun asked.

'I believe so, sir.'

'You know your wines, Commodore Calhoun,' said AA.

'What I don't know is why we're meeting here. There are official channels—'

'Some would say that we four represent the most powerful forces in the country,' AA interrupted.

'Apart from the navy,' Calhoun said. 'And the army, the Blackshirts perhaps.'

Julian surmised there was little comradeship between the two established intelligence branches.

AA gave a long exhalation. 'The four security services. The army and the navy don't get involved in politics and never have.'

'You didn't invite Special Branch?' Calhoun asked.

'The Commissioner couldn't be here tonight, but he's firmly on our team. My point is that information is power, and we four in this room, plus the police, have information at our fingertips.'

'Look, old man, I'm just Z3,' Julian objected.

'Don't underestimate yourself, Thring. You lead the active part of Department Z, the covert intelligence section. Dr Valentine's role is to have everyone in your party looking over their shoulders, and his man Parker just chases the Jews, but your section is free to do so much more.'

'I understand.'

'Z3 has more agents than the two of us combined,' AA said to Calhoun.

'And I hear you have two fewer fascist policemen,' Calhoun said directly to Dougie.

Dougie's face coloured. 'It was *his* friend—'

'Now, this is the point,' AA asserted. 'Calhoun, you keep tabs on Stalin's men at home.'

'We do,' Calhoun replied. 'And your men stay outside the three-mile limit.'

'Quite. Now, the role of the Fascist Police is to maintain order on the streets.'

'Political order, that is,' Dougie added. 'We're not chasing pickpockets. That's for the ordinary police.'

'You didn't invite Commandant Allen of the Women's Auxiliary Police,' Calhoun observed.

'They're just for show,' Dougie said. 'It keeps the suffragette battle-axes happy.'

The club servant arrived with the wine, uncorked, and served it. Julian suspected it was an excellent and very expensive vintage but could barely taste the liquid touching his lips.

'Which leaves Department Z,' AA said. 'It's supposed to be the *internal* intelligence unit of the British Union.'

'You're not a member of the Party,' Julian said. 'Nor are you, Commander Calhoun. And Dougie, you only joined in December?'

'I expect you have files on all of us,' AA said. 'Bravo. Where we live, how many dogs we have.'

'Dougie has a dog,' Julian said. 'But Calhoun doesn't.'

'You make my point very well, about information and power. But all this snooping by Z3 is just not necessary,' AA said. 'Hugh Clifton is becoming a law unto himself, picking enemies at random when there are enough enemies right in front of our faces. *Britain's Gestapo,* they are saying. Shooting people, stabbing men to death on trains, burgling who he likes, smearing influential men, ruining careers.'

'It's just not British,' Calhoun said quietly.

'This could change with you in charge, Thring. After all, you're one of us.'

Julian nodded, which could be taken any way the others wanted to take it. The whole room must know how he was conflicted between his party, his department, his club, and his friends. And above all there was Melissa, hoping for his advancement in step with the inexorable rise of British fascism. After all that, his own hopes and dreams also came into consideration.

AA raised his glass to toast the camaraderie of the Club, and Julian played along. He *could* be the Director of Department Z if he correctly played the hand he was being dealt; he'd be one of the most powerful men in the country by the time he was thirty. It was what his father had groomed him for; it was what his wife dreamed of.

'If we're not Britain's Gestapo, then what are we?' Julian snapped. 'Are we supposed to just pack up?'

'No, no, but put Department Z's focus back where it should be—clearing out the black sheep of your party, if you excuse the pun.'

'And if I do so, will you stop attacking Department Z?'

'*I'm* not attacking Department Z.'

'Then who is? Dammit, AA, you said we were the most powerful forces in the country. So one of us round this table should know.'

The other three looked from one to the other.

'And JEB Baxter is back. Who is he working for this time?'

'Ah, Baxter.' AA turned to Calhoun. 'I had to separate him and Clifton back in 'thirty-five. They were locked in some Shakespearean feud.'

'Baxter does spend most of his time abroad,' Calhoun mused. 'Outside the three-mile limit.'

AA ignored the barb and turned to Julian 'Why not ask your father? I'm sure I've seen them together. Your father has shipping interests, spends a lot of time on the continent.'

'Has links with the Nazis,' Calhoun added.

'We all have links with the Nazis!' Julian burst out. 'Admiral Domville even runs an organisation called The Link with that very purpose.'

'We will be inviting Domville into the fold,' AA said.

'Another seat at this table?' Calhoun asked. 'Or back leading Naval Intelligence? We all have contact with the Nazis, but Domville is blind to their ambitions.'

'Don't misinterpret Domville' motives. He's forging links because he's a patriot. Britain comes first, and he knows that keeping good relations with Germany is essential. If there are Nazi agents sniffing around, I'm sure you keep an eye on them.'

'I'm sure we do.'

'So you'll know the admiral's dealings with Germany are proper and above board.' AA swept a couple of fingers across his forehead to contain a wayward fringe. 'Now I hear the mutton is very good tonight, but before it arrives, we need to be clear. We need to agree that this infighting stops. The Commissioner has already agreed to clip the wings of Special Branch, so we don't overlap. We must not get in each other's way.'

'We don't kill each other's men,' Dougie grumbled.

'Each to his own. Do you agree, Julian?'

After a moment, he said, 'I can see the sense of it.'

'And when Clifton crawls out of his hiding place—'

'He's ours,' Julian asserted. 'And he'll be dealt with as an internal party matter.'

'Balderdash, he's a bloody murderer!' Dougie sent a spatter of wine-tinted spittle onto the tablecloth.

'And possibly a communist agent.' AA added.

'Which means if you find him,' Calhoun said. 'I want him.'

'No!' said Julian.

'I need him alive,' Calhoun said. 'Not tortured, not interrogated, not beaten to death because your Fascist Police want revenge—and not smuggled away because he's your friend, Mr Thring. If we're going to argue who bats and who bowls and who sits in the pavilion, then Hugh Clifton is mine.'

Chapter Thirty-One

Back hiding in my London hovel, I spent my idle hours reading all the newspapers I could buy. The aviatrix Amelia Earhart had vanished while flying across the Pacific, and Princess Elizabeth had been hurt when she fell over at a garden party. While I sat in my room, the world continued to turn.

A box advert in the *Evening Standard* announced yet another meeting of the National Socialist League that coming Monday, and it woke me from my torpor. We had touched a lot of nerves in the past few months, and one of those must have been the trigger for the attack in Sark and the manhunt that followed. All the paper Lucy was assembling offered a ragbag of clues, but we had no proof that anything we had stumbled on made Z3 a target. The Radio Plan was trivial, and my assault on the fringe fascist groups had been as much about keeping my team occupied as making a real difference. Dragon North was the big news, but we were not party to any information that could derail or delay it. Lucy's paper shuffling amounted to little more than a rustling noise when the whole nation was holding its breath.

We needed to know more, and given the number of hats he wore, Peter Wise must have amassed a great deal of information. He would be at that meeting.

*　*　*

Hills had the presence of mind to mix a can of green paint and apply it to the bakery vans, making them anonymous again; they had become calling cards for the section. Walsh arrived from Kent soon after lunch on Monday and immediately came back into service as my driver. On a warm evening in July, he sat at the wheel while Hills and I with our new recruit Drysdale loitered on the pavement beside the van.

'When is the best time to pull off a robbery, Hills? Or burgle a house, snatch a wallet.'

'When nobody's looking,' he said. 'Or when they're busy with something else, like watching a football match.'

'So if you wanted to get away with a really ambitious crime, you'd wait for something big to be happening in the background.'

'A cup final.'

'Or an assault on an English city by British troops.'

'That would do.'

'So what's being robbed?' Drysdale asked.

'It was a metaphor. We are being distracted, but what from?'

Across the road was the Brixton school hall where an NSL meeting was in progress. It was approaching dusk when a prolonged bout of applause signalled proceedings were at an end.

'That's the car he uses,' Hills said as a maroon Humber swept past and parked in a side street.

The audience began to leave. A familiar man emerged from the building in the company of another I knew to be an old flat mate of his.

'Is that William Joyce?' Drysdale asked.

'It is.'

'We can't grab him,' Hills said. 'Our lives wouldn't be worth a candle.'

'I dream about it,' I said. 'But let's net a smaller fish first.'

I climbed in next to Walsh, and he started the van's engine and turned across the road to park behind the maroon Humber. Peter Wise was hurrying towards his car, then paused as I got out and approached him.

'Peter Wise,' I challenged.

'I'm sorry, who are you?' He made to side-step past me before noticing Hills and Drysdale at his elbows.

'Department Z. We just want a little chat, then you'll be free to go about your business. If we wanted you dead, you'd now be dead. Go to the driver of your car and tell him you'll be taking the Tube home. Walk around the off-side, and please don't try anything foolish. It won't be in your interest for the driver to know you're talking to us, and you know why.'

The driver of the Humber didn't have his engine running, so for all this talk of robbery there was no chance of Wise making a Bonnie and Clyde getaway. I walked a few paces behind him, hands pushed into my pockets, just to make sure.

Wise did exactly as ordered, then stood back a few paces as the driver started his engine and drove off into the night.

'You're Hugh Clifton, aren't you?' he challenged.

'Well done, pleased to meet you. Come for a ride, and if you're a good chap, you'll be home by morning.'

'Home?'

'Or deposited at a certain address in Highgate.'

Hills helped Wise into the back of the van, seated him behind the driver, applied a set of handcuffs, and then removed his shoes for good measure. I sat by the doors and handed Drysdale the Luger I'd purloined so it couldn't be grabbed. Perhaps this reassured Wise. The other three squashed into the front, and the van's engine shook into life.

'Where are you taking me?'

'Highgate,' I said, 'The home of Daniel Cooperman.'

He slumped back on the side bench, perhaps eight feet away from me, too far for him to make any sort of move I wouldn't anticipate. He didn't look like a brawler, more an office worker, though he'd once served in the army as so many of his generation had.

'So, Captain Wise,' I said. 'Here we are, just you and me. My men won't be able to hear us over the engine, so you can be totally frank.'

'You're wanted for murder,' he said.

'And that should concentrate your mind. Tell me, have you joined the National Socialists to betray them to the British Union, or are you betraying the British Union by joining the National Socialists?'

He remained impassive.

'Or are you betraying both of them to the Chief Rabbi?'

'Don't be ridiculous.'

'I know that agents working for the Board of Deputies have penetrated the BU. And I've good reason to believe that you are one of them. The address we are headed for is a prime piece of evidence against you. If anyone else in the BU, National Socialists, or any other crackpot antisemitic group knew this, you would be a dead man. Beaten and tortured first for good measure.'

He inclined his head. I must play my hand carefully.

'Fortunately for you, and despite whatever you've read, that's not my way of doing things. In an hour, you are going to walk away with all your fingernails intact and your testicles still attached.'

'Who do you want me to betray?' he asked with a hint of sarcasm. 'You'll get no names.'

'I don't care who you are spying for, but I want to know what the National Socialist League is up to. You're the treasurer, for goodness' sake. Is money coming in from Germany?'

'I need a promise. More than that, I need a guarantee I'll walk away as you said. You're the Blackshirts' chief assassin, leaving a trail of bodies wherever you go.'

'Wise, if I was the man the newspapers paint me as, we'd be headed out to the Essex marshes and digging a shallow grave. We wouldn't even be having this conversation.'

'The newspapers say you're wanted by the Fascist Police,' he said. 'Have they turned on you too?'

'Put two and two together, and you will see we have a common interest.'

He gave another little twist of his head, in a way a parrot does when curious. I talked frankly as the van trundled through the city at night. Wise said nothing as I explained the crisis facing the country; he just eyed me and weighed my soul. He'd spent several years living a lie, just as I'd done, and he was not going to break silence on a whim.

'Is your heart with the BU, the National Socialists, or the Jews?' I asked. 'Who are you working for, ultimately? And I'd like to assure you that I'm not an antisemite, and the idea there's a Jewish conspiracy to take over the world is nonsense.'

'Easy to say.'

'Bluntly then. Where does the NSL get its money from? I need an address where I can find the paperwork.'

'Most of it comes from Nordic Link, and I believe you already have their paperwork.'

'We've seen German bankers mentioned in correspondence, but nothing more than that.'

'You know Nordic Link was set up by Nazi agents?'

'The Nazis don't have any spies in Britain.'

'I didn't say spies; I said agents. The Abwehr is sowing the ground. There's a man who goes by the name of Bruno Vogel who would be worth your attention.'

'Bruno Vogel,' I repeated, keeping poker-faced.

The little electric bulb flickered as the van hit a pothole.

'So you're saying that the Nazis set up Nordic Link, which in turn establishes a set of fringe organisations such as Militant Christian Patriots to spread pro-German propaganda.'

'Yes.'

'And the National Socialist League?'

'No, that's home-grown. It's only a few months old—I joined in its infancy.'

'And are William Joyce and John Beckett and others of their ilk the founders, key members, passengers, or spies like you?'

'It's hard to tell. You fascists play games.'

'I know there's a conspiracy building up, and it's not the Jews behind it.'

He shook his head. 'Not a conspiracy, just politics. You've played your part in setting the tone, destroying the White Knights and the Imperial Fascist League. Oh yes, it's not gone unnoticed.'

'Is that why people are out to kill me?'

'I've no idea. But with all this tension between one group and another, Joyce has called for a meeting next week to clear the air. All the fascist and national socialist groups are going to meet with Mosley, the King's Party, and the Cabinet. This little war over who is the better fascist will be brought to a close.'

This was the correct shape to be an important piece of the jigsaw, not a boring patch of sky.

'Everyone together, all Mosley's enemies?'

'And his allies.'

'Where will it be?'

'Nobody can agree,' Wise said. 'Everyone wants it at their own headquarters. Mosley, of course, wants it to be at Westminster or Downing Street. Joyce doesn't want it to be in London as he fears supporters of one faction or another will turn up and cause trouble. Or socialists, or those wicked Jews.' He narrowed his eyes. 'Or a battalion of Blackshirts.'

'Neutral ground, then,' I said. 'Away from London—so in the north?'

'Well, obviously not in the cities held by the socialists. And Blackshirt support is too strong in the small towns.'

'Too few Jews to blame things on,' I said.

'Exactly.'

'So down south?'

'Churchill has suggested his house at Chartwell, but nobody trusts Churchill.'

'Has the Foreign Office made any suggestions?'

'Why should they?'

'Or the Security Services, say AA Thorne?'

'Somewhere south of the Thames, I'm told.'

'So Chartwell would have been good.'

I had to be there, I had to see who came and had to win Wise's trust.

'Are you in a position to make suggestions? I mean, you sit next to Joyce at these NSL meetings.'

'I could.'

'Suggest Highwood, in Kent. It belongs to Baroness Rockwell. She's a friend of the BU Treasurer, but she and Mosley have differences. She has a far more old-fashioned vision of England-as-it-never-was than he does, and intelligence suggests she's joined English Mistry.'

I knew because Sissy had asked her to do it.

'In addition, I believe she knows both Admiral Domville and the Chief Constable of Kent socially. And she doesn't approve of me, either,' I added. 'Too common, too provincial, new money. And I nearly got her daughter killed.'

'Where is it?'

'The Medway Valley, about an hour from London by car, and there's a couple of train stations within a few miles. It's close to Chatham, so Admiral Domville should feel at home, and not so far from Chartwell if I know my geography.'

He nodded.

'What will the security arrangements be?'

'Everyone wants their own stewards, which is impossible. We can't be ringed by Blackshirts, and…' he paused. 'Nobody wants Department Z.'

'Fascist Police, perhaps.'

'It has been suggested.'

'How about real police? Special Branch detectives?'

'The Commissioner of the Met was appointed by Mosley.'

'But plenty of their middle-ranking officers have survived from the pre-Mosley era. They're not political; they just care about their pensions. I'll give you the name of an inspector who took delight in arresting me a couple of times. And he doesn't like Department Z at all.'

Wise took a deep breath. 'I could suggest it to Joyce directly.'

'And I could make sure Mosley receives the same suggestion.'

He nodded. 'You're an interesting person, Hugh Clifton.'

'And so are you, Peter Wise.'

Chapter Thirty-Two

'ho are we tonight?' I asked Sissy.

'The Friends of Spain. It's five shillings for two hours, and the caretaker said he'll lock us out at nine sharp.'

Z3 converged on a church hall in an unfashionable part of Southwark, south of the river and not so far from my drab lodgings. Two dozen of the section sat in rows like some hastily assembled parish meeting, with Julian and me sitting behind a little table and Lydia Vectis-Hunt poised to take down notes. Julian's Welsh aide and another of the younger men stood guard outside until we were done.

'For the purpose of the record, I don't command the section,' I said.

'Well, old man, just make like you do,' Julian said.

'Thank you. Was anyone followed?'

Drysdale looked at Hills.

'We were,' Hills admitted.

Hills lived only a ten-minute walk away, and Drysdale was staying with him.

'You threw them off?'

'Not exactly,' Hills said, withdrawing a wallet from his pocket. 'But he won't be following anyone for some time. Not unless he uses crutches.' He nudged Drysdale. 'This one's useful.'

Drysdale grinned.

'Seven pounds, eight shillings, and ninepence. I think drinks are on him tonight.'

'But no identification?'

'He's one of Valentine's.' Hills held up a Department Z brass badge.

I put my head in my hands, then realised it made me look weak.

'Well, he's lucky to be alive,' Eleanor said. 'Hugh—sir—is the story of the train true?'

'Yes, sadly. Two FP men got more than they bargained for. And Agent Drysdale here covered for me.'

'He's a good lad.' Hills slapped him on the shoulders.

I listened to reports from one agent, then the other, with Mrs V-H taking notes as fast as she could and only as detailed as necessary.

'Be assured we have an enemy out to destroy us,' I said.

'But who?' Hills said. 'If we knew, we could take them on, bring 'em down.'

'We would.'

Eleanor raised a finger. 'But they're not strong enough to bring us down. No, no, I'm not boasting. If it was, say, the First Division opposing us, they'd fall on us like avenging angels. We'd have been wiped out a month ago.'

'And if it was the Jews,' Julian began. 'Well, they'd go after Parker first.'

'And it's not the communists,' I said. 'Because they've plenty on their plate fighting Dragon North. It's not Mosley, because he could simply order us to be closed down and be done with it, but it must be someone close enough to him to stop having those charges against me waved away.'

'How about Francis-Hawkins?' Eleanor asked. 'Because there's something fishy about Dragon North. First, it's on, then it's off. My man is at his wit's end, assembling his men, dismissing them again. It's like they're not serious; it's all for show.'

'Military operations often turn into a shambles,' I said. 'The army was no better when I served in India. Most of the stormtroopers have never been in military uniform, and most of their officers have never commanded anything beyond a Blackshirt action squad.'

'It was just an idea,' she said.

'And what about Baxter?' Julian said quietly. 'You need to tell them—you've never even properly told me what you're planning.'

After a moment's pause, I announced, 'If nobody has any more reports to offer, we need to clear the room.'

I looked from one face to the other, naming eleven of my comrades.

'The rest of you go home and return to work as normal tomorrow.'

Everyone shuffled. One or two of those not chosen rose to go, then hesitantly sat back down again.

'Thank you for your support, but if you're not on the list, you need to go. I need security for the next operations, it's not a case of the more the merrier.'

Given a second opportunity, half the warm seats in the room became vacant. The room became deathly silent as I held up a photograph.

'Jeremiah Erskine Baxter, who prefers to be called Jeb. Explorer, adventurer, mercenary. He's served British interests in various parts of the World: Arabia, Iraq, Russia, Ireland. Wherever things were at their ugliest, there he was. Back in 1935, someone recruited Mr Baxter for a very special mission.'

'My father,' Julian said bluntly.

'Forget anything you've been told or you've read in the papers about a socialist plot to disrupt the general election in thirty-five. It was all down to Baxter, backed by German money and a plan expertly compiled by Commissioner Thring.'

My audience remained quiet.

'The fact the Party holds power is to some extent a consequence of that plan.'

'So,' Drysdale ventured. 'This Baxter is on our side?'

'You might think that. In fact, it's likely even Commissioner Thring thought that at first.' I addressed Julian directly. 'Do we know whether they're still in touch?'

'No,' he said quietly.

I described how the adventurer had operated: stealing explosives, arming disaffected ex-soldiers with communist leanings, murdering two policemen, even killing his own associates when my investigation drew too close. Fascists or not, my audience was unsettled.

'A gentleman's club called Young Britain is little more than cover for a group of self-serving individuals pushing themselves into positions of influence. Somehow, they gained control of Baxter and his operations.'

'He's the bastard who killed Julia!' Eleanor exclaimed.

'We don't know that,' Sissy objected.

'But yes, Eleanor, you could be right,' I said. 'That operation as good as had his fingerprints all over it. Recruiting French killers just as he recruited British killers before. Serving the interests of the Young Britons, just as he did before.'

'We need to take him out,' Hills said.

'Yes, we do.'

Chapter Thirty-Three

It was well advertised that renowned explorer Jeremiah Erskine Baxter was to speak at the Royal Geographical Society on Thursday evening. Their new lecture hall was a bleak brick affair at the corner of Exhibition Road opposite Hyde Park, its angled-off corner giving it more the look of a military bunker than a centre of learning. A statue of Livingstone looking over Kensington Gore and a statue of Scott on the east side were the only concessions to heritage.

We were twelve, all my best people. Against my dearest wishes, I brought Sissy, as even though she'd been looking rather grey these past days, she would not be left behind. Against my better instincts, I brought Eleanor as I needed her vigour, and Julian, as he was in formal command now.

Baxter arrived in a car that delivered him to the main entrance on Exhibition Road. He bore a distinctive stoop and, even when on show to the public, moved furtively. A man left the car with him, clearly a close associate or bodyguard, but a wholly anticipated complication. We'd wait until the explorer emerged after the lecture, as there would be a hubbub of departing guests to hide our approach and less traffic to impede our escape. It would be a reprise of the way we'd snatched Peter Wise, but on a grander scale.

The junction with Kensington Gore was continually busy with traffic and the trees and parked vehicles offered plenty of cover for agents. Students from Imperial College and the Royal College of Music passed by regularly, meaning my young men and women did not look out of place. A concert was being played at the Royal Albert Hall, so taxis were frequent, and concertgoers flooded out of the tunnel leading from the Tube station.

My plan needed sharp timing. Once Baxter's car drew up again, we'd pounce. Ideally, we'd bundle the explorer into one of the former bread vans, as we did with Wise, but it would stick out like a sore thumb in that genteel area, and using one of the black BU 'armoured' transports would simply scream our presence. Instead, we'd seize his own car, Walsh taking the driving seat after he, Julian, and Eleanor had darted across the road and forced the driver out. Hills and Jenkins would rush Baxter from the top, with another man covering their backs. Drysdale and I would attack uphill, with Sissy covering our backs.

A repainted bread van was parked several streets to the west and another among the mews to the east. Both had drivers at the wheel. Our final man covered the entrance to the Tube station tunnel in case we needed to escape that way.

It was still only dusk. The car drew up, a large Bentley in two shades of grey. Audience members started to leave the hall. Sissy and I walked arm-in-arm up from Princes' Gate with our heads down, Drysdale a few paces behind. Hills and Jenkins appeared around the angle of the lecture hall, while Julian loitered on the opposite pavement conducting a pantomime conversation with Eleanor. Walsh stood in front of a parked car, hands on hips as if contemplating buying it. Out came Baxter, glad-handing men in suits and ladies in furs, his man glancing round. Time to strike.

Three young women walked jauntily down the opposite side of the road. Possibly, they were students, but they walked with purpose. Almost marching.

Walsh waited for a bus to pass, then sauntered across the road, hands in pockets. Julian moved to follow, but someone else moved out of cover beyond him. Not one of our men, and Julian knew it. We were being watched. This was not our ambush; it was someone else's.

Hills and Jenkins were rapidly closing on the group outside the door. Sissy had dropped back, and Drysdale was by my side now. We were only a few yards short of Baxter, yet he was making no effort to get into his car. Walsh reached the driver's door. Julian hesitated, edging away. Eleanor spotted the three women and drew a pistol.

Baxter looked me in the eye, grinned, and reached into a coat pocket. His driver's door flew open, and Walsh recoiled into the road, was struck by a taxi, and fell out of sight.

'Run!' I grabbed Drysdale's elbow and dragged him around. A man stepped out in front of us, but I shoulder-barged him out of the way, his hat flying into the road. We dodged into the crowd. I heard a shot from behind us, then three from a different weapon.

'Hugh!' Sissy shouted as a black-painted transport with the British Union lightning-in-circle badge painted on the side veered out of an access road.

It braked to a halt astride the pavement, blocking any escape towards the Tube tunnel. I reached Sissy, and we took a chance with the traffic and raced across the road, Sissy shouting 'sorry!' at a car that braked to avoid her. Drysdale dodged off in a different direction. FP men shouted orders for us to stop, but sufficient bodies blocked any shot they might attempt.

Exhibition Road was long and straight, but leading off the east side was a network of mews and small gardens where we might more easily escape pursuit. Women in Auxiliary Police uniforms were pouring down the steps of a building and Eleanor vanished in a scrum of flying hats and punches. Julian was running to join us, and our ragged trio ran into Princes' Gardens.

I began to cough. I could never keep up this pace, and Sissy was flagging. Two FP men were in distant pursuit, but a man wearing civilian clothes was rapidly gaining on Julian. As soon as we were clear of innocent civilians, I'd have to shoot someone.

'Guns!' I panted.

We swung into cover behind a parked car. Sissy and I let off shots at long range, and our pursuers ducked into cover. We heard bullets ping off metal and shattering glass. Julian ran past us.

'Move! Back to the van.'

There was no traffic here in the quiet side streets of Kensington, so we scuttled down the offside of the parked cars. A man's hat bobbed up, but I didn't fire again.

With squealing gears, the green van that should have been our salvation streaked away down the mews behind us, immediately followed by a black car that surely must catch it. Our getaway vehicle was gone, but so was the guard preventing our escape.

'What's happening, Julian?'

He hunched his shoulders and threw his hands wide. 'They've guessed. They've seen through it.'

'Come on.'

We were soon rushing past the first row of mews houses, then turned down another side road.

A taxi had just deposited a fare, and Julian pulled its door open. 'Chelsea!' he shouted. 'King's Road.'

Sissy followed him, then, with a glance back, I was last aboard. The taxi trundled off down the cobbles of the Mews, and behind us, that man in civilian dress simply watched us go.

'Did you see what happened to Walsh?' I panted.

'Hit by a taxi,' Julian said.

'Run over?'

'No, he bounced off it. But they'll have him.'

'And Eleanor?'

'She shot one of those women—they must have been Auxiliary Police. Then there were dozens of them. She could never have got away.'

Even if everyone else escaped, that meant at least two more of my team were lost—two of my mates, as Lucy called them. And I'd have to explain what happened to Lucy in person. I coughed again.

'Drysdale doesn't know London, which means he's stuffed if he doesn't make it back to the other van,' I said. 'And if Hills didn't get away, Christ, that's everyone. Baxter bloody well got us this time.'

Sissy vomited onto the floor of the taxi.

'Aw, missus!' the taxi driver exclaimed. He slammed on his brakes.

'Keep driving!' I ordered, praying I'd not have to draw a gun again.

'Someone's got to clean that up, you know.'

'It's worth a quid, just keep driving.'

'Two quid.'

'Two quid it is, just go. And I'm sorry about the mess.'

'Where are we going?' Sissy groaned.

'Black House,' Julian said.

'It won't be safe,' I objected.

'Driver, take us to Putney.' Julian rattled off his home address.

Defeated, vomit-stained, out of ideas, there was nowhere else to run, barring my bare rented room. As I sat in the back of the taxi, panting and coughing from my own exhaustion, cradling Sissy, it felt like the end of the line.

And if they could use Charles Viscount Wickersley against me, they could use Julian. How better to set a trap than to employ a friend, dangling the carrot of my vacant post. A friend who had first alerted me to that lecture by Baxter. Quite who was spider and who was fly was no longer clear. And spiders did eat other spiders.

Julian was a friend, I told myself repeatedly, and at that moment, our only friend. There was only one way to find out.

Chapter Thirty-Four

As the taxi rattled westwards, I tried to clear my mind. Stormtroopers were massing for an offensive, Department Z hunted itself, the bloody Young Britons dropped more of their men into senior posts, and Baxter was back at the heart of the plot. The movement of the chess pieces could appear random from close to but should fall into a pattern if I could step back far enough. And, of course, there would be many moves invisible to me. I'd no idea what the Germans were doing, or the NKVD, or what Calhoun's men were up to, or what the triple-agent Peter Wise's orders were.

After the debacle in Exhibition Road, I needed manpower, but just possibly I could obtain woman power. Sissy only had a handful of armed ladies under her command, and these were scattered now. Melissa, on the other hand, led a section of thirty. All had been trained to use rifles and pistols, and though I wouldn't rate their chances against the regular army or even green stormtroopers, they would give the Fascist Police pause for thought. Melissa had a chance to clear her name and become a hero of the party in her own right. For once, her unthinking, unblinking dedication to the cause could be turned for the good. She might even save her soul.

Julian had recently bought a semi-detached house in a smart area of Putney. With bay windows, a little front lawn, clipped privet hedge, and a short gravel drive it was an estate agent's vision of a young couple's dream home. Light peeked from behind the lounge curtains.

I paid the taxi driver. 'Sorry for the mess, mate.'

He grunted.

'I really am terribly sorry,' Sissy said.

We scuttled down the side of the house and Julian led us in by the side door. He strode into his kitchen and Melissa appeared before he'd even called out.

'Julian…and Hugh, Sissy.'

She looked surprised, flustered.

'Sorry for the intrusion,' I said.

After a moment, Melissa regained her composure. 'Julian, you should have told me we'd have guests.'

'Sorry dear, but it's all getting rather frantic.'

'Oh, Sissy, what a mess!' Melissa looked about herself as if seeking a cloth, a towel, anything to help clean the stain from Sissy's coat front but offered nothing. 'They can't stay here, Julian. Sorry, Sissy but you can't, you're wanted. Or he's wanted.'

'He's wanted for a murder I committed,' Julian said.

'You? You're saying that to protect him.'

'Hugh's never killed anyone. It was me and Eleanor who shot the Frenchmen. Hugh took the blame so you and I could get back to England.'

'I don't believe you. Married, not six months, and you're lying to me. I had to lie to the police for you, and I had to sit in that horrid black room being threatened. For you. And for him.'

'Calm down.'

'Don't tell me to calm down. What about those policemen on the train? You weren't on the train, Julian.'

He cocked his head towards me.

'Melissa, we need you,' I said. 'We need you and all your section.'

'What for?'

'Shall we sit down?' Julian said, taking a place at the kitchen table. 'We can offer tea, or coffee? Or something stronger, Hugh?'

'Clear heads are needed. Coffee, please.'

Sissy and I also took seats at the table.

'Now Melissa—'

'I can't help your secret mission, because I'm making coffee,' she said, setting about filling a kettle with water.

'We've got some biscuits,' Julian said.

Melissa passed the tin over with poor grace. 'So, why do you want my women?'

'To stand by. To be a force, nobody takes account of. You could buy enough time to thwart whatever is in the offing. The communists are up to something, planning their moment, and the people who tried to kill us in Sark are picking who will die and who will be in power. Foreign agents are active, and we could have civil war. The Leader is in danger.'

'From you.'

'No, not from me. Mosley is seen as weak, and his authority is being undermined by a myriad of groups all claiming to be better fascists than he is.'

'So tell him,' she said. 'Just you go and tell Mosley, like you've just told me.'

'It's not as simple as that. We've been painted as criminals; there's no reason for him to believe us. This is your chance to shine, Melissa. To do something for your country.'

'Oh, cups, cups,' she said, moving through into the dining room.

'We don't need the best ones!' Julian said.

'Some of us have standards,' she sang from the other room.

Julian gave a shrug of apology, and I couldn't resist a laugh. No matter how deep the crisis, suburban etiquette must triumph.

Melissa returned, face hard as marble, a snub-nosed revolver gripped in both hands. 'You're under arrest, Hugh Clifton.'

Julian half-rose from his seat. 'Melissa, what are you doing?'

'I know what I'm doing, but what is *he* doing?' Melissa thrust the muzzle towards me. 'You want my women for what, your latest plot? To kill more people and blame me for it?'

'Dearest, come on.'

'Sit down, Julian. He's right, this is my chance to shine.' The gun muzzle stayed pointing my way. 'I always knew you were a spy, Hugh Clifton. Like that Verity was, until she was stopped for good. This time, I'm going to stop you.'

CHAPTER THIRTY-FOUR

'Melissa, please.'

I'd trained her to shoot a pistol. She wasn't a bad shot, and I couldn't gamble on her missing a target as large as me at a range of four feet. Then also missing Sissy who sat at my elbow.

'You've never believed in national socialism. You're a Jew lover,' she spat. 'Over and over again, I gave you the chance to prove me wrong, but you stick with your holier-than-thou act. Well, I'm not one of your *comrades*.'

'Darling,' Julian made to rise again. I hoped dearly he was not the kind of man who'd throw himself into the path of a bullet meant for a friend.

'I'm saving you, Julian. I'm saving your career. I'm saving you from becoming a traitor like him and getting your head blown off.'

I raised one hand as if trying to calm a horse, 'Melissa—'

'The Fascist Police know you're here. They're surrounding the building.'

Julian's eyes met mine. Did he know, did he plan this, was this the ultimate betrayal? Could I truly not trust anyone anymore?

Julian glanced back at his wife, hesitating, calculating the odds. All Melissa's attention was on me. He dived from his chair, grabbed his wife around the waist, and pulled her pistol hand down with the other hand. The shot blasted our eardrums, and Melissa screamed. As she fell to the floor, Julian fell with her.

Sissy grabbed my arm. 'Run, Hugh.'

We were out of the kitchen door in moments.

Chapter Thirty-Five

'No, no,' Julian crouched over Melissa's limp body as she slid down the kitchen sideboard and onto the floor.

Time hung still as he tried frantically to dab here and there, trying to unscramble year-old first aid training.

'Silly old girl, silly old girl.'

Melissa began groaning and sobbing in equal measure. Two men piled in through the open kitchen door, pistols in hand.

'Department Z!' One yelled.

Julian took no notice.

'Stand up!'

Now he noticed the men in the gaberdine raincoats. 'Help her.'

'Stand up.'

'Help her, please. She needs a doctor!'

'Stand up, you bastard, or we'll shoot.'

Julian recoiled away from Melissa. The lower part of her pale skirt was soaked in blood, and a crimson wave surged across the grey-mottled linoleum floor.

'Help her, for God's sake!' Julian sobbed, half-raising his hands.

One of the men kneeled beside Melissa, picking up her revolver and passing it to the other. Julian recognised one of Blake's men, but his mind spun too fast to recall a name.

'Help her. Or let me help her then.'

'Who shot her?'

'It was a bloody accident.'

'Cliff…Clif…C…C,' she mumbled.

'Hugh Clifton? Is he here?'

'He's gone, he's gone,' Julian said.

Now, the kneeling Z-man took an interest in Melissa's wounds. 'Does a doctor live nearby?'

'I don't know. There's a dentist, two houses down.'

'Which way?'

'He's a dentist, idiot. What can he do?'

'Where are the traitors?' The standing one demanded.

Someone else began banging on the front door.

'Hugh's not a traitor!' Julian shouted. 'Oh, let me.' Julian pushed the kneeling man aside. He pulled Melissa's skirt up beyond her waist. Her whole pantie line was soaked in red, and a deep crimson jet pulsed from her thigh.

'Oh shit, oh damn.' Julian pressed his hands over the squirting wound. 'Get a bandage. A towel, anything. Tablecloth, in the dining room.'

Three FP men joined the chaos in the kitchen and the other Z-man led them outside, raising a hue and cry. The first man took an age to find a cotton tablecloth and hand it to Julian. By then, the squirting was easing, and Melissa's muttering faded away. Her eyes opened once, fluttered closed, then her chest stopped moving.

'Oh no, oh no, you silly girl!'

The last Z-man abandoned hope and left to chase shadows around the streets and gardens, leaving Julian kneeling and sobbing beside his dead wife. Minutes slipped by uncounted.

'What's happened here, sir?' A uniformed police officer was standing inside the kitchen doorway.

'Melissa is dead.'

The constable kneeled and felt for a pulse on her right wrist. 'I'm sorry for that, sir.'

'I killed her.'

'Are you sure of that?' The constable stood back.

'No, she shot herself. It was an accident. How can you die being shot in the leg, how?'

The constable spotted the revolver, which now rested on the kitchen table, and pushed it further from Julian's reach. 'I'm sorry, but I'm placing you under arrest. I'm going to have to take you to the station, and I hope you'll come quietly.'

'Get a doctor first. Then call Scotland Yard.'

'It's hardly a case for Scotland Yard.'

'It is. Call Inspector Renton. I'll even give you his number. We've a telephone in the hall. No, stay with her. I'll do it.'

'Sir,' the constable warned.

'I'm an important member of British Union, and my wife is dead. This is political. Now let me phone.'

Melissa remained curled on the floor as the police officer put a handcuff on Julian's right wrist, clipping the other end around his own left.

'You be careful, sir.'

Julian dialed awkwardly with his left hand, making the call in a halting voice, needing to repeat himself several times. The constable took up the telephone and confirmed the address, then led Julian into the lounge and cuffed him fully without meeting resistance. Julian sat on his new sofa, transferring blood from his hands to its fabric without caring. The police constable sat in the armchair opposite him, trying to coax a statement. Time slowed to a halt before an FP commander appeared and tried to take charge. Men were still running about the neighbourhood. Doors banged, dogs barked, and a dustbin fell over. Cars pulled up and roared away again.

Julian said little in response to the constable's questions and ignored the FP officer's badgering.

'Talkative, aren't you, killer boy? What you waiting for, a lawyer? Because that's the last thing you'll get.'

Time remained frozen until the FP officer lost interest and left the house, shouting orders. Another car pulled up outside, and the officer returned, cursing.

'Has he talked yet?'

'Shall I handle this?' said a voice with a touch of a Scottish accent.

CHAPTER THIRTY-FIVE

The constable stood up.

'Who are you?' challenged the FP officer.

'Detective Inspector Renton, Special Branch.'

'This is a matter for the Fascist Police.'

'Sir, I was the first uniformed officer at the scene,' the constable said. 'These FP blokes were nowhere to be seen.'

'This is now my case,' Renton stated.

'We have authority,' the FP officer bit back.

'And I'm bloody Department Z, and my wife is dead!' Julian shrieked. 'So we have authority.'

'What an effing circus,' Renton said. 'Are the bloody girl guides going to turn up next?'

The FP man tried to step between Renton and Julian. 'Under the Public Order Act—'

'Shut your stupid mouth,' Renton snapped. 'I was cracking murders before you were born, sonny, and I'll be cracking them long after you get kicked out on your arse. You're no more police than I'm an archbishop. Fuck off and leave it to the professionals.'

'You don't know who I am.'

'I don't need to know who you are.'

'This man is helping a fugitive. Hugh Clifton, the murderer, he's on the loose out there.'

'Well, go and chase him then.'

Two of Renton's detectives edged towards the FP man, who straightened up to restore his dignity, then left the house, yelling orders out into the night. The uniformed constable grinned.

'It's not funny, constable.' Renton indicated Julian should follow him into the kitchen. 'Let's have a look at what happened.'

Renton knelt by Melissa just long enough to verify the absence of a pulse for himself, then gently shifted her skirt back into place. 'Where's the weapon?'

'On the table,' said the constable.

Renton regarded the little revolver for a moment. The Department Z gang had fallen into the habit of carrying German automatics, so the choice of weapon made him wonder. He took a handkerchief from his pocket, then gingerly lifted the revolver. He opened the cylinder, confirmed just one round had been fired, and shook the rest into the palm of his hand.

'Wait outside,' he said to his detectives. 'Constable, man the front gate and stop any of those FP jokers coming back in.'

Julian stood in the doorway between dining room and kitchen, wearing handcuffs he'd barely noticed being applied. Not an hour before, he'd suggested his wife make coffee.

'Mr Julian Thring, I'm placing you under arrest.'

'I'm already under arrest.' Julian held up the cuffs.

'You're coming with me back to the Yard, and in case you've other ideas it will be better than waiting for that shower to return. We still enforce the law of the land, but they make it up as they go along. Are there any more weapons in the house?'

'My Walther is in the writing desk, as is the spare ammunition.'

Renton collected the automatic and dropped it into his pocket. 'I'm sorry I can't let you spend a few minutes with your wife.'

Julian nodded. 'Help me move her into the lounge, at least.'

Renton lifted Melissa by the shoulder, and despite the handcuffs, Julian managed to grip her blood-greased ankles, and together they lifted her onto the sofa, then adjusted her pose so her head rested on a cushion and pulled her skirt into place. A tablecloth served to cover her face.

'It will ruin your sofa.'

'It's already ruined. Everything is ruined.'

'Was Hugh Clifton here?' Renton asked.

'Hugh didn't do it.'

'This smacks of him all the way. So tell me, honestly, was he here? Is Hugh Clifton back in London?'

Julian was silent.

'Good,' Renton said.

Chapter Thirty-Six

Our second escape in the same day was less dramatic than the first, and we slipped away with more ease than we deserved. We scrambled over a couple of back garden fences in the dark; a dog barked at us when I kicked over a dustbin used as a step-up, then we were free and half-walking, half-running down a suburban side street. I stepped out in front of a slow-moving saloon car, waving my arms, Sissy flashed her Department Z badge, and we were driven into the night by a commercial traveller expecting no more than a cup of cocoa and the welcome of his own bed. We released him once he dropped us at West Acton underground station, and he drove off quickly, crashing the gears and making a wild U-turn to take himself home.

Only once we were riding the Central Line carriage did we dare look into each other's eyes.

Sissy gripped my hand. 'We just ran out on them. They could be dead, both of them.'

'I know.'

'Melissa…was it a trap?'

'Two traps. One ready if the other failed.'

'Did Julian betray us?'

'We must assume he did—unless it was all of Melissa's devising. Someone got to her, or made threats, made promises. You know how they work. You know what fascist Britain looks like now.'

She nodded.

'And it will get worse the longer Mosley is in power and allows his minions to behave as they wish.'

'Do you still think you can stop him?'

'If I could, I would have before now.'

'And I'd have stopped you. Before now.'

I squeezed her hand.

'And now?'

'Oh God, Hugh, I've been such an idiot falling for all that…all that nonsense. And it's all too late, it's all too late.' She began to cry.

The knife-sharp young fascist I'd met just two years before had seen her dreams crushed, and all I could do was hug her tight.

'We just have to make things as right as we can, the best we can,' I said.

'But what's happening isn't Mosley, he's better than this.'

'Are you sure? Because it's Hitler, and it's Mussolini, and it's the way Franco is going. There's no reason Britain is so special.'

'It's…' she grasped at the straws she could reach. 'It has to be those Young Britons, twisting things to their own advantage. I mean, why would the Party turn on us? Why turn on you? Their hero, my hero.' She gripped my hand again.

'I wasn't very heroic tonight.'

'Well, tomorrow is another day, and you'll bloody out-hero them all.'

'It can't just be you and me,' I said, close to despair.

'What about your shady friends, the ones you used to work for. Whose side are they on? Are MI5 after you too?'

'Not that I know,' I said.

'Well, jolly well get them on our side.'

I nodded. 'Could you round up Melissa's section? At least some of them. Make any excuse you like, a wake or whatever.'

'I can try, but they won't all trust me now. I can get the Wives to work on them; Priscilla was one of them. She must know them.'

'And I'll talk to MI5,' I said. 'But you are going to need to choose a side, Sissy. If what we are seeing is Mosley shifting into a higher gear, then Britain is headed for dictatorship.'

* * *

It was a risk to contact Calhoun, but he was the closest to an ally I had left. If MI5 was party to the plot, then the jigsaw was complete. If they were working against it, then we had a chance to tip up the box.

Calhoun knew better than to try to trap me. And after all, I was just one man and the agents who were still at my call could be rounded up or driven into hiding until I was truly alone. We were to meet in Selfridges department store, by the cosmetics counter. Plenty of people thronged the store, most of them women, and one of the women was mine.

'Buy something nice for your wife,' I said as I came up behind him.

'Who says I have a wife?'

'Well, we know where you live.'

'Of course you do.'

'So we know you don't have a wife.'

A sales lady marked us as potential customers and sidled along the perfumes counter.

'Stop playing games.' Calhoun moved away.

'It's not a game.'

We found space with our backs to a wall.

'I'm sorry it came to this,' he said. 'You were a good man.'

'Were? You've written me off?'

'Everyone has written you off,' he said. 'If you're not killed, you'll be arrested. And if you are arrested, I never knew you, and we never had conversations such as this.'

'Hung out to dry completely.'

'Yes.'

'Did you hear about what happened at the Thring house last night?'

'She's dead, and he's in custody. Your friend Inspector Renton has taken special interest in the case. I imagine he's putting together all the pieces.'

'And are you? MI5 can't be totally blind to what's going on. What have you been doing for the past three months?'

'Saving the country from one of Moscow's plots. It will be in the newspapers soon, so I can risk telling you. We've been watching a spy ring. NKVD agents working with Communist Party members to steal naval secrets.'

'So the house in Holland Road was what, a trap?'

'We organised a safe house, and they fell right into it.'

'Arrests?'

'We're still watching what they're up to, so please, please, keep your people away from this. If you still have any people.'

'My people are too busy. Meanwhile, all your eyes have been completely fixed on that house.'

'M Section at least.'

I let out a long sigh of frustration. 'How far up the chain did the information about your operation go? Did AA Thorne and SIS know your best agents were fully engaged in a spy hunt?'

'Why?' Calhoun asked, suspiciously.

'Because everyone is being kept very busy. What's happening while you're not looking, and I'm running for my life?'

'Says the man who is abducting people right, left, and centre and leaving bodies in his wake. You've bagged a man named Peter Wise.'

'He's supposed to be propaganda officer for the north, and yet he finds time to also become treasurer of the National Socialist League.'

'Let him go.'

'We have. And why the worry? Is he one of yours?'

'Just leave him alone.' Calhoun rolled his eyes at me. 'I've had a request.'

'From who?'

'Just know that Wise isn't an enemy, not unless you've wholly gone over to the Nazi creed. Leave him alone.'

'And you need to step up to the crease,' I said. 'Nobody is chasing you. Nobody is out to kill you. Yet. A game is afoot, chairs are moving, and when the music stops, will you still be head of MI5? Or will you be in the basement of Black House or some other basement, knowing you'll never see the light of day again? Forget the communists. It's the Nazis you need to worry about. Or a military coup and that civil war you keep telling me you want to avoid.'

'Now you're being dramatic.'

'My friend betrayed me, and his wife died in his arms. I threw two bodies off a train and left more in a holiday hotel dining room. I've seen the fascist forces building up to storm Hull and been chased halfway round the country. Dramatic is underplaying it.'

Calhoun looked from one passing customer to another. 'Julian Thring is not your friend. He's been bought.'

'And you?'

'I'm worth more than a bottle of fine wine and a larger desk. But your bête noir, AA Thorne, thinks otherwise.' Calhoun rolled his eyes at me.

'I used to be your informer. Open your ears, and I'll feed you enough information to save the country.'

'I'm listening,' he said.

I told him about the proposed conference. 'I think it's on Wednesday.'

'Thursday,' he corrected. 'Mosley has been ill, an attack of that phlebitis he suffers from time to time.'

'That's his war wound,' I said, wondering if the illness was a convenient ruse. It was certainly a complicating factor if the date could slide around. 'Have you been invited?'

'No.'

'I bet AA Thorne has, so you'd have an equal right to be there.'

'I can make my case. The venue hasn't been decided yet.'

'Highwood, Kent.'

Calhoun raised his eyebrows. 'Baroness Rockwell's modest home?'

'And if your view is canvassed, support the idea.'

'It would be very interesting to hear what is said.'

'It would indeed.'

'Will you be there?'

'Of course not.'

'Of course not,' he echoed.

Chapter Thirty-Seven

I waited until the late edition of the *Evening Standard* came out before I tried to contact any of my team. Mrs Melissa Thring of Putney had been shot dead, read the lead story. Her husband was being held in custody and a manhunt was on for police-killer Hugh Clifton in connection with the incident. It made sobering reading in my lonely one-bed room.

Turning to page two, an auxiliary policewoman had been shot and severely wounded in a terrorist attack in Exhibition Road. Two fascist policemen had also been hurt, but a man and a woman had been arrested at the scene and were now in hospital under police guard. Another man driving a green van had also been arrested after a police chase.

I had to conclude the others must still be at liberty, and if there was any compensation in the stories broadcasting my failure at least Walsh and Eleanor were alive.

Dressed down as far as I could manage, I found a public house in Southwark where the remnants of my section could meet. Drysdale was a positive asset, a working-class lad who played a working-class lad with ease. He slapped a pint of warm southern beer down on the table beside me.

'On me, sir. Sorry, not supposed to call you sir.'

'No, and certainly not here. Unless served with a heavy dose of irony, as in *your pint, good sir!*'

Drysdale gave a nervous laugh. 'I've been to Black House today.' He slid a small case across the floor. 'Your uniform; Danny Hills thought you might need it. He said it was worth a shot me going there, seeing as nobody knows who I am. And I've got my Leeds branch card, so I'm not tarred with the same brush as you.'

'And?'

'There's next to nobody left. Mr Thring's wife died, so he's not around. Commander Parker has taken all his men up north. And Z3, well. Dr Valentine has posted a list of who's to be arrested.'

He passed it over. A dozen obvious names were included, with mine at the top and Sissy second.

'You're not on the list, Drysdale.'

'Nobody knows who I am.'

'Which we can use to our advantage, but don't go back in case you're added as an afterthought.'

'No.'

'Are you still with us, or would you rather go back to Yorkshire? There's no disgrace.'

'I'm fine, sir.'

'Even with this list?'

'It must be a mistake.'

'It's politics. There's a lot going on, and it will get even uglier. You've seen people die, and there will be more before the end. Still happy to stay?'

He licked his lips. 'Yes. I mean, sir, I've never done anything this exciting. We're changing Britain, aren't we? Defeating the communist plots wherever we can find them.'

'Yes, we are.'

'Ah, another important thing, there's a message from agent Athens. It makes no sense to me. It's just a number.'

I left Drysdale with a shilling to buy another round of drinks and went to find a telephone box out of the public eye. I repeated my trip three times during the evening, with one pint of beer between each, because nobody picked up at the far end the first two times. Verity's hoarse voice came through at the third attempt.

'Verity?'

'At last, what have you been doing?'

'I might ask the same.'

'And was that Julian in the paper, killing his wife?'

'Afraid so.'

'Poor man, he didn't deserve that. But this is urgent, we don't have time and we don't know who is listening. Are the Blackshirts still going to attack Hull on the twelfth?'

'The order to the First Division is to muster on the twelfth,' I said, 'and the attack won't start without them. Your old antagonist, Parker, and the whole of his Z2 bully boys are already up there, perhaps a hundred of them.'

She exhaled. 'Good, the train strike to prevent the move will be called on Monday.'

'They're assembling on Monday, but the movement order is now for Tuesday. Mosley has been ill, so everything has slipped a day.'

'Nothing painful, I hope?' she said.

'He's got a gammy leg, but it could be a political illness.'

'What for?'

'To buy an extra day—or throw us all out of gear. Your strike would be predictable; they must have planned for it, and there will be enough Fascist Union drivers to man the trains they need.'

'No, no, the fascist scabs have secretly agreed to join our strike. They'll refuse to drive the trains, man the signals, or anything.'

'So Francis-Hawkins will simply requisition motor buses. It will slow him up by a day or two, but no more.'

'No, no, you're not listening. Why have the FUBW scabs been ordered to block the move? And by who? You find out, and then tell me.'

She put down the telephone and left me wondering.

The First Division were the cream of Francis-Hawkins' men, the descendants of the infamous I-Squad, and as close to fanatical as BU men could be. Once they were in the north, a meeting of the fascist groups could take place without the fear of the sudden arrival of Mosley's men by the truckload. However, a well-timed train strike would mean a couple of thousand stormtroopers would be assembled and armed in the capital, kicking the heels of their jackboots. The margin of comfort for those groups would be gone.

Perhaps Hull was not the city the stormtroopers would be ordered to capture. Ostensibly, those stormtroopers would be waiting for trains, but in reality, they would be able to respond to a click of Mosley's finger. With the Fascist Police on his side, the Metropolitan Police neutered, and the Guards no doubt restrained by the king, the capital was in his hands. Nobody would be on the alert, and every political office and every political opponent could be removed in an afternoon. Forget Joyce and the intellectual wing of the party. Forget play-along King's Party men like Churchill and those who wanted to retain the vestiges of a democratic system. The militarists would be in control.

I must be at Highwood for the conference. Whoever was left of my section, whoever I could find who was reliable, we had to be at Highwood on Thursday.

Chapter Thirty-Eight

We had only a few days to set the stage.

'Hello, Mother,' Sissy said.

'Sissy, are you using a telephone box?'

'I am.'

'But I saw–'

'Yes, Hugh is wanted for murder. He didn't do it; he's innocent, but he's in hiding anyway until the Party clears things up.'

'He's not with you? Where are you?'

'I'm keeping out of the way of the police in case they think I had anything to do with it.'

'They've already been here, asking for you. Are you wanted, too? It's a good thing your friends have gone from the boathouse. And poor Melissa Thring—Howard is heartbroken.'

'You've talked to Julian's father?'

'Yes, he called by today. He couldn't stay long, I think he needed the air, just somewhere to walk around, don't you know?'

'He walked around what—the house, the park?'

'Yes, to take the air. It's been a horrible summer, and for a change, it's quite pleasant down here–'

'Did he say why he was there?'

'It was a *social call*, darling. Not everyone is a spy or a secret agent.'

'Was he alone?'

'His driver came, but he just went off for a walk.'

'A walk…Mother, I want you to do something for me.'

'Not another pitiful band of politicians for me to join?'

'No, I want you to hide me. Just for a few days until the hullabaloo about Hugh has died down and the misunderstanding has all been cleared up.'

'Just you? Not Hugh Clifton—I'm not having a murderer in my house. Even an innocent one. No, you'd better not Sissy. For the good of the family. Stay away until all this… hullabaloo is done with.'

'Very well. I'll go north, somewhere.'

It was not a complete lie. Sissy drove down to the north gate of Highwood late on Tuesday. It was only used by a few of the groundsmen and by the Women's Section when coming to camp. Once we were free of London, I emerged from under the rug where I'd been squeezed behind the seats. Just before midnight, we pulled into the kerb of a wooded lane and waited.

A green van drove up, and Hills stepped out.

'Boss?'

'How many have you found?'

'Two dozen, but I'm going to have to bring them up in three trips.'

'Get it done before dawn.'

'Is this going to work, boss? Last week was a complete cock-up, and who says this isn't another cock-up just waiting for us.'

'You're on the wanted list, Hills. How long do you think you can hide from them?'

'Are you sayin' they may as well catch me tomorrow as next week?'

'Make sure they don't. Everyone needs to keep their heads down until Thursday, so I hope you brought sandwiches.'

* * *

Sissy carried a key for the big back gate and drove into the parkland without lights. It was a moonless night, so she had to rely on the silhouettes of trees to guide her to the dark outlines of the four training camp huts. She concealed her car in a lean-to built for that specific purpose, collected her electric flashlight and we set off on foot carrying a light bag each. Stealthily we moved from trunk to trunk through half a mile of parkland, avoiding using the flashlight, then had no choice but to keep our heads low over the wide grassy bank to the north of the formal gardens. Our hands finally touched the hard, cold brick of the walled rose garden, and its gate was never locked. From there, the flint chipping on the paths glowed pale between the rose beds. I stayed within the arch of the rose garden as Sissy nipped across to the north wing. Finding a side door locked, she disappeared round the back.

I sat on a bench under starlight and patchy clouds until she returned half an hour later.

'The kitchen door was unlocked, so I got in. Everyone is asleep.'

'Dogs?'

'Mother hates dogs.'

'Well done.'

'We're not putting Mother in danger, are we?'

'Everyone in the Party is in danger if there's a coup. We're not the only people who keep lists.'

'I suppose you're right. But Hugh…'

'Yes?'

'It's just…when this meeting is over—if it ever happens—we need to have a talk.'

'Agreed.'

Sissy had unlocked the service door on the north wing, so we slipped through and took a half-flight of stairs down into the basement. One route led to the chapel, another to the north service stair, but a dimly lit passageway led straight under the house. We moved quickly along it, and Sissy collected a couple of keys from the hooks outside the kitchen. Then she led up the south service stairs to the second floor.

What had been the Nursery was in the southeast corner at the top of the house, with a sloping ceiling on two sides. After locking us in and removing the key from the lock, Sissy used her flashlight to point out the cute but too-small bed she'd known as a child. It was unmade and looked dusty.

'That's mine,' she said. 'But you sleep in here.'

The ceiling on the south side sloped down to shoulder height by the time it met the wall.

'Hold this.' She passed over the flashlight. 'Can I have your pocket knife?'

She fumbled with her fingers until she found a seam beneath the wallpaper, then cut a neat slit down it. Using the blade, she wiggled until a panel about a yard square fell free.

'I used to hide in here as a child. It was my den. My brother and I used to play Peter Pan and Wendy, and this was our secret cave where we'd hide from Captain Hook—our nanny.'

I peered into the triangular-sectioned recess. 'I sleep in there? For two nights?'

'Nanny could never find me until she at last worked out where I must be.'

'The FP are sharper than your nanny.'

'No, they're not. And this space goes all around the roof towards the back so we can crawl right across the wing if they come nosing about.'

I saw a water tank intruding on the space which explained why there was a hatch here, but also might make rapid escape difficult. The mustiness made me sniffle, and I started to cough.

'You'll have to stop coughing; do try, Hugh. I'll bring bedding up from the store in the basement and raid the kitchen on another trip. If any servants see me, I'll shush them. They won't know I'm not supposed to be here.'

It all sounded like a schoolgirl jape, but its simplicity was alluring.

'And the closet is next door. Don't worry about the noise; the servants use it all the time. They sleep along the corridor, in little rooms to the back and front. Nanny's room was through there.'

She cast the beam of the torch over what was once a communicating door, now replaced by a solid panel and wallpapered over.

Sissy slipped around the house like a ghost, and when she brought me breakfast, also brought news that Lucy's assistant Jenny had stayed on at the house after Lucy left, filling the vacancy of a maid who'd given notice. Women were not taken seriously by the top fascists who saw the world as being run by white Christian men of substance, and for their benefit. It was one of those principles of self-defence, which our women learned to use the enemy's confidence in their own strength to advantage.

'I spoke to Jenny,' she said quietly.

'That was a risk.'

'This whole escapade is a risk, so don't chide me. I trust her. As far as she knows, I'm the only one hiding here.'

'Have the staff been told about the meeting?'

'No. I don't think anyone has.'

Sissy had also helped herself to a maid's uniform. We remained in the Nursery throughout Tuesday, keeping the door locked, the bed unmade, and the hatch ajar, ready to retreat. As quiet as one of Calhoun's submarines lurking on the ocean bed, we communicated by whisper and touch. Never had we been so close as this as a couple, hiding our blushes when using the chamber pot in the tiny room. Timing a dodge across to the closet was farcical, but we were not seen, and we always shared a silent laugh afterwards.

At dawn, a finger of sunlight stabbed through the part-open curtains, and Sissy roused me. The Nursery was at the top of the projecting part of the south wing, and its tiny dormer window offered an aspect down the formal drive so, affording a good view of arrivals. I stood back from the window, close enough to see between the curtains but not so close I could be seen from down below.

A car pulled up precisely at nine o'clock in the morning. I was at the window in time to see Howard Thring, Julian's father, step out. He was alone and strode into the house with purpose.

'I think your mother is about to hear the happy news.'

Officers of the Kent constabulary arrived within the hour, with a senior officer heading into the house, presumably to brief the Baroness. Half a dozen officers moved to take up positions out of sight from me. Next it was the turn of Special Branch. Calhoun was clearly playing his part in stacking the dice, as of the many inspectors available to Scotland Yard, Renton had been given the assignment. Just four plain-clothes detectives accompanied him, sweeping the ground for terrorist snipers and moving through the house from room to room, presumably checking for bombs and lurking assassins.

As heavy feet clumped upstairs, we retreated to our triangular haven. Men banged on doors, challenging servants. Someone tried the Nursery door.

'Key,' came a muffled voice.

A clatter of a key turning in the lock was followed by footfall on the wooden boards of the room, which softened as they reached the rug. They wore shoes, not boots, so I surmised these were Renton's detectives.

'Child's room, sir,' one said. 'Not used, is it? You can see right down from here, though. It would make a good observation point.'

'The room down below is better, and the window's bigger.' It was Renton's voice.

'Yes, yes.' The detective rapped on wood. 'And this is all blocked up.'

He must be examining the board that sealed the connecting door to Nanny's room.

'This just leads into the next room. Or did once.'

Renton's voice was only just audible. 'And yet another toilet.' He closed a door. 'Lock up and move on. Is there an attic?'

'No, this is the top. They shove the servants up here.'

'And their children.'

As the policemen locked the Nursery door, I heard the soft click of Sissy slipping the safety catch of her Walther back on. It would have been a desperate moment if the police officers had found the hatch. After twenty minutes, we eased our way out and stood to full height.

Sissy sank her head on my chest. 'Hugh, Hugh. When did we last dance?'

I slid both my arms around her. 'We'll dance again soon.'

Servants clattered along the corridor outside the Nursery, and we heard the housekeeper assigning rooms to eight Women's Section volunteers we'd watched arrive in a little motor coach. Next came two black vans carrying Fascist Police. I counted twelve, which was a lot to account for, but they had an extensive perimeter to patrol. They couldn't be accommodated in the house, but possibly they would use the huts at the training camp. More might be posted at the gates, but I never counted more than the original twelve.

I tried to read James Cain's *Double Indemnity* between spells watching from the window, and Sissy took turns with the book a few chapters behind me. It was not a good choice; we needed less tension, not more. Magazines with fluffy articles about travel or film stars we shouldn't care about would have been better. Sissy requisitioned a copy of *The Daily Telegraph* from a few days before that had been left in the closet. The outside world was as dangerous as our inner world—China had been invaded by Japan, and the British mandate of Palestine was to be divided into an Arab and a Jewish state. I thought about Arnold Leese and his crazed Madagascar plan, then wondered if this new proposal offered a more hopeful future.

Police of all descriptions streamed from the house towards late afternoon, presumably satisfied. The gates and the perimeter would be sealed; nobody could come in, and nobody would go out. The Fascist Police van headed out towards the training camp, but I noticed two FP men walking back, so perhaps they were sentries for the front door. Sissy and I enjoyed a midnight feast of cold chicken and bread from the kitchen once the house was asleep. A bottle of Bordeaux came to hand, and I treated myself to a glass or two in the small hours.

Sissy declined to join me. 'Frankly, I don't feel wonderful.'

'I know, it's the tension, it's the waiting. I find a glass helps, but perhaps I shouldn't.'

'Oh God, Hugh, it's tomorrow. This plan, I mean…everything must go right. And it won't because plans never work like they're supposed to.'

'Let's hope their plan doesn't work either.'

'Hugh, I'm—'

'Scared, I know.'

'No, you don't know.'

She slept a little and I slept a little, but the wind was rising in the night. We risked final trips to the closet, because goodness knows when we'd have chance again and consumed stale bread and cheese as a spartan breakfast. Rain began to hammer on the roof above us, and to the side of our refuge. It had to be coming from the west as our windows remained clear.

Soon after dawn, the Fascist Police returned in force, slamming the doors of their vans and hurrying to assemble in a double line with heads held down and wearing greatcoats with the collars turned up. I counted a dozen again when they formed up for a miserable parade, plus an officer who strode about jabbing his arm, pointing here and there as his men fidgeted, just wanting to be under cover. The FP men gave the fascist salute before dispersing to their posts. Renton and his men came in two Wolseleys driven by uniformed drivers. Clad in tan gaberdine raincoats of various hues, the detectives formed a huddle, checking their surroundings with far more awareness than the FP men. Renton's orders were more subtle, issued quietly and receiving only nods in response.

Thunder rolled down the valley before us, and the rain grew heavier. Weather complicated any plan, and I was unsure whether it would help or hinder us. Towards noon, an assortment of cars splashed one after the other through the stream which had formed across the drive. The first carried Joyce, together with a man I didn't know, and Peter Wise climbed out of the back to hurry inside. Next came Mosley's allegedly bullet-proof Bentley, preceded by a pair of Blackshirt motorcyclists that drew up so close to the main door I lost sight of them. A First Division bodyguard held a door open for Francis-Hawkins, who was in the next car.

F-H looked about himself, taking note of the cars that had arrived and the positions of the police, braving the rain as Mosley scurried into shelter. For a moment, my heart caught in my mouth. *Mosley is weak*, Bruno had said. If Neil Francis-Hawkins thought he was the stronger man to rule Britain, this was the day to show his hand. Stormtroopers were deployed at his command, as in theory, were the Fascist Police. The bodyguards might be loyal to Mosley, but who else would be?

And Tuesday's strike would have kept the cream of the stormtroopers in London.

Winston Churchill arrived in another Rolls, his driver shielding him with a brolly, then came a naval man with an assistant, possibly Admiral Sir Barry Domville. Calhoun and AA Thorne travelled together in another Wolseley, chauffeured by a police driver. Whether they were friends, colleagues, fellow conspirators or rivals I did not know—I could only stake my hopes on the last option. If I was right, it would have been a stiff and uncomfortable ride.

Thorne made straight for the house, but Calhoun paused momentarily to look to the heavens, letting the rain strike his face like sea spray.

Still, they kept coming, a rogues gallery of the men vying to run the country, for they were all men. I spotted EH Cole from the Nordic League, and even Victor Roe from the White Knights, but I didn't see Arnold Leese, so perhaps nobody had bothered to invite the Imperial Fascist League. One large terrorist bomb would not have been out of place; where was Verity when she was really needed? And there was General Fuller in British army khaki, ribbons on his chest, and aide de camp at his side. An enterprising officer of the regular army would find this a fine moment to stage a coup.

A man in the Action Press uniform of a Blackshirt officer stepped from the latest car to arrive, and put on his cap.

'Julian,' I breathed.

Sissy came to my side and hugged close as we watched. Julian's father stepped out from the opposite side of their car, wearing a unform which was a rarity for the austere party treasurer. Both looked grim. Black silk bands glistened on their right arms, balancing out the party brassards on their left. Julian opened a brolly as lightning split the sky.

'Glad they're not planning a garden party.'

She squeezed my hand. 'It's time to dress up.'

I put on my full uniform; black Action Press style jacket, dark grey cavalry-style jodhpurs, calf-length boots, peaked cap, and the party armband in red, white, and blue. An assortment of uniforms would be on show, so from a distance, I might just go unrecognised among all the black and grey. Sissy donned her maid's uniform, which was rather too large and swamped her figure but added to the downtrodden image. With her hair pulled up into a little white hat, without make-up or earrings, even I'd have to look twice to recognise the vivacious socialite who'd brought me under her spell. If glanced along a corridor, she was unlikely to be identified as an imposter. She allowed her scar to show, and it glowed an angry red as I cast the flashlight across her.

As the servant's staircase was quiet, Sissy crept to the basement to find Jenny again, then crept back without being detected. We sat on the bed, and she whispered the news.

'The butler and cook are tearing their hair out, and the staff are run ragged. Mother is close to having hysteria, but, of course, couldn't say no when Julian's father told her of the meeting. He's got all the planning worked out, though, there's food arriving, and the extra women are pitching in.'

'Any of ours among them?'

'Melissa's section,' she said. 'I know some of them, but I don't want any to recognise me.'

'Are they in uniform?'

'No, dressed as maids, like me.' She made a show of her costume. 'It's a woman's place in the Party, don't you know?'

I smiled. 'Can you take charge of them if it all goes to pot?'

'I'll try, but there are whispers that Melissa's death was all your fault.'

'Which, in many ways, it was.'

'She brought it on herself. Melissa betrayed us, and she might have been the one who betrayed our attempt to grab Baxter, too.'

'That was Julian.'

'No, it could have been Melissa,' she asserted. 'Jules probably told her the plan; you know how soft he is.'

'Is he? Is he really soft? Or underneath it all, is he his father's son?'

'He's nothing like his father!' Sissy raised her voice louder than was wise, then ducked her head in apology.

Thunder drowned whatever she said next.

'What else did Jenny say?'

The staff had been given the minimum amount of information and a list of instructions. Delegates would enter the Great Dining Room from the Grand Staircase at the north side. The door to Baroness Rockwell's suite led off the west side of the dining room and would be locked, as would all three doors to a parlour called the Red Room on the south side. Staff would need to use the passageway under the house and come up the north service stairs when needed to bring refreshments or clear the tables.

One curious aspect of this eighteenth-century home was the way access from south to north along the first floor relied on moving through bedrooms, which may have been fine back in the day, but not anymore. The Red Room looked out from the front façade of the house, one floor down and one room north from where we stood making our plans in the Nursery. It had been converted from a bedroom into a parlour, and in normal times servants coming up from the kitchen could go through it to reach the Great Dining Room beyond. We could reach it in a knight's move in a three-dimensional version of chess.

Now came the dangerous part.

Sissy slipped out of the nursery to scout the route to the Red Room, and in moments she was back. 'Coast is clear.'

Taking the chance, we trotted swiftly down the south service stair, and Sissy unlocked the Red Room and let me in. It was gloomy without lights, but I could hear servants laying out a cold lunch in the Grand Dining Room beyond the next door. The delegates must all be still downstairs, talking in the Salon or smoking out under cover of the wide veranda. Ten or fifteen minutes later, I heard a familiar rhythmic tap on the door and let Sissy in.

'Half the men are being served sandwiches in the Salon; the bodyguards, the secretaries, all the little men. They're all men, every single one of them.'

'So much for modern Britain.'

'The rest are coming upstairs now, the important ones. Can you hear through that door?'

'Not brilliantly, but your mother's servants are quiet, and fascists like to hear the sound of their own voice.'

She offered me a pained smile.

'Sorry, Sissy, but this is what it's come to.'

'I know.'

A hammering came from the door to the hallway. Sissy cocked her head. I nodded and touched the Luger, which fitted my pistol holster awkwardly. It was far too early for drama; this could so easily go wrong. I put my cap on and pulled its brim low.

'Who is it?' Sissy challenged the door.

'Mam, that's not you?' asked a voice curtly. 'Baroness?'

'This room is private,' she said.

CHAPTER THIRTY-EIGHT

'We've got to guard it. We've got orders. Open up, Fascist Police.'

Sissy unlocked the door and opened it half-way. 'I can guard the room.'

'You're a maid. How are you guarding a room?'

'Very well, you guard it.'

'From inside. We've orders to guard it from inside.'

One pushed at the door, and Sissy allowed him in. I gave the smartest Roman salute I could manage, and after a moment's surprise, two FP men returned it. They looked at the maid, then at me. I gave a shrug, Sissy put her head down in shame, pretended to fasten a button near her collar and they could make what they wanted of the situation.

'Sir, no Blackshirt officers are allowed upstairs. For any reason.'

One leered at Sissy, and she slipped out of the room, keeping her gaze down.

'Very well.' I was not going to draw attention to myself, and they'd already drawn their own conclusions as to why Sissy and I were locked in the room together. I straightened my jacket and left.

Out in the corridor, we stood useless and exposed.

'Damn.'

Chapter Thirty-Nine

In what was known as the Tapestry Room, William Joyce was dressed in a cheap suit with a black shirt and tie. His scar was accentuated by his expression of pain and suspicion as Detective Inspector Renton explained how Melissa Thring met her death.

'She and her husband were arguing over a little pistol, and somehow, she shot herself in the thigh. A bullet cut an artery, and she was dead in minutes.'

'Are you sure it was an accident? Thring is here —we can't have killers here.'

'I'm surprised to see him too, considering. But the thigh is not where you'd shoot someone if you were meaning to kill them.'

'His father may want him as his aide, but I don't want him here.'

'I'd agree, he's the last man I'd want as an aide. He was very emotional when I last saw him.'

'I don't want him because he's a friend of Hugh Clifton.'

'I always thought Clifton was your Party's biggest hero.'

'You thought wrongly.'

The commander of the Fascist Police detachment opened the door. 'Er, Mr Joyce. We've a problem. And the inspector needs to hear it too.'

'Spit it out, we're busy,' Joyce snapped.

'Two of my men are missing.'

'Missing? How, why, how do you know they're missing?'

'They didn't come back for their lunch break.'

'Lunch, lunch, you give them breaks for lunch? Is this a holiday camp?'

'Which direction were they patrolling?' asked Renton.

'Up that track to the north, then back along the river. They might have got lost in the trees and with this storm.'

'Go and find them!' Joyce ordered.

The man saluted and left.

'I don't like this,' Joyce said. 'With Julian Thring being here it stinks of Department Z. Arrest him again, just get him away from here.'

'I can't just go around arresting who I please.'

'You can, it's an order. Find him, arrest him, and take him away immediately.'

Marcus Calhoun from MI5 had been listening and joined them.

'Calhoun, isn't it?' Joyce sneered. 'Why are you even here?'

'I was invited.'

'You invited yourself. And it's starting,' Joyce said. 'I need to be upstairs. Renton—arrest Julian Thring. And if Baroness Rockwell's daughter is here, arrest her too. And if Hugh Clifton turns up, shoot him on sight. You, Calhoun, are needed upstairs.'

'With you in a moment,' Calhoun said.

Calhoun waited for Joyce to go. 'Missing men?'

'The FP are amateurs,' Renton said. 'And half of them have got charge sheets of their own. I wouldn't bet they've not found the wine cellar and are drinking away the afternoon.'

'And Melissa Thring's death—an accident?'

'Hugh Clifton's friends and accidents don't fit easily together.' Renton lowered his voice. 'Is he here?'

'We have to assume he is. And his girlfriend, and now Julian Thring.'

'But you're not telling Mr Joyce.'

'Inspector.' Calhoun adopted a warning tone, then glanced towards the door to the hall behind them. 'If Clifton and his first eleven are close by, I expect trouble. Get your men out of sight and call more. As many as you can—and as quickly as you can. And be very careful they don't tangle with Department Z, or there will be a bloodbath.'

'Trigger happy baker's boys. Are they here, too?'

'Who knows?'

'You know,' Renton stated. 'What's Clifton planning?'

'He has an interesting theory which boils down to us being about to witness a coup.'

'Is he right?'

'The whole basis of his theory is wrong.'

'Then we have to stop him doing whatever he is trying to do. We need to enforce the law, Calhoun, or what passes for the law these days.'

'Sir?' It was one of the maids. 'Are you Commander Calhoun?'

'*Commodore* Calhoun.'

She glanced at Renton. 'Sorry, but this is just for Commodore Calhoun.'

'I'll go about my business,' Renton said.

Calhoun held his hand out for the paper she carried. 'What's your name, my dear?'

'Jenny.'

The note she passed bore one word: Chapel.

* * *

It was a large meeting, with only senior men present. The government was heavily over-represented, with all its key players at the table. Joyce was acting as peacemaker with the half dozen larger fascist and far-right groups. Mosley laid down the law, Francis-Hawkins reiterated that it could be the *only* law, but the parties outside government demanded seats at the top table. And more action against the Jews, and closer ties with Germany. An alliance, in fact.

A fascist policeman came into the room and spoke close to Mosley's ear. He waved away the news with a curt 'Yes!'

'Sir?' Joyce asked.

'You have a man down with appendicitis. Of all the times to choose! An ambulance is on its way.'

A mutter rippled around the table.

'Make sure it goes round the back!' Joyce ordered the FP man. More softly, he added. 'Let me know when it's here.'

'Yes, we should care about our men,' Mosley intoned, and the audience nodded. 'I fought in the Great War.'

'As did many patriots,' Admiral Domville added.

'Well, most of us did,' F-H inclined his head towards Joyce, who had been far too young.

'There must not be another European war.' Mosley rapped his knuckle on the table. 'But as for an alliance with Germany, that's another matter.'

Discussions resumed. *Interminable*, thought Calhoun, and strangely pointless. It was rather like sitting through a play by some experimental young playwright who hadn't studied classical drama; all monologue with no obvious direction. A team of middle-order batsmen, playing for time in the hope of a draw. No star bowlers, no bold strokes over the boundary, just a room full of men pumping up their own importance. Dr Valentine, the man who had schemed his way to head Department Z was seated to his right, looking by turns bored and restless. Calhoun needed to slip down to the Chapel. A call of nature could be the excuse, but now the FP man had returned and whispered to Joyce. And Joyce whispered to Mosley, who frowned, nodded, then interrupted proceedings.

'Gentlemen, matters have come up that we must discuss privately.'

This could be it. The boring playwright had sparked up the script by introducing the *Deus Ex Machina*.

Joyce stood and began to speak. 'If I give your name, please adjourn to the Salon.' Almost as if he had a list in mind, he recited a number of names and looked each man in the eye. Almost as if prepared for this, the assorted fascists acquiesced. AA Thorne was among those asked to leave. He'd been there ostensibly to represent the Anglo-German Fellowship, but few of those present were fooled. Calhoun was asked to stay, as was Valentine.

Calhoun leaned towards him. 'Dr Valentine, I presume,' he said in a low whisper.

'MI5, what are you doing here?' Valentine whispered back, barely moving his lips.

'Keeping on my toes.'

'What do you know?'

'I'd ask you the same question. I thought Department Z was all-knowing. Or have you been too busy poking your own eyes out?'

Francis-Hawkins, Churchill, Fuller, and Joyce were among those who remained. Admiral Domville was one who left.

'Excuse me, Prime Minister, but what's happening?' Calhoun asked.

It was Joyce who replied. 'News from the north. The assault on Hull.'

Calhoun stood up and grimaced. 'If you don't mind, I'll seize the moment. Quick trip to the heads.'

'Stay where you are; this can't wait,' Joyce said.

'I'm sorry, but nature calls.'

'That's not such a bad idea, Calhoun,' Mosley added. 'A five-minute break, gentlemen.'

Chapter Forty

A laundry store in the basement was our next refuge. Sissy stood with her back to the narrow door, and I slumped against the wall opposite, beneath a slit window that opened at what would be ankle level to the world above. We had to allow time in case the FP men reported seeing us, but we couldn't hear the hue and cry of the house being searched.

'Now what?' Sissy asked. 'We're not going to learn anything down here.'

'I just needed a clue,' I said. 'I thought this meeting was set up so Mosley could bring all his opponents into one place, then have them arrested to consolidate his power. All the leading fascists who don't support him will be taken off the board.'

'That's what I'd do,' Sissy said. 'But the others would have seen straight through it, and they wouldn't have come.'

'Yes, but there's the bluff of sending the First Division north.'

'But the train strike has stopped that.' After a moment, she added. 'So Mosley can go ahead?'

'Don't sound so pleased. Remember you had doubts the other day.'

'They were not doubts, more…I don't know, worries.'

'Well, keep those worries in the forefront of your mind.' I tapped my forehead. 'The house is guarded mostly by the FP, and they're commanded by Julian's chum Dougie, so whatever happens next has the sanction of the Young Britons.'

'Well, F-H is above Dougie.'

'In theory.'

'So how about F-H planning to depose Mosley and clear out the others at the same time?' She suggested.

'It's fifty-fifty either way.'

'Or it could just be a meeting. You know how those men love to talk. Once it's over, we can surprise Mother and see what she heard and see if our ladies or the staff picked anything up. We can check the wastepaper from the baskets, things like that.'

'But in the meantime, we learn nothing hiding down here.'

The sharp tang of starch pervaded the room, and I tried to resist coughing. I stood on tiptoe but could see only grey rolling clouds through that high window. The rain may have eased a little. At least Calhoun was on the inside and may share what he'd learned. He should have received my note about the Chapel before the meeting convened and know only one person would have sent it.

'Well, as we're stuck here,' she said. 'It gives us a chance to talk.'

'Talk? We get plenty of chances to talk.' I was trying to think.

'But you don't listen to me, do you? Not really listen. You don't pick hints up.'

'Sissy, it's not the time—'

'It's the perfect time, it's the only time. We've been chased around the country and got away with it so far, but we know that man Baxter is involved now. He kills people, and he'll kill you if he can, Hugh. What other reason would they have to bring him into…whatever is going on?'

The laundry was located beneath the Smoking Room and just south of the terrace. A slit window six feet from the floor opened into a light well, which ran between the terrace and the south wing. I heard the crunch of boots on gravel and took the chance a look. The basement had been designed so servants couldn't use its windows to spy on their betters, but I pulled down a heap of folded sheets to offer an extra six inches of height so I could peek through the slit window. My improved view was of stonework, and a slit of grey above, but the window would open fully enough to allow me to squeeze out.

'Help me up,' I asked.

'We still need to talk.'

With a leg up from Sissy, I crawled out and splashed down into an inch of water running along the mossy stones lining the trench-like light well. A little tunnel, half man-height, carried the trench under the terrace. It offered cover for me to stick my head over the lip. A few men had taken advantage of the pause in the downpour and stood in casual groups, talking and smoking. Some looked rather bored, glancing wistfully back at the house where the important discussions would be in full flood. Half the conversations mentioned the weather, but I heard a snatch of conversation about poor Johnny falling ill. And something about an appendix. Half a dozen FP men in very wet greatcoats and wilting caps were brought together by one of their officers, their heads turning as a man to give attention to something out of sight.

My knees and legs were soaked, and a persistent drip struck me on the head, then my shoulder, then my back.

Crouching, half-crawling, through the slimy tunnel gave a better view. What looked like a St John's ambulance came to a halt on the gravel, half concealed by the north wing. A whole squad of ambulancemen poured out, bearing two stretchers between them and enough medical bags to patch up a platoon of casualties. It was a lot for one sick man called Johnny, no matter how well-connected he was. And far from helping, the FP men were marching away. The back of the house was completely unguarded. Apart from Sissy and me.

I crawled back along the light well to the window of the laundry room, stuck my head inside, and summarised what I'd seen.

'Ambulances?' she asked.

'Two of them now.'

'For one man? It must be Baxter, he's up to something.'

'Baxter, Baxter, of course! You're right. You're so very right.'

'So what's he doing? I mean, if F-H is bringing his stormtroopers down, he doesn't need Baxter.'

'No. And Mosley doesn't either.'

Chapter Forty-One

Julian Thring caught his father in the Marble Hall, directly beneath the room where the meeting was taking place. 'Father. Shouldn't you be in the meeting?'

'It's been adjourned.'

'What is it really for?'

'Reconciliation.'

'Not just that. Far too many things have been happening…' he paused. 'Have happened, just to bring about a talking shop.'

'Reconciliation, and some re-ordering of affairs. Don't worry, Julian, our rise within the party is assured.'

'Assured by who? And is it you who brought Jeb Baxter back? You wound him into your plans in thirty-five, so it all points to you again. What's he up to?'

His father shrugged. 'I haven't the faintest idea.'

He tried to walk away, but Julian grabbed his arm.

'Don't lie to me. I've been working in intelligence for two years; intelligence, so don't treat me like a child. Melissa is dead because you forced her to spy on me, on Hugh.'

'She wanted to. Melissa was loyal; *loyal*, Julian.'

'It was she who told you we were going to detain Baxter, wasn't it? She's dead because of your plots and plans. We're going to rise in the Party because my wife is dead.'

'Stop acting like you loved her. It was always a marriage of convenience.'

Julian gripped his father's arm tighter. 'And you had Verity killed too.'

'Nonsense.'

'Or you tried,' Julian pushed his father away. 'Did you know she's not dead? Did Parker tell you the truth about how he failed?'

His father blanched.

'One day, she's going to come back and settle scores.'

'Rubbish.'

'Yes. Everything you've told me is rubbish.'

'I only brought you here today because I felt sorry for you. I wanted to stop your moping.'

'And I only came to find out what the bloody hell is going on.'

Inspector Renton and two of his detectives appeared from the Salon door. 'Ah, Mr Thring, both Mr Thring's to be sure. I'm afraid I need to have a word with Mr Julian.'

'Has he done something wrong?'

'His wife was shot dead, sir. That's pretty wrong in my book.'

'It was an accident,' Julian said. 'You have my statement. You let me go, I'm on bail. Why do you want me now? When are you going to release my wife's body so we can have a funeral?'

'All in good time,' Renton said.

Thring Senior nodded to the detective. 'It's tiresome, but you need to go with the inspector, Julian. If it helps, I can call my solicitor again—'

'I don't need your solicitor.'

Renton laid his hand firmly on Julian's upper arm. 'Julian Thring, I'd suggest you come quietly.'

Chapter Forty-Two

More commotion demanded I return to my lookout point in the light well. From the terrace came a growing hubbub. Many of the assorted aides and secretaries who'd been sitting on the terrace began filing out on the lawn. Two of the ambulancemen were herding them towards the summer pavilion way down on the left. Now staff were leaving; cooks, maids, chauffeurs, all being rounded up by another ambulanceman. Some of those maids were our women, and I hoped they'd not try something brave. The house was being emptied, and a kind of prison being created out in the pavilion. Baroness Rockwell came into sight down the terrace steps, protesting loudly to an ambulanceman urging her on her way.

'Unhand me. This is my house!'

He swore at her and pushed her physically.

'Uncouth brute—bring me an umbrella, I'll catch my death!'

He jabbed a pistol into her midriff, and her protests gave way to stolid compliance. She was marched away with her nose in the air, raising her hands in theatrical surrender as the rain commenced once more.

Part of me hoped those ambulance men were Verity's guerrillas come to cut the head off the fascist snake, but I knew it would not be the case. One of the men in disguise seemed to be in charge as he was shouting orders. He held his head low, his back bent, his arms dangling when not pointing or gesturing. If rats could grow to human form, this was the posture they would adopt.

I wormed back to the window. 'You're right, it's Baxter.'

'One of those days I hate being right.'

'They're herding everyone out to the summer pavilion. Including your mother.'

'Oh God, Hugh, get down here.'

I turned onto my belly, posted my feet through the window, wriggled inside, and dropped onto the linen. Sissy grabbed hold to stop me from toppling backwards off the pile.

'Thanks.'

'God, you're soaked.'

The room was replete with towels, and she found one to dab at me after I'd stepped off the heap. I took it up to wipe my face and hair, then rubbed at my knees.

'We need to get away,' she repeated. 'We should go now while they're busy rounding people up.'

'I feared for a moment you'd suggest we go and try to rescue your mother.'

'Just us, against all of them?' she pleaded. 'There's more at stake now.'

'Yes, the fate of the whole bloody country.'

'No, we're having a baby, Hugh. There, I said it.'

I was stunned. With everything going on around us, I could hardly absorb the news.

'God knows how it happened, but there we are. We must have been careless when I came back from France.'

'I'm sorry about that.'

'Sorry? Is that all you can say—you're sorry? Sorry about what, that I'm preggers, that you ever met me, that we're bloody well adding scandal to scandal.'

'No, no, I mean, I was so pleased you were alive, so pleased to see you…And you've been trying to tell me this for weeks, and I've been a dope.'

'You have. For an intelligence officer, you're not very intelligent. And now, the three of us need to escape. Forget trying to save the country, just save our family.'

'Oh, Sissy. I said I'm sorry, but I'm not sorry about a baby. This can be wonderful.'

'I'm ruined,' she said. 'Totally ruined.'

'We'll make it work—the world is different now. We've got money, we've got friends. We'll get through today then—'

'We're going to die,' she said.

'No, no, we're not. But if we're going to survive, all of us, all three of us, we have to come out of this on the winning side. We need to get to the Chapel.'

'Yes, if we use the cellar door under the library, we can sprint to the rose garden when nobody is looking.'

'But we need to go to the Chapel first.'

'Well, one is next to the other.'

I drew the Luger, wondering if I could trust a weapon stamped with the date 1917. I pulled back the toggle to load the first round, leaving six more in the magazine and took off the safety. If we were discovered, Sissy and I might still be able to shoot our way out, given the number of activities occupying the attention of the plotters. But we needed to survive for longer than just one afternoon, we had to secure our future. I put my cap back on, though I was a muddy disgrace of a Blackshirt now. Pistols in hand, we made a short rush along the passageway to the base of the north service stair, hoping there was no guard posted at ground floor level.

A sharp turn to the left brought us to the door of the Chapel, half-sunken to the basement level so offering extra height. Calhoun was already there, one hand in his pocket, visibly shaken when Sissy thrust a Walther into his face.

'Aha,' he said. 'And you must be Sissy. Perhaps the bravest woman in Britain.'

'Excuse me?' she exclaimed. 'Who are you?'

'Sissy, this is my boss,' I said. '*Was* my boss.'

'Marcus Calhoun, Security Service.'

He held out his hand, but Sissy refused to shake it. She did at least lower the pistol.

'So whose side are *you* on?' she demanded.

'The national interest,' Calhoun said. 'And the nation doesn't have much time,'

'No, there are fake ambulancemen clearing civilians from the house,' I said. 'They're led by Jeb Baxter, so the coup is already underway.'

'It can't be a coup,' Calhoun said. 'This tale you've been spinning about a military take-over is wrong. The stormtroopers have gone north.'

'That's what everyone here is supposed to think. But there's a convenient strike arranged to keep them in London, with full participation by the fascist unions. Can't you smell that rat, Calhoun?'

'No, I smell a different rat. It will come as news to you, hiding here in a cubby hole, but the strike was called off, and the stormtroopers went north on Tuesday, as planned. The strike has been rearranged for today to make sure they stay there. Whatever is underway, it is *not* a military take-over.'

I looked at Sissy. She looked at me. How could I be so wrong – and stake our lives on being so wrong?

'Meanwhile, Joyce is sorting the sheep from the goats. He's got some big piece of news, so I need to go back and find out what it is.'

'Joyce?'

'Is there any connection between Jeb Baxter and Joyce?'

'No, not that I'm aware of. But Baxter has worked for Howard Thring, and he must be working with AA Thorne.'

'And neither of them is still upstairs,' Calhoun said.

'Baxter's here to kill Mosley,' Sissy said abruptly.

Calhoun nodded. 'I fear you are correct. So, Clifton, I hope you've a lot of men with machine guns hidden out in those woods.'

'A few,' I said.

'You'll need more than a few. I need to get back upstairs.'

'Are you armed?'

'We don't play by those rules,' he said. 'Time your entry well. If this is going the way I think it is going, we've got one chance—and you're it.'

Chapter Forty-Three

Inspector Renton took his four detectives and their prisoner to a room at the end of the stable block. On normal days, it was used by the groom to make tea and sit and read the newspaper when he was not needed by the Baroness or her horses, which was much of the time. Julian sat silently in the corner, handcuffed and head bowed.

'What's the plan, Mr Thring?'

Julian simply looked up.

'Someone on high requests that the Yard send a detail here, and someone else asks that its led by me. Nobody else but me, and protecting nobs isn't my patch. Just like I don't normally get called out to accidental deaths in the suburbs.'

After a moment, Julian spoke. 'I called you because I thought you'd understand.'

'Oh, I understand, all right. Did you also ask for me to be here today?'

'I'd guess that it was Hugh. He trusts you for some reason.'

'But it wasn't him who requested me, which makes me wonder who he's been talking to. And then another order from on high says to take no more than four officers. We'd be here for show, but without enough men to make a difference if things turn ugly. What is happening, Mr Thring?'

A St John's ambulance trundled slowly past the window, kicking up gravel.

'Did any of you hear someone call for an ambulance?'

Renton's men shook their heads. A second ambulance ground past.

'Two ambulances, Thring?' The Inspector demanded. 'That's not your Department Z friends arriving, is it?'

'I don't know.'

'I suppose bread vans are more your style.'

'There's a plot,' Julian blurted out.

'Involving ambulances?'

'I don't know what the ambulances are for.'

'Why didn't Clifton just warn me, rather than have me sitting here a spectator?'

'He doesn't know any detail about what's planned.'

'And what is planned?'

'Hugh doesn't share everything he knows.'

'He's here, isn't he?'

Julian shook his head.

'Is that a yes or a no or a refusal to answer?'

From outside came a growing hubbub.

'The ambulancemen are armed, guv,' said one of the detectives. 'They're not ambulancemen.'

'Of course, they're not.' Renton turned to Julian. 'Whatever Clifton told you is about to happen he's got his facts wrong, so if he's got a plan to stop this coup, it's already down the jobby.'

'How do you know?'

'A little bird told me, the same little bird who arranged for me to be here. And he's also mysteriously well-informed about what Department Z is up to. A Military coup, Mr Thring?'

'No, that's not likely.'

'What is likely?'

The detectives watched discreetly, but buildings blocked the view of the gardens behind the house where all the activity seemed to be taking place. Only an open gateway allowed a window on what was happening. The house was being evacuated, or people were being taken prisoner. It was hard to tell.

'Nothing happens without money.' Julian said after some thought. 'It's the Germans, the Nazis. It's where the money is coming from; they're the paymasters.'

'The Germans, oh, happy day. And they gave me just four men, so I had no chance of stopping this.'

'My father must be involved,' Julian said soberly.

'Putting you on which side?'

'I'm not going against my country.' He put his chin up. 'Call me a murderer, Inspector Renton, but I'm not a traitor.'

'Good,' Renton said. 'I'd like to even the odds. How many Department Z boys and girls have you got in hiding?'

The prisoner remained silent.

'Let's do this another way. Two FP men went missing an hour or two ago, off to the north or down by the river. Is that where Clifton and his men are? Sonny, it's kick-off time. Who is supposed to blow the whistle?'

'I don't know.'

'If you wanted to run for help, would you go north? Down by the river?'

'There's a boathouse out of sight of the main house. It's run down, old.'

'We went down to search it yesterday, but there was already an FP man on guard,' said one of the detectives.

'An FP man, or a man in an FP uniform?'

The detective pulled his face into a taut grimace.

'We used to practice shooting there,' Julian added. 'I taught Meliss—'

'So Clifton posts a fake FP man to guard it yesterday, and today two FP men get too inquisitive and get knocked on the head for their pains. How far away is it?'

'A quarter of a mile from the main door, perhaps a little further. But from here–'

'Could you get there without being seen?'

Julian knew there was a fair chance Hills would be in the boathouse, together with others who looked up to Hugh with a sparkle in their eyes. To Hugh, not to Julian. But Julian was a Blackshirt hero, too.

'We practiced attacking the house,' he said. 'Three times, one weekend when the Baroness was away. We pretended it was a communist headquarters, and the servants played along.'

'Can you get to this boathouse?'

'If I go out the back of here, then down through the trees… they might see me as I cross the drive, but the rain will help. And from a distance, one black uniform looks like another. Yes, yes… After the drive there's a ha-ha I can creep behind. Then it's downhill towards the lake, but it's pretty open until I reach the trees on the north side. I might be spotted on my run, but once I reach the woods, there's an easy track down to the boathouse. Then things would kick off, as you say.'

'Free him,' ordered Renton.

'Are you sure about this, sir?'

'So sure, I want you to follow him as far as the drive, then get to the main gate. Be very careful, keep to the trees as long as you can. Find the Kent officers, not the fascist arseholes. We need as many decent old-fashioned coppers as we can get.'

Chapter Forty-Four

'So that was the man you were working for?' Sissy asked once Calhoun had left the Chapel.

'Yes.'

'And still working for?'

'Working *with*. And the villain of the piece must be Joyce. He sent us to Sark, planned our murder, and kept the hunt for me alive.'

'Not the Young Britons? But they must be involved somehow. And if Baxter is here, that means—'

'Julian's father.'

'And Julian?'

I shrugged my shoulders. 'The time for guessing is done. You need to get to the boathouse. We need numbers, and we need them now.'

'We should go together.'

'No, you'll slip past easier than I will; you're *just a maid*.' I gave Sissy a wink. 'The FP will see one scared woman dashing for safety, that's all.'

'I can't lie, I am scared.'

And I was scared for her too. Baxter would not want any surprises spoiling his next move, no guards or detectives or Department Z agents popping out to ambush his men. Highwood boasted nearly fifty rooms and would take a lot of clearing by the handful of ambulancemen not already marching prisoners out to the pavilion. There was a good chance none had been posted to the rose garden or were patrolling the path in front of it.

She pecked me on the cheek. 'We'll dance again.'

'We will. Boathouse.'

Beneath the north service stair was an arched passage leading to the external door we'd entered by on Monday night. Its bolts were well-oiled and slid back quietly. If there was a guard outside, he was going to be shot before he even saw us; I'd finally break my duck and become the killer everyone portrayed me as. That ugly Luger led the way out.

A quick glance through sheets of slanting rain confirmed there was an FP man stationed at each corner of the north wing, far enough away that a running woman would be very unlucky to be hit by a pistol shot fired in haste.

'If they fire on you, I'm not going to shoot back, because it would give the game away,' I said. 'And don't you stop to shoot either, just run, run for your life. For both your lives.' I touched her shoulder.

Sissy breathed in, exhaled heavily.

'Love you.'

'Super,' she said, without even looking back. She took another deep breath. then burst into a sprint. Sissy was across the gravel of the path in moments and had passed the first little conifer beyond before a man shouted. He shouted again as she hurtled down the little path to the welcoming brick arch.

'Run, run,' I breathed.

Both the FP men were shouting now. I could hear the scrunch of their boots, but Sissy was through that arch, dodged left into the walled garden, and vanished. I closed the door, praying I didn't hear a shot. I imagined Sissy rushing past the roses and reaching that green door at the far end. No sound of a shot came to shatter my life, but I knew I couldn't linger in case the FP came to check that door. I left it unbolted as friends might find it a handy way inside, and I ventured cautiously up the stairs to the Chapel Gallery. I moved into the Library, where I'd enjoyed browsing the brass-grilled shelves on visits past. The door to the Smoking Room was on the left and I could hear loud voices beyond it.

A closer voice made me pull back against the bookcases.

'I need to use the telephone.' It was Peter Wise, the man who so many people thought was on their side.

'No one is allowed in the study.'

'Mr Joyce has sent me down. I need to ring Buckingham Palace.'

'Step back, mate. Nobody is allowed in there.'

'Mr Joyce—'

'Yes, Mr Joyce's orders. Nobody but him is allowed in there.'

The house had only two telephones, and one was in the Study. Perhaps Joyce was in there now, leaving a guard outside to argue with Wise. I could rush him now and learn the truth, but perhaps Joyce was elsewhere and just wanted others kept away from the phone.

Footsteps were coming my way. Wise entered the library, heading for the Smoking Room door, but I gave a loud double-click as one might use to summon a dog. He froze, and his eyes met the muzzles of my automatic. If he panicked now, or was playing for the Nazis all along, the game was over.

Without making any signal to the invisible guard, who must be able to see him from the Study door, Wise moved very slowly into the body of the Library. Once out of the eyeline of the guard, he glanced behind him.

'So, whose side are you on, Mr Wise?'

'I would ask the same.'

'We haven't time. Who were you going to call? And don't tell me the king.'

'I've been told to place a call to the palace.'

'Why?'

'By the end of the afternoon, we will have a new national socialist government and an alliance with Germany.'

Deep down I knew, everything had pointed this way.

'Were you really going to call the palace?'

His eyes judged me. 'No.'

'How long have you known about Joyce's bid for power?'

'For a while, but I still don't know how he'll achieve it.'

'So you don't know about the ambulancemen?'

'I have seen a couple of ambulancemen. One of the men has fallen ill.'

'They're not ambulancemen, but mercenaries led by a man named Jeb Baxter. Have you seen him? Weather-beaten, tanned, slightly stooping?'

'Just now. In there.' He indicated the Smoking Room.

CHAPTER FORTY-FOUR

'That's how Joyce will achieve it. Who's left upstairs?

'Mosley, Francis-Hawkins, General Fuller, Churchill, and the spy chiefs.'

'Including Dr Valentine?'

He nodded.

'They'll be arrested or killed in the next few minutes. How many guards are on the stairs?'

'A fascist policeman by the Study door and another three at the bottom of the staircase. Mosley's two bodyguards are outside the dining room at the top.'

Oh, for Eleanor now. I could take down the man by the Study, but three more could run through from the hall in a second or two, and Mosley's bodyguards might even thunder down the stairs to join in, not knowing what way the wind was blowing and not giving me time to explain. If one of my shots missed, or the Luger jammed at a critical moment, or those ambulancemen were the breed of killer I'd expect Baxter to recruit, I'd be dead within the next minute.

'If the National Socialist League takes power, it's bad news for Britain's Jews, isn't it?'

After a moment, he admitted his true allegiance. 'It would be a catastrophe.'

'Find Baxter. Delay him if you can.'

I left Wise and hurried down the service stair again and into the subterranean passage. The lower kitchen ahead on the right was deathly quiet. I glanced into the doorway and saw how hurriedly it had been cleared of staff. Carefully, now I went up the south service stairs. Thank God I'd been to the kitchen a few times and even used it in training before we raided the White Knights. Highwood had been well designed to allow servants to move about unobserved by their masters, and I stayed unobserved by the new masters of the house.

As I reached the first floor the time of decision had come. One of the FP men who disturbed us earlier was standing guard outside the Red Room. I wondered if the Fascist Police knew which side they were on, but the secret plot could not have been shared with too many, as the risk of betrayal rose with every mouth that could share the secret.

I let my Luger dangle by my side and strode towards him. 'You're relieved,' I said.

He looked down at my soaked and spoiled trousers. 'What's the password?'

'The password is: *unbuckle your belt, or I'll blow your balls off.*'

For good measure, I tossed aside my cap. There was no point in disguise anymore.

'Do you recognise me?'

After a moment, he nodded. 'You, you—'

'So unfasten your belt and let it slide to the floor. One twitch towards your gun, and you're as dead as those men on the train. Don't think I won't do it.'

He complied with fear in his eyes.

'Now, very slowly, unlock the door and go inside.'

I pushed the FP man into the Red Room before me. A second was sitting in one of the chairs, reading a newspaper.

'It's him,' said my captive.

'You, stand up. Drop your pistol belt, then move over by that door.' I indicated the one which communicated through to the Grand Dining Room.

Neither of the men were typical young FP recruits, fed by lies, exploited for their poverty and ignorance. These were old hands who must be in on the act. I collected their belts, weighed down by heavy military revolvers. I'd need every round I could get. I wondered whether a moment existed where we could take back democracy if the far right was about to tear itself apart. Mosley's 'kosher fascism' was odious enough, but Nazis were a deeper shade of black. The solution had to be brutal, and I needed both Valentine and Calhoun alive to achieve it.

'Now you, yes you. Unlock the door there and pull it wide open, slowly. Then we are all going to join the party.'

The FP man unlocked the door, his eyes barely leaving me for a moment. The other kept his hands half-raised. I didn't relish seeing the deaths of two more FP men.

'In, now!'

The men jerked into motion with hands raised fully for maximum dramatic effect, and I followed. My line had been rehearsed many times before.

'Department Z, nobody move!'

Chapter Forty-Five

Two-thirds of the seats at the great dining table were empty. Mosley sat at the far end, earnestly talking with Joyce as I made my entry.

'Clifton!' Mosley exclaimed. 'What the blazes?'

Joyce turned pale as I shifted the muzzle of the Luger from the cowering FP men to him.

'You two, get over by the windows, away from the door.'

I edged into the body of the room, switching my gun from Joyce to the FP men to Joyce again. It was a large room, and he was a distant target.

'Explain yourself!' Mosley barked.

'You may be wondering why you've been called here today,' I said. 'A rag bag of national socialist racialists assembled at the very moment the cream of the stormtroopers have been sent to crush resistance in Hull. And when MI5 are engaged in breaking an NKVD cell.'

Calhoun took an intake of breath as I looked his way.

'And Department Z is busy hunting its own.'

Valentine nodded, perhaps now finally understanding.

'Meanwhile, Special Branch and the Fascist Police are chasing me, and I'm all wound up in being chased. Who wins?'

'What the bloody hell do you think you are doing?' Joyce said.

'Spoiling your day. Right now, your national socialist friends are busy downstairs forming a new government, correct?'

'Joyce, is this true?' Mosley demanded, grabbing his arm.

Joyce shook him off.

'Traitor!'

'*You* are the traitor,' Joyce replied.

Mosley cursed, F-H yelled out in anger, Churchill growled disapproval, and General Fuller thumped his fist on the table.

'You're all traitors to the white Christian race! Jew lovers like Clifton.'

I should have shot him right then, but Fuller's head partly blocked a clear shot, and Churchill's bulk offered excellent cover. Fuller could hardly be accused of being a Jew-lover either, so more was afoot here. I edged closer to shorten the range and improve my angle. Joyce was not a big man and now he slid behind Mosley, then F-H, then Valentine.

'My men have this building under their control,' Joyce exclaimed. 'If you let him shoot me, you'll never get out of here alive, none of you. Valentine, bring your dog to heel. This cretin is right in just one respect: today is the first day of the new national socialist Britain. We have a new national socialist government, and we have very powerful friends. So you reflect on that, Dr Valentine. And you, Commodore Calhoun. We don't need Department Z, MI5, Special Branch, and all your apparatus for spying on the people.'

'Men like you always need men like us,' Valentine said, keeping his eyes on me and without even turning to address Joyce. 'You need us to keep *the people* in check.'

Calhoun now chose to speak. 'You may think the house is under your control, Mr Joyce, but it is surrounded, and you are outnumbered. The Security Services know every detail of your plot: MI5, Special Branch and Department Z.'

Valentine's eyes shifted towards the man sitting next to him, then back to me.

'You're lying. You're bluffing. It's just Clifton and his mistress. And she's not even here. Oh, Clifton, you're on your own with one little gun.'

'Guards!' Mosley yelled, standing up so sharply I almost shot him on reflex.

My aim swung back to Joyce, but my hand trembled. I was angry, and angry didn't make for clear thinking or accurate shooting. From the corner of my eye, I saw one of the FP men bolt for the Red Room door. I shot him, and he crashed into one of the great windows. As glass cascaded down, his friend rushed past and had almost reached the door before I put my second shot between his shoulders. At least, I thought I did, but he kept on running. I switched my gun muzzle around, but Joyce was no longer a target and must be grovelling on the floor somewhere.

One of the great oak doors swung open as Mosley's bodyguards responded to his call but shooting broke out in the stairwell behind them, and one tumbled into the room and fell on his face. The second turned and fired down the staircase. A submachine gun fired rapidly, and a shotgun barked, and he fell out of sight. Men shouted and screamed and yelled incoherent words.

I slammed the two pistol belts down onto the table and whipped them along the polished teak. Hands grabbed for the weapons.

An ambulanceman stepped over the fallen bodyguard, submachine gun in hand, and it was my turn to duck below the table. Everyone else cascaded to the floor.

A sudden silence fell.

JEB Baxter pushed his way through the doorway, his tanned, leathery face creased by a long life of adventure and danger.

'Get Clifton!' cried Joyce. 'He's on the floor.'

I sought a clear line on Baxter as he sought one on me. I pulled the trigger, but the Luger refused to fire.

Sometime explorer JEB Baxter twitched his muzzle towards me. Sometime submarine commander Marcus Calhoun fired without hesitation. Baxter's shots went wild, and as I was still fiddling with my ancient weapon, my target was falling, falling from sight. Men scrabbled in all directions. I surprised myself when the Luger decided to fire into the floor. Missing Mosley's head by inches, I shot another ambulanceman in the shoulder, and he spun against the wall. Firing could now be heard from outside the house.

Where was Baxter? Joyce scooted out of the door behind the legs of another ambulanceman, then he too vanished. Everyone who now held a weapon fired towards the open door, and shots that came back were wild and unaimed. Another ambulanceman fell dead in the doorway.

'Police, Scotland Yard!' The voice was Renton's, sounding from the Red Room doorway. 'Can someone in Christ's name tell me what is going on?'

One of Renton's men pushed a scared FP man into the room, the one I thought I'd shot in the back.

'I hope you've sent for help, Renton,' Calhoun called.

'Wasn't that your job, you dodgy bugger?'

I edged past the crouching Churchill.

'Any more revolvers to hand out?' he said, breathless. 'I'll take some of the bastards with me.'

Just one of the attackers remained by the door, wounded, holding up one hand in submission. I scurried across and picked up his weapon.

Valentine stood over me. 'I'll have that, Clifton.'

I weighed the revolver in my hand and Valentine's trustworthiness in my mind.

'Who are you working for?' he muttered.

'Britain,' I said, passing over the revolver. 'Watch the stairs.'

Mosley himself took Baxter's fallen sub-machine gun. The explorer lay motionless, arms spread wide, a red circle marring his forehead. Renton took a long look at the body.

'Your police killer, from Kensington in thirty-five,' I said.

He gave Baxter a tap in the ribcage with the toe of his shoe. 'He won't be killing any more policemen.'

Everyone began shouting at once, inevitable when a room is occupied by men used to their orders being obeyed without question.

Calhoun came my way.

'A very good shot, sir.'

'I keep my eye in.' He didn't seem shaken at all. A man who had sent goodness knows how many sailors to their graves with torpedoes must gain a turtle's shell.

'Is this our moment, Calhoun?'

'To do what?'

I lowered my voice almost to a hiss. 'Take back control of the country.'

'You're one man, Clifton, one man. One wrong step, and you'll be dead and forgotten.' He gave a little shake of his head.

'Well done, Clifton!' Mosley's features twitched, and hands that gripped the submachine gun shook with rage. 'And Inspector...and Calhoun. Where's Joyce? Has the bastard got away? And you, Clifton. I want a list; everyone responsible for this.'

I already had one, and I nodded. There would be score-settling in the days to come. If I'd been the suicidal type, I could have sent Mosley to join Baxter in Hell's waiting room, but Joyce was still on the loose, and civil war reared its ugly head again.

One of Renton's men fired two shots down the grand staircase. I took a glance over the two bodies blocking the door and saw the second of Mosley's bodyguards sprawled on the landing and an FP man curled up at the turn of the stair, clutching his stomach. More shots sounded from downstairs, outside. From a grand window, I saw two fascist policemen running across the gravel in front of the house, one throwing his pistol away as he ran. A bullet cracked through the glass above me and splintered the plaster ceiling. Everyone warned everyone else to keep away from the windows, and the first FP man I'd hit now started stirring amid broken shards. I could hear a tommy gun firing out on the lawns somewhere. A car engine roared into life outside, then another, as friends or foes or innocent neutrals began escaping for the gate.

Like settlers huddled in their cabin while bandits swirled around, an unlikely grouping of allies awaited rescue. General Fuller had been hit at least twice yet lay on the floor proclaiming he was fit and able to fight. He declared that we had enough weapons between us to fight our way out, but I probably had, at best, one or two rounds left in my treacherous German antique.

Francis-Hawkins' left arm was bleeding heavily, but he still gripped a pistol in his right, swearing repeatedly. 'We're going to kill them, kill them all.'

Caught between mercenaries disguised as ambulance men, Fascist Police, real police, Department Z, and whatever reinforcement Renton had summoned, people would die in the confusion. And two dozen or more national socialists were somewhere downstairs and possibly armed; old men with war experience and younger aides fired up by Nazi philosophy. Rats would fight if cornered, and Sissy was out there, and others who put their faith in me and their very lives were in my hands.

Renton raised his voice. 'Calhoun, Clifton! We must get this bloody fiasco under control.'

I backed away from Calhoun. 'Time to go,' I shouted to the room. 'That way!'

'Sir!' Renton shouted at Mosley. He clenched his jaw firmly shut, as if holding back his emotions at serving this Leader.

I led the way through the Red Room, down the south service staircase, and into the Breakfast Room. Bursting into the Green Parlour, we found three of the fascist plotters hiding behind furniture, and our gun muzzles pushed them ahead of us into the Salon, where more were milling in confusion. Peter Wise was there, and AA Thorne beside him.

'You are all under arrest,' Renton boomed. 'Get on the floor and stay there.'

Smoke bit into my nostrils. Something was on fire.

Peter Wise moved towards us. 'Joyce has gone, Domville has gone—'

He collapsed as a muffled shot silenced him. Thorne darted out of the group and through the door into the Marble Hall, but I was after him in a trice. He slipped on the well-polished floor, and as he recovered, I saw he held a pistol.

'Don't!' I commanded.

'Yes, don't.' The voice was Julian's, advancing through the main door, Thompson submachine gun at his hip, hair slicked flat, and drops of water running down his face.

'Bravo, bravo,' Thorne said, dropping his pistol and raising his hands. 'The Blackshirt heroes do it again.'

And Sissy was unhurt!

She came up beside Julian. 'It's him, Thorne, the one responsible for Julia.'

'And Melissa,' Julian choked back the words.

'Don't do an Eleanor,' I warned them.

'You won't harm me,' Thorne said. 'You've no idea how much support we have.'

'We know exactly how much support you have. Names, addresses, the lot. Where's Joyce?'

'Run away, gone, he's escaped you, Clifton.'

More thunder rumbled from outside.

'We couldn't stop the cars,' Julian said. 'We had no idea who was in them. There are police and servants running all over the park.'

'Afternoon, boss.' Hills entered through the front door, holding his submachine gun jauntily in one hand, muzzle towards the ceiling.

Young Drysdale came in next, clutching his left ear from which blood dripped into the cuff of his black leather coat. He was panting with exhilaration, and his pistol joined the half dozen weapons aimed at Thorne.

'Can I put my hands down now?' Thorne asked.

'If you do, the only question is who will shoot you first.'

Chapter Forty-Six

A Thorne was on his knees in the centre of the Marble Hall, both hands on the top of his head. More satisfying still, Sissy was still alive.

'You did it, Sissy.'

'Jules beat me there by a whisker.'

'So well done, Julian!'

His expression didn't thaw, but Julian was back on our side. If he'd ever left it.

'How are our people? Have we lost anyone?'

'One dead,' Hills answered. 'And a few nicks, like Drysdale 'ere.'

'Ear,' said Drysdale, forcing a smile. 'That's a joke—you've been practicing that.'

Hills smiled.

'Jenny's hurt,' Sissy said. 'She was running to join us and fell. I hope Lucy gets to her in time.'

'Lucy reached her,' Hills said. 'Looks like she was hit in the gut, but Lucy'll do her best.'

'You, Clifton,' Renton called from the door. 'Get your circus together and keep 'em inside the house. This is police work now. There are men with hostages out in the park and the last thing we want is more death. They hold the Baroness, so they think they have the crown jewels to bargain with.'

Sissy glanced at me. 'Perhaps now we can rescue mother.'

'No,' Renton asserted, 'I've seen your rescues. We talk them out, not storm in shooting. It might take a day or two, but we've time, and we've the manpower now.' He lowered his voice. 'There's a superintendent from the Kent force outside, and he'll be taking command.'

'But you're Scotland Yard,' Sissy protested.

'He outranks me, ma'am, and all the uniformed men are his. We have to work by the book, follow the law.' He looked hard at me to drive home the point. 'Even now.'

'I see,' Sissy said. 'Well, there must be real medical equipment in those ambulances. I'm going to get it and go back to help Lucy.' She touched my hand. 'Take care.'

'And you. Both of you.'

We herded the prisoners into the Chapel. It had only one entrance, its diamond-pane lancet windows were high, and guards could be placed on the ground-floor gantry in a position where they couldn't be rushed. The racial supremacists, the would-be Nazis, and the men who sought a shortcut to power crowded onto the pews, facing the altar and an uncertain future. Julian prodded his father down the steps.

'You ungrateful…after all I've done for you.'

'You made me what I am,' Julian said in the coldest tone I'd ever heard him use.

A makeshift hospital was set up in the Salon for the wounded, and a smouldering curtain needed to be torn down and thrown outside before a fire ran out of control. I moved around the building, making sure all my party from the boathouse were accounted for. Of the Blackshirt women other than Jenny, five had been herded out to the pavilion. The crisis was far from over.

I saw Sissy drive past behind the wheel of one of the ambulances, her hands grasping the wheel, leaning forward for a clear view of the drive, and not looking my way. Oh, how our lives had changed. Nothing would be the same again.

Returning towards the Chapel, I found Calhoun sitting in an easy chair in the library with a glass of brandy in his hand. AA Thorne sat opposite him, handcuffed and with a bleeding nose. He may have caught a jab from Hills' elbow, but it was less than he deserved. The intelligence men were talking quietly.

'No deals,' I warned.

Calhoun turned his head. 'There are always deals.'

'Not with him.'

'There are always deals.'

'Clifton!' bawled Mosley from the door of the Study.

I trotted over dutifully, my mind clearing now and knowing what it was I'd achieved. Britain had escaped Nazi rule by a hair's breadth, but the price would be military dictatorship. Francis-Hawkins was using the telephone, barking orders, his left arm dangling, his black uniform sleeve torn and stained red.

'Have you found Joyce?' Mosley asked.

'Not yet.'

'Find him. I'm going to wipe the floor with his blood.'

'Yes, sir.'

I turned away and followed the Leader's order without dissent, as any good fascist would do. It was no longer a case of drifting with the current, I was being dragged along by a raging torrent.

'Hills!' I shouted. 'Hills—you're with me. We're not done yet.'

After an argument with the Kent policemen, we trudged out to retrieve Sissy's car as thunder rolled above us and a regular monsoon battered the woods. Leaves and sticks cascaded down.

'Nice day for it,' Hills laughed.

Not knowing what was happening at the north gate, I drove the yellow T-type cautiously through the park, wary of flying shots. Only falling sticks thunked against the roof. Police officers stopped us again, and a sergeant had to be called before we were allowed down to the main gate for further argument and delay. Two cars had crashed during attempted escapes, unarmed officers had been shot by fleeing FP men, and everyone was on edge. Ten more minutes were wasted in argument. We were dirty, soaking wet and Hills wore trousers ripped at the knee. Both our caps were gone. Hills had used his uniform jacket to cover one of our fallen, and I'd already discarded mine as it was stained with blood, spilt wine, and had glass shards in its seams. And I did not want to look like a fascist any longer than I had to. It took a messenger to run to the house and back before we were free to leave.

In the lanes leading away from Highwood, we squeezed past police vans, cars full of detectives, and genuine ambulances heading in the other direction. I drove through flooded dips and impromptu streams running down the roads. Once I turned onto the A2, I pushed my foot to the floor and sped for London.

Joyce had thrown away everything in one reckless gamble. Everything apart from his new wife Margaret and perhaps new friends in Germany—if the Nazis didn't simply disown failures. Napoleon was not a defeatist, but he always planned for setbacks, and, more than once, had snatched victory from disaster. A man with a similar ego but lacking Napoleon's strategic sense might not even have contemplated failure and now be scurrying for any bolthole he could find. Joyce might run for home.

Margaret and William Joyce lived in a flat at 83 Onslow Gardens, north of London's Fulham Road. Margaret had confided in Sissy at one of their few meetings that she'd expected to move somewhere larger, more comfortable, now her husband was a government minister, but he boasted no interest in middle-class trappings. The fact the neighbourhood had trees was sufficient for him, which struck me as an odd affection.

The A2 had been laid down by the Romans, and west of Rochester ran arrow-straight, so I pushed the T-Type as fast as its engine could manage and the weather allowed.

'It had to be Joyce who betrayed us over in Sark,' I said to Hills. 'It was his idea I accompany Julian, and probably his idea that Julian went in the first place.'

'Not Dr Valentine?'

'No, he was never party to the plan.'

'He's been chasing you though.'

'He was doing his job, following orders. But until the weekend, he left the rest of you to run free because he wanted to find out what was going on, too. The Leader has recruited a lot of fools, but Valentine isn't one of them.'

'So Joyce wanted us out of the way because we were locking his mates up?'

'And coming too close to discovering what he was up to. A raid on the right address and we'd have had letters, diaries, bank accounts, the lot.'

I wouldn't mention how close Peter Wise had come to being the hero of the hour, and few would ever know.

'So who brought them Frenchies in?'

'AA Thorne, the one you gave a bloody nose to. He was big in the Foreign Office, runs the Secret Intelligence Service, and must have links to French extremist groups. And JEB Baxter—'

Hills put his index finger in the centre of his forehead. 'The one you shot right there.'

'It wasn't me.'

'You always say that, boss; it doesn't wash. There's no court going to convict you for it.'

And so my reputation would continue to grow. I shivered, damp from my neck to my toes.

'Baxter was a mercenary, perhaps working for Thorne in the end but recruited in the first place by Julian Thring's father.'

'And this Thorne just wanted power?'

'Yes, we bagged a room full of men who just wanted power. Whether Joyce was using Thorne, or he was using Joyce is academic now.'

'But Mr Joyce was the Leader's number two.'

'And most number twos want to be number one.'

'Well, I don't,' Hills said. 'I'm happy being number four, or number seven, or whatever I am. Reckon they'll give you Valentine's job now, as you spotted Joyce's game, and he didn't?'

'I hope not.'

'That's you with your modesty again. Get it, boss. Grab the medals and the pay rise. And if you've any going spare, there's plenty of others earned it today.'

Onslow Gardens was typical for affluent areas of Chelsea. Its houses were white-painted affairs with four stories, plus basements and flats in the roof.

What looked to be a black Ford Popular was parked directly in front of one colonnaded porch. Bruno drove a version manufactured in Germany called the Eifel. I parked directly behind it, and Hills made no attempt to even hide his Thompson as he climbed out of the passenger door and strutted forward to investigate. I approached from the pavement.

Bruno sat behind the wheel of his car, placing both his hands on the steering wheel as he noticed us.

'Good afternoon, Bruno.'

'You look like gangsters,' he said.

'Well, the real gangster is in there.'

'No, he's not,' Bruno said. 'I've been watching for half an hour.'

'How about his wife?'

'I've tried the doorbell, and nobody replies.'

'You're very polite for a Gestapo man.'

'I don't work for the Gestapo, my friend.'

'So why are you here?'

'Orders. May I step out, I feel I have been stopped by traffic police.'

We made room for him to join us on the pavement. The rain had abated to a drizzle, but the sky promised more.

Bruno looked upwards at the clouds. 'England in the summer,' he said.

'Did you know what was planned for today?'

'I do not know what has happened today,' Bruno said. 'I trust Sissy is well.'

'Never better. Excuse me, but I have to search you.'

'I am not carrying a pistol.'

'Forgive me if I check.'

I began to pat Bruno's pockets.

'While you are searching me like a criminal, please tell me what has happened. I can see you have been in a battle. Or was it a swimming race?'

I summarised events at Highwood, and Bruno nodded in time with my words, betraying no emotion.

'So, sorry, but Hitler won't have a puppet government in Britain,' I concluded, stepping back.

'No.'

'You're not disappointed.'

He smiled. 'I just follow orders.'

Hills jabbed a thumb towards me. 'He doesn't follow orders. That's how we cracked this plot.'

'Your man is impertinent.'

'Hills, you're impertinent. Get us into Joyce's flat. Is there a back exit, Bruno?'

'No. One door, no escape.'

Hills rang the doorbell to Joyce's flat, then rang several others for good measure. After only the briefest pause, he hammered on the door, yelling, 'Open up!'

'Now *he* could work for the Gestapo,' observed Bruno.

A resident answered after two minutes of incessant ringing and hammering, and Hills pushed the door wide open. The resident started to protest but went silent as he saw the guns.

'Next time, answer the bloody bell!' Hills led the way up the communal staircase.

'A Luger, Hugh?' Bruno observed as I drew it. 'What happened to your Walther?'

'A tedious story.' I should have swapped it for something better, and fully loaded, I realised. 'And if you're only following orders, what are they?'

'To escort Herr Joyce back to the Embassy.'

'Preventing us from questioning him about how much support came from Berlin? I don't suppose you'd spare me the time and just tell me.'

'If I knew, I would not tell you. You know that.'

Hills reached the door of Joyce's flat and hammered on it, keeping to one side in case his knock was answered with a shot. 'Department Z. Open up, or we come in shooting.'

'Wait, wait,' said a man's voice.

A chain rattled off, then the door opened.

Hills pushed it aside. 'Does nobody answer their bloody doorbells round here?'

A man retreated before us, and I recognised him as the flat mate Joyce shared with before he got married. Another teacher, another young right-wing radical. His name came to me.

'Macnab, isn't it? Where's Joyce?' I demanded.

'He's not here,' Macnab said as we pressed past him into the living room.

'His wife?'

'No.'

'Whose is that valise?' I pointed to the bag resting on the settee, ready to be lifted at a moment's notice.

'His.'

'Is he coming back for it?'

The man hesitated. 'I…I'm to take it to him.'

So, there was a plan for failure.

'But I can't now because—well, you arrived. Sitting out there. You're not going to kill me?'

'Only if you don't tell these men where Herr Joyce has gone.' For some reason, Bruno accentuated his German accent. '*Schnell.*'

The flatmate's eyes wandered over our dishevelled state, the congealed blood in my scalp, our unshaven chins, and he must have picked up the scent of death.

'Waterloo Station,' he said.

'The boat train? Where's he heading, Germany?'

'Yes.'

Bruno responded to my accusing look with a shrug. 'I was told he'd be here.'

'You'd better go back, Bruno. Report to your superiors that your plot didn't work.'

He smiled. 'It wasn't my plot.'

'Their plot, then. Come on, Hills.'

All this had taken far too long. By the time we reached Waterloo, abandoned the car in the taxi rank, and rushed inside, the train had long since departed. If Joyce was aboard, it was without his valise, if he'd ever intended coming back for it in the first place. Perhaps only his wife had fled by train. If he'd planned an escape, it would make more sense for him to catch the train at some point along the way or drive straight to Dover. I glanced at my watch. He'd had three hours to make good his escape, plenty of time to reach the port and jump on the first ferry to anywhere. With luck the unexpected storm had made the sea too rough to sail on. It was St Swithin's Day, and the rain just fell and fell.

I found a telephone box and bullied my way to the front of the queue. It was impossible to put a call through to Highwood as the line was permanently engaged. I made other calls, but lines were down in the storm and whole exchanges had ceased to operate. The country was in confusion. Nobody I managed to speak to was sure who was in charge, or who I was, or what authority I carried.

William Joyce was going to get away.

Chapter Forty-Seven

For all the Leader's boasts about order, there was little order in Britain in that summer of 1937. Mosley's grip on power may appear to have been strengthened by the unmasking of the plotters, but more than ever, he relied on the massed ranks of stormtroopers. Rounding up the conspirators removed some problems but simply cemented another. The militarists were now the puppet masters.

I'm not proud to have presided over mass roundups. Those lists so carefully compiled by the agents of Room Z now came into play, as did those made separately by Valentine, and by Calhoun and by Renton. The full force of what was now the law came down on the conspirators, their friends, allies, financial backers, wives, and nephews. Next, we moved on to people who printed their pamphlets or hired out rooms, or anyone Mosley simply didn't like. I'm ashamed to admit I added wide swathes of the Young Britain Club membership to the lists to be sure we caught all the guilty. I also named many genuine whole-hearted Mosley supporters who had nothing to do with the plot, but who I decided the streets would be safer without.

I decided. It was an arbitrary and vicious form of cleansing, far removed from true justice. One newspaper playfully referred to it as the 'night of the small knives.'

I wanted to wash my hands ritually once it was all over, but such a stain could never be removed. I had no clear plan what I'd do next, beyond an intention to retire from Department Z and live a quiet family life. My idea that Sissy and I could run away abroad had gained a baby-shaped complication, which was far from baby-sized. And if we ran, our names would just be added to the list of traitors.

Eleanor and Walsh had been released from detention with bruises, a couple of fractures, and more scars to add to the tally my friends were racking up. The gallant Jenny faced a long stay in hospital, but doctors were confident she'd recover in time. It seemed wise for me to accept an instruction to attend a meeting at the Palace of Westminster. I was specifically asked to wear full uniform—for the last time I hoped—and I had to borrow most of the components.

Wearing that uniform had the effect of making me march rather than walk. After I'd handed over my new Walther at the door, I was led upstairs by a Blackshirt aide and strode in step with him along the historic corridors. He stopped and rapped at a door bearing a plate marked Prime Minister.

Mosley was also in uniform, sitting behind an enormous desk flanked by flags. Seated to one side in front of the desk was a familiar man in a far more formal three-piece suit than he normally wore.

'Clifton, have a seat!' Mosley boomed.

I took the second chair, noticing a signed photograph of Adolf Hitler occupied a prominent position on the desk.

'You've met Vice-Admiral Calhoun.'

Calhoun smiled. The jump in rank would make any ambitious man smile.

'But not in the best circumstances,' Mosley added. 'Commander Clifton needs no introduction, Calhoun, and I've no doubt you already hold a thick file on him.'

My former handler reached across and shook my hand. 'Pleased to make your acquaintance in more civilised surroundings.'

'Calhoun is my new Director of Security Services. You'll be working together, so have lunch, get acquainted.'

'But sir—'

'Now, Clifton. The press is most amused by what they're calling the night of the small knives, but there's serious work to do. You are promoted to Inspector and my Director of Intelligence. You'll be leading Department Z.'

'Sir—'

'Your military service record is being corrected, and your court martial erased.' Mosley referred to a typed sheet. 'You'll receive back pay due from 1933, the Indian General Service medal, and you'll be one of the first recipients of the new Edward Cross for gallantry in a time of peace.' He paused and smiled. 'The king has finally recognised the great service you did for him. And for me.'

I was speechless. My objections had been stifled. Was I ambitious? Had I ever been ambitious? Were these trinkets worth the cost?

'Sir, I really—'

'Clifton,' Calhoun intervened. 'We should have lunch and discuss the way forward. The country faces threats on all sides; we have much to do.'

And the doors of my cage clanged shut once more. If the bars were now gilded, it was still a cage.

'What about Dr Valentine?' I asked.

'I've appointed him as Commissioner for Police and Security to bring all the strands together,' Mosley said. 'His role will be largely political.'

'And you're disbanding the Fascist Police?

'Certainly not.'

'So will I command them too?'

'No,' Mosley said. 'I think it is best to keep powers, ah, separate.'

Divide and rule would be the policy.

'The FP were misled by Joyce and the other traitors. Inspector Parker has been transferred to knock them into shape and bring them into line.'

And to counterbalance me, no doubt. I could walk away now, abandoning Hills, Lucy, Drysdale, and the others to the leadership of someone like Blake, or indeed Parker, and to be pulled down the slope into becoming Britain's Gestapo. Or I could stay and try to ride out the storm, keeping both Nazis and communists at bay until the electorate of Britain realised they had been hoodwinked by the fascists' promises. Desperately I wanted to escape with Sissy at my side and not become a desk-bound tool of a dictatorship, the most feared and most hated man in Britain. And one day, there would be a reckoning, and I'd be in the dock with the guilty.

'May I make a counter proposal?' I ventured. 'Make Julian Thring the head of Department Z. He's proved his loyalty, and he's more of an administrator than I am. Give me some fancy title so it doesn't look like I'm walking away—ah, Special Investigator, or something ambiguous like that. Allow me to roam. I don't want to sit at a desk.'

No matter how big and shiny and how many flags were draped around it.

'I see,' Mosley said. 'But you would still be the power behind that desk?'

'If people wanted to see it that way.'

'I'll consider it.'

The meeting lasted for almost an hour, where Calhoun briefed Mosley on the latest security threats, and I confirmed Department Z's roundups were complete.

'For now,' Mosley concluded.

A dictator always needs enemies to provide excuses for repression. He went on to justify his latest political moves, purging the whole leadership. General Fuller was dismissed due to his membership of the Nordic League.

'It would have been better if he'd died on that floor.'

Any member of the new Controlling Committee must be a member of British Union and only British Union. Mosley had given the King's Party men such as Churchill a month to either join him unequivocally or resign from politics, and their time to agree was running out.

I was sitting in a fog, a strange reality I never imagined. All the time Mosley spoke, I wondered what I should have done differently, whether I could have pulled history in a different direction by making different choices, but as Calhoun had said I was only one man. Perhaps all my moves were predetermined, and I flattered myself to think otherwise. Most would say I'd planned every rung of my climb to the top.

Calhoun and I emerged together, turned down the corridor, and walked in silence, not sharing our thoughts. A portly figure emerged round a corner up ahead, walking towards us without haste and taking the centre line so there was no question of our politely slipping past. This was no coincidence, no accidental meeting. The man who was for a few more days First Lord of the Admiralty stopped and waited for us to close the last few steps.

'Good morning, Mr Churchill,' I said.

Churchill shifted his eyes from me to Calhoun, then back again. 'So,' he growled. 'Which one of you rascals is running the country now?'

Coda

'Jaiirmany calling, Jaiirmany calling. Here are the Reichssender Hamburg, station Bremen.'

Rundfunk's English news service employed a handful of natural English speakers, clearly all encouraged to sound the same, just as BBC announcers also affected a particular form of speech. The odd haw-haw accent and the strange pronunciation of Germany lent the Nazi propaganda station a personality all its own.

In Room W at the top of Black House, Department Z staff monitored the short-wave radio news output of a variety of European stations. Although the Rundfunk announcers strove to sound similar, there was clearly a new haw-haw voice on the air. William Joyce had found a job in Germany that suited his talents. We hadn't heard the last of him.

A Note from the Author

Blackshirt Rebellion is alternative history, building on the events depicted in *Blackshirt Conspiracy* which changed the course of 1930s Britain as we know it. In reality, King Edward VIII abdicated at the end of 1936, the 'Kings Party' was no more than a fleeting idea and Mosley never took power. British Union remained on the fringe of British politics until broken up on Churchill's orders in 1940 when several hundred of its leaders and prominent members were rounded up and interned without trial.

This said, much of the detail within this story is rooted in historical fact. Bruno articulates Hitler's disdain for Mosley as being too aristocratic, whereas German national socialism was born on the streets. In 1937 William Joyce became disillusioned with the man he called 'the Bleeder', thinking him weak and insufficiently antisemitic. The 'kosher fascist' tag was real. The militarist wing of the BU headed by Francis-Hawkins successfully schemed to eclipse Joyce and the populist intellectuals, so in the spring Joyce and the leftist intellectual John Beckett left BU to set up the National Socialist League. Mosley was incensed, declaring he'd wipe the floor with the traitors' blood. Some 60 BU members also defected but the breakaway party failed to attract much support and was wound up just before the outbreak of WW2. Joyce himself feared arrest on the eve of war in August 1939 so he and his second wife Margaret fled to Germany. In need of work, he found a job as a radio announcer and became infamous as the traitor 'Lord Haw Haw'. Both British Union and NSL were penetrated at an early date by agents working for the Board of Deputies of British Jews and the character of Peter Wise is based on an actual agent about whom I could not find enough information to include as a historical personaility.

Apart from the Young Britain Club all the smorgasbord of fringe right wing organisations depicted in this book existed in some form during the 1930s, although I've taken some liberties for the purpose of fiction. Many more haven't been mentioned, as I didn't want to dizzy the reader and Hugh could not pick fights with them all. We would today characterize them as 'far-right'; reactionary, ultra-nationalistic, and driven by rabid antisemitism. Some had occult leanings and overt white supremacy agendas. Individuals could often be members of several organisations at once. The Nordic League was established by German agents and its web of front organisations and affiliated groups had strong connections with the Nazis. So too did The Link, established by Admiral Domville the former head of Naval Intelligence. The smaller political parties and dinner clubs tended to attract stereotypical right-wingers including military personnel and landed gentry. In contrast the National Socialist League was the main adopter of what these days is called a 'populist' agenda, following Hitler's model of street-level politics.

The Radio Plan was a money-making scheme pursued by Mosley and his associates up to the outbreak of war. Negotiations were pursued with Belgium and Germany for the establishment of a network of commercial radio stations and an agreement was signed with Sark in June 1937. Setting up a radio station on the island contravened the Post Office Act, so Air Time never got off the ground, joining other failed ideas such as Blackshirt cigarettes and a Diana Guinness cosmetics range. Diana didn't adopt the Mosley surname until 1938 when the Leader finally announced they were married. Ostensibly he'd concealed the marriage to protect her from being attacked by his opponents, but it also protected the couple from the disapproval of the chattering classes.

Alderney was mooted as a potential internment centre at one point and was infamously used by the Nazis for brutal work camps run by Organisation Todt and the SS during the Second World War. Mosley did propose in 1937 that mortars were a legitimate weapon to use in urban combat against communists. The British weather in 1937 was often grey and wet, and almost by coincidence the plot climax takes place during the St Swithin's Day storm which battered the country that July. This was remarked upon as seeing the heaviest rainfall in a single day for several years.

Maxwell Knight, 'M', of MI5 spent the summer of 1937 working on a sting operation against a communist spy ring. Resourceful agent Olga Grey penetrated the Communist Party of Great Britain, gained their confidence, and set up a supposed safe house. A Soviet plot to steal naval secrets was unmasked, though the Russian 'illegals' involved were allowed to escape.

Hugh has been placed in the dilemma shared by millions of people in Germany, Italy and Spain in the 1930s; should they hitch their wagon to the fascists and profit from their rise or oppose them and suffer the consequences? The agents of Room Z have learned the price that comes with supporting a dictatorship, and they have not heard the last of the French extremist group Francisme. As talk of war increases, how will the Agents of Room Z fare?

If you enjoyed this book, please post a review or rating.

Acknowledgements

In writing this book, I am grateful to many friends in the Crime Writers' Association, and to thriller enthusiasts running blogs and e-newsletters who supported the launch of this series and continue to show interest. Thanks are also due to Yan Marquis for guidance on the Sark Language Serquais, to other friends in Sark, plus Tom and Rob for advice on 1930s trains. I must also thank the Dames of Detection, in particular, Verena Main Rose and Shawn Reilly Simmons, for bringing this book to completion.

About the Author

Jason Monaghan's life has provided plenty of inspiration for writing historical thrillers. He trained as an archaeologist studying Roman pottery, but his career took unexpected twists, including investigating shipwrecks, a spell in offshore banking, working as an anti-money laundering specialist, and ultimately becoming a museum director. Now a full-time writer living in his native Yorkshire, he travels as often and as far as he can.

AUTHOR WEBSITE:

www.jasonmonaghan.com

SOCIAL MEDIA HANDLES:

Website, Blog and Newsletter: www.monaghanfoss.com
Facebook: Jason Monaghan Author
X/Twitter, and Bluesky: @Jasonthriller
Pinterest: Jason Monaghan
Youtube: Jason Monaghan (Studio Monaghan)
Instagram: docmonaghan

Also by Jason Monaghan

Agents of Room Z
  Blackshirt Masquerade
  Blackshirt Conspiracy

Jeffrey Flint Archaeology Mystery Series
  Darkness Rises
  Byron's Shadow
  Shadesmoor
  Lady in the Lake
  Blood and Sandals

Historical Novel
  Glint of light on Broken Glass

Historical Short Stories
  Islands that Never Were

www.ingramcontent.com/pod-product-compliance
Lightning Source LLC
Chambersburg PA
CBHW020604110726
47899CB00002B/363